I0823448

MERIDIAN RISING

MERIDIAN RISING

a novel by

PAUL BURCH

NEWSOUTH BOOKS,
an imprint of
THE UNIVERSITY OF GEORGIA PRESS
ATHENS

NSB

Published by NewSouth Books,
an imprint of the University of Georgia Press
Athens, Georgia 30602
www.ugapress.org

Printed and bound by Sheridan Books
The paper in this book meets the guidelines for
permanence and durability of the Committee on
Production Guidelines for Book Longevity of the
Council on Library Resources.

Most NewSouth/University of Georgia Press titles are
available from popular e-book vendors.

Printed in the United States of America
25 26 27 28 29 C 5 4 3 2 1

EU Authorized Representative
Easy Access System Europe—Mustamäe tee 50, 10621 Tallinn, Estonia,
gpsr.requests@easproject.com

Library of Congress Cataloging-in-Publication Data
Names: Burch, Paul, author.
Title: Meridian rising : a novel / by Paul Burch.
Description: Athens : NewSouth Books, an imprint of the
University of Georgia Press, 2025.
Identifiers: LCCN 2025003999 | ISBN 9781588385550 (hardback) |
ISBN 9781588385567 (epub) | ISBN 9781588385574 (pdf)
Subjects: LCSH: Rodgers, Jimmie, 1897–1933—Fiction. |
LCGFT: Biographical fiction. | Novels.
Classification: LCC PS3602.U7297 M47 2025 | DDC 813/.6—dc23/eng/20250307
LC record available at https://lccn.loc.gov/2025003999

For Henry and Meg

Nothing in his life
Became him like the leaving of it

—Macbeth

Meridian Rising is inspired by the life of musician Jimmie Rodgers, the Blue Yodeler, born in 1897 near Meridian, Mississippi, and died in New York City in 1933. Today, Rodgers is called the "Father of Country Music" and is the only artist to be honored in the Blues, Country, Songwriters, and Rock & Roll Halls of Fame.

From this point forward, the reader will be asked to believe that one part of the story comprises Jimmie's previously unknown memoir, while the other part of the story comprises recollections by the people who knew him best.

Though this imagined tale is adorned with details of Jimmie's extraordinary life, from his touring itinerary to his favorite brand of cigarettes, any true resemblance to persons living or dead is purely coincidental.

PB

MERIDIAN RISING

A Word from the Heirs of This Manuscript and the Editor

The editor wants you to note that for the portions of this story attributed to Mr. Rodgers, the punctuation, dialect, and unusual spellings have been recreated from the original manuscript of his memoir, which is, by its very nature, incomplete. Though his is more complete than most.

The events, people, and scenarios both public and private herein might closely resemble real events, people, and scenarios both public and private as they were known by Mr. Rodgers himself.

But to err is human. So, repeating portions of this book, publicly or privately, as anything other than hearsay, is hereby done at the reader's own risk of great embarrassment for having the mendacity to speak of these things as true even though you know otherwise.

Folks,

I was halfway through writing this story—my story, that is—before I realized I should say something about my intentions.

Just so you know, I'm dead and have been so awhile. And now that you know I'm dead, and taking into account that I'm likely the only fellow who ever set out to write a book that didn't actually own one, it's my hope you didn't pay nothin' for this. I'd like to think you found it in the back of a cab or got it as a gift from a hobo. If you procured this in a proper book shop, consider yourself swindled and go back and steal all the copies you can and throw them every which way as you run amok. This wasn't supposed to be for sale.

Naturally, my inspiration to write a book that everybody owns but nobody pays for is the Bible, which also happens to be a book I never read. I've been told I should try. And I have. But always in a crowd who's stuck on reading the same line over and over again. I do admire how it shows up everywhere. Hotel rooms. Hospitals. Creep joints. Subways. Outhouses. I found one on a horse once. I don't know how many mornings I've leaned halfway off a mattress, steadying a new-lit cigarette, my head a creaky cage of kickin' elephants, and been threading my Hamilton out of some sweet thing's heel straps all the while trying not to ash the carpet on fire, only to find that goddamned book under the bed.

Somebody is paying somebody to keep them plentiful. So I'd be gum pleased if the next time you're in a hotel room, layin' about while your old lady or old man is bubble-bathing, you might find my book alongside the Bible and haul off with both. Maybe if it's a cold wintery night, you'll read mine and throw the Bible on the fire instead. It burns just fine. The more folks steal this, the more popular it's bound to get. And I hope whoever's printing my tome gets paid handsomely by all the louses who told me I wouldn't amount to nuthin'. If my life had been all fried chicken and roses maybe I wouldn't bother. But I have some bones to pick. And once I pick 'em all, you'll 'bout have my skeleton and most of my guts, too. But you won't have my heart. I gave that away. It's still out there somewhere.

My quibble with the Bible is that it seems like the folks who know it by heart are also the sorriest, most bug hearted, glomming, cruelest bastards ever made. Find me somebody who'll club a man to death for being hungry or small or walking funny or brown or black or hot or cold or slow or fast or sharp or dull or hairy or bald or from somewhere unpronounceable, and I'll show you a man who knows his Bible. This book is for everyone who's been on the wrong side of that swinging stick and got away.

I once had a book by Houdini. (I didn't say I never owned a book.) And in it, Harry put all his imitators out of work by spilling the secrets behind his escapes. The milk can, the hand cuffs, the straitjacket. Just so those lazy bums couldn't make a living copying him. So think of this book like Houdini's. After you're done, you'll know every shucker from here to Hollywood and where they buy their suits. And when you shut this for good, if you think you can make five bucks with a yodel and a C chord, good fuckin' luck to you.

The longer I live, the more I realize we all have a desire to see what it's like to fall. Funny though. Once you get knocked down a few times, that desire to be tricked turns on itself and you become a little wiser, a little more understanding of just how vulnerable we all are. That's called humanity.

Folks, gather 'round now. Within these pages I'm gonna tell you how to part the Red Sea, how to raise the dead, and how to turn your enemies to stone. It's human nature to pay for the privilege of being fleeced. So, for my last trick, I'm gonna tell you everything I've learned and give it away for free. Think of this book as a Bible for people who don't trust the other Bible has their best interests at heart. Life is like three-card monte. The dealer has two chances to your one. I aim to even the odds.

A few more things while I'm thinking of 'em. A lot of authors want you to identify with their characters. (I did learn that in school.) Well, I don't care if you like me. I've been liked by plenty. But if you don't like me now, give me time. I might grow on you. Also, not everything I write here will be exactly true, but it will be honest. If you find out later I was wrong, it was because I was wrong, not because I led you astray.

I should also warn you my fuse is lit and it's burning fast. I'll take you far as I can go but I have no idea how far that will be. I don't have much time and this being my first and only book, I'm sure I'm gonna miss a lot. I'm not the best describer. But I will tell you what caught my eye. And a few other parts. If you find you need to know more, make it up yourself. You get what you paid for.

Lastly, if you're the kind of person that wants to be surprised by a pretzel plot that keeps you curled up on the couch for hours at a time, this is not your book. If you want a tearjerker where the noxious get what they deserve and the hero rides into the sunset, this is not your book. What's at the end of a sunset anyway? Pitch black, that's what. And if you're riding into it, well, you've arrived at the end. I don't care if you're in high cotton in Hazelhurst or freezing your ass off in Minnieapolice begging to be cuffed on a misty meaner to get out of the frost. Dark means the end. Happy is the middle. Happy is right now. Or at the beginning, when you're hopeful.

I'm no moralist. I had to give up on this world and I don't believe in the next. You won't hear me say love your brother or do unto others before they might do to you. Go trespass wherever you want. I have robbed on occasion, but I am not a thief. All the pool sharks and swindlers I met along the way were upstanding citizens in my eyes. They behaved as advertised. If you come to play, you will be played. Don't bellyache about it. It's the other folks you've got to watch out for, the ones you're told to look up to. If you're not careful, you'll be looking up to them all your life with your hand out. I do advise that if you're gonna break a law, don't break more than one at a time.

I better go back to where I was before I got on this detour (which was driving over miles of toads in a Cadillac, Chapter 3 or 4, but who knows now). If you're one of the folks who stitched this together on my behalf, I encourage you to make all the money you can. Just get it up front. One thing about the entertainment business, which you'll come to find was my profession, is there is no better pay day then the one you're not around for. Lastly, if anyone reading this knew me for real and anybody asks you what I was really like, tell 'em while I was here, I tried hard as I could to let everybody know it.

JR

Chapters

TEST PRESSING

A-SIDE

My Home in San Antone

TRANSCRIPTION

Carrie R., at home in San Antonio, Texas, February 6, 1959.

Reel 1 (Reference Disc A)

(Sound of microphone being adjusted)

Carrie R.: Will that dog be too loud? (Inaudible) Jimmie used to cut to wax. He'd call them beehives.

EJC: That's why I brought a tape recorder. We can talk as long as you like.

CR: Would you look at that.

EJC: Try it now, Mrs. Rodgers.

CR: Testing . . . This is Carrie Rodgers of San Antonio, Texas. (Pause) What else do want to know? (Laughs) You don't seem like your everyday Jimmie Rodgers fan.

EJC: Oh, but I am. I'm so happy to finally meet you.

CR: You know I can't tell a little story. Once I get going, I'll have to say everything 'til it's all out of me.

EJC: Let's just talk then. Tell me what Jimmie was like. What comes to mind?

CR: Well, right next to you there, those are Jimmie's cigarettes. He called them Pick-a-Tunes (Note: Picayune). They were his brand. When he couldn't smoke anymore, he'd just put one on his lip and say: "Mother, as long as I can feel that sting, I know I'm alive." He used to sing around the house. (Sings) "I'm goin' homeses to my Picayunes and Four Roses." That was his favorite whiskey. Not sure Ralph ever heard that one.

EJC: Mr. Peer, his producer?

CR: A&R man. If he didn't like "Prohibition Blues" he wouldn't have touched that one.

EJC: Was "Prohibition Blues" a song of Jimmie's he rejected?

CR: He cut it but Mr. Peer didn't care for it. All that talk about dope in the lyrics. Too close to home, I guess. Jimmie's fiddle buddy Mac McMichen made the record instead. Jimmie ran it down for him. Mac sang it just like him, too.

EJC: There's quite a lot of interest in Jimmie now. I bet people would enjoy hearing that.

CR: I had a copy of Jimmie singing it. I gave it to Ernest Tubb.

EJC: Jimmie passed away in New York City. Were you with him?

CR: No. I wasn't. My brother Covert was living with us at the time. He had cancer of the lungs. Jimmie did write me quite a bit. He told my brother to go ahead and smoke if it makes him feel good. I had a letter waiting for me when I got back from the funeral. Posted the day he died. He wrote a lot of people from there.

EJC: When was the last time you saw Jimmie?

CR: I drove him to Galveston to get on the boat to New York. April or May '33. Whenever it was. He was going to meet Mr. Peer to make some recordings.

EJC: Did you know the end was coming?

CR: He was in bad shape when he left. I had a feeling.

EJC: And he traveled to New York with a nurse, Cora Bedell. . .

CR: Yes. He hired her. She liked to take care of show people. Ole Pleasin' he called her. I don't know where they met. Maybe Houston. He spent most of winter there at Methodist (Note: Methodist Hospital). They had him in an oxygen tent.

EJC: Was he still performing up to then?

CR: Not much. He was workin' for the J. D. Morgan Show when he fell ill. One of those bottom of the barrel type jamborees, whatever you call them. He was their sole attraction.

EJC: Did you visit him in the hospital in Houston?

CR: Oh yes. You'd think the whole floor was his. He invited everyone he'd ever met, seemed like. He had this Boston Terrier, Mickey. The nurses let it run around the floor, messing everywhere. Can you imagine? There was one fella, Billy Terrell, who came and talked him into one last show that spring. I think that's probably the last one he did. Billy was an old running buddy. I'm sure it helped Billy out of a jam. Jimmie would sooner help somebody out of a jam than his own.

(Pause) I never cared for that dog.

EJC: Jimmie lived with TB for almost a decade.

CR: That's right. He found out about the time we lost June.

(Note: June Rebecca was the Rodgers' second child who died at six months.)

EJC: It must have been hard for the two of you with his condition.

CR: (Pause) It was so hard. He worried for Anita (Carrie and Jimmie's oldest daughter). He took a room at the Gunter Hotel (San Antonio) for a long time until they asked him to go. He never acquainted himself with this house, not really. We had a house in Kerrville. He called it Yodeler's Paradise. But it got too expensive to run, you know. He'd say: "This is your home now, Mother."

All that fall before he died, he could hardly get out of bed. That was the longest he'd been home in a long time. Now he did some radio for KMAC. But mostly he was in bed. I think the last time he went anywhere during that time was for my parent's 50th wedding anniversary in Meridian. He enjoyed that I think. He grew a mustache. (Laughs) But I knew he was melancholy. I remember we stopped to get some gas and some catfish sandwiches. He saw somebody he knew and talked to them for quite a while. After that, seemed like he was melancholy all the way home.

EJC: Do you know who he spoke with?

CR: Some musician friend of his. He was always taking care of some business.

EJC: You said he kept a room at the Gunter Hotel.

CR: If he was working his radio show, he might stay rather than drive all the way home. He liked to socialize. He threw Will Rogers a birthday party there. You see that hide on the floor? That came from the buffalo they roasted that night.

EJC: You were saying Jimmie was home a lot in the fall of '32, before he passed . . .

CR: . . . Sunday's he'd put on his overalls and get up early with the dogs. Make drop biscuits. He'd cut up the butter and the flour in a bowl. Then he'd say to Anita: "Here's how you mate them together." You could hear them giggling all over the house. That mug behind you, Will Rogers gave him that, too. Belonged to Buffalo Bill. See what it says there . . .

hand it over. (Puts on her glasses.) Rochester, New York, 1911. He'd use this for sweet milk and dip his cornbread in it.

He liked those honorariums. Men's club type things. Anytime somebody wanted to present him some award he'd drop everything. And charge them for the privilege. (Laughs) He played for a Bible group down in Florida for, I think it was, $200. A lot of money in those days. And he sang "Frankie and Johnny" and "In the Jailhouse." Can you imagine? But then he'd go over to a Black theater and play for nothing. He'd say, "You don't charge family. The railyards raised me."

EJC: Do you think that's how he got TB? Working in the railyards?

CR: I suppose. His father was a foreman for many of the lines that came through Meridian. That was James' playground. I don't think he was much of a railman, honestly. But you didn't hear me say that.

I'll tell you a funny story. On the table behind you, that police siren. It came off our old Packard. The Texas Rangers gave him that when they made him an honorary sheriff. And he'd crank that up when he'd get 'bout a mile from the house. That's how we knew he was coming. He got so mad once when he came home and found all his dogs outside. 'Cause it had gotten cold so fast. And me and Annie, who kept house for us, we heard his siren, you know? And we knew he'd be cross if we kept the dogs in the cold. So we ran out there and put blankets on them in their kennels.

He come running in the house. Didn't even say hello. Just started pitchin' a fit. "How dare you leave those dogs out there in this cold. What's the matter with you?" He runs upstairs and rips the blankets off our bed, which were white. But then he got outside and saw the dogs were standing on the wool blankets we had already brought out there. Jimmie spent all night apologizing. He loved those dogs. And his cars.

EJC: What kind of car did he drive?

CR: Plural. The first good car we had was a Buick. And then we had a Chrysler 8 Imperial. And the custom Cadillac. Gray with Mandalay blue trim. That was a special order. And his Ford Phaeton. He called that one Thirsty the Christmas Tree. It was green. He painted the top red. It had all kinds of secret pockets and gadgets. He and some fellows would drive to down to Mexico in it. When he came home from the road, he'd say "Mother, I'm goin' Cadillacin." He loved to just drive around town so people could see him. We pulled up someplace in Dallas going to get supper, you know, and this old fellow come up to us and said, "Jimmie, your throat pay for this?" He just loved that.

One time I went to meet him down here at Sunset Station (San Antonio). He'd been in Hollywood with Mr. Peer. Sessioning, he called it.

EJC: I believe he recorded with Louis Armstrong there.

CR: I don't remember. I know he met Laurel & Hardy. He was out there for a couple of weeks. So I did my hair up like it was when we met. I waited and waited. We were gonna have a reunion, you see.

(Note: CR not making eye contact here. Had they been apart?)

CR: . . . And he wasn't on the train. I was crestfallen. I walked out of the station so mad. And there he was out front, honkin' at me in a new 7-seat black Packard.

EJC: Wow!

CR: Good looking car.

(Note: Paid for with advance on royalties from RP. Packard 740, custom eight, seventh series, 8-cylinder, 106-horsepower, 140.5-inch wheelbase, 7-person sedan, body type #414)

CR: And he showed me the title, which was in my name. I never had a car in my life. I was so mad. 'Cause I'd been waiting, you know? I almost told him to take it back. I wanted yellow! (Laughs) When I finally took off my hat he said, "Oh, look, you done your hair!" And he reached in the glove compartment and pulled out a diamond broach.

(Tape paused. CR goes to the kitchen. Returns)

EJC: Jimmie is always so well dressed in these photos.

CR: It would take us forever to get out of the house. He'd say, "I'm not leavin' 'til I'm fit to kill." That one was taken in New Orleans. Whenever he drove there, he'd stop by Meyer the Hatter's on St. Charles and get himself a new hat. He'd say, "It's got to match my ride." So, he was there a lot, you know. (Laughs) I think Meyer gave Jimmie a free one when he was down and out and he never forgot that. He had all kinds of funny habits. When he'd answer fan mail, he'd lick the envelope and then he'd take his fist and pound on it, like he was punching a rail ticket.

EJC: Where did you meet?

CR: At my parent's house. I was 16. How old are you?

(Note: CR is sharper than RP gives her credit for.)

EJC: We're here to talk about you.

CR: My sister . . .

EJC: Elsie . . .

CR: Annie. She brought him over with a friend of hers. My father was a minister, so we were the only ones on the block with a telephone. There was always people coming over. On this particular day, I thought I had the house to myself. I was in the bathroom with Ponds on my face and I heard this racket in the living room. From the bathroom I could see right in. I heard a banjo playing and all kinds of carrying on. And I ran out and there he was. And that was it you know. Like the movies. He had his arms like this on his hip.

(Note: CR puts both hands on her hip like a tea kettle with palms out, fingers splayed)

And even then, he had on that Black Narcissus perfume to cover up the coal smell. And he had on a straw boater, vest, and a starch shirt. And a red tie tied up real short. That was the style then. A pencil in one pocket and a chain watch in the other. Probably broken. And round specs too small for his face. I had on a little old gingham dress that zipped up the side. Nothing fancy. I was just playing dress-up around the house. He took off his glasses and looked at me, seemed like forever. (Puts hand on her chest.) I forgot to breathe. And before I could say anything he says to my sister, still looking at me: "Annie! I see you keep the prettiest member of the family locked away. Otherwise, no one would pay attention to the rest of y'all."

And he winked at me I remember thinking, uh oh. And the water's still running in the sink and I got this stuff all over my face. I was just stunned, you know? Maybe I said something like, "Who are you?" He got right in my face and sang, "I'm the daring young man on the flying trapeze." His breath smelled like cough syrup. Then he touched my nose with his nose and got cream on it and said, "There. Now we both been swimming in the same pond."

EJC: Did you get married soon after?

CR: Not long. He came over with a friend of his. And, you won't believe this, his friend was talking on the phone and had his back to us. So, while he was talking, Jimmie held up his hand. And he had this teeny weensy gold band on his pinkie. He pointed to it and kind of nodded and smiled. With his eyebrows up. Like he was asking me. I nodded back. He took the ring off his pinkie and put it on my finger. And by the time his friend got off the phone and turned around we were engaged. I'm not sure I ever said yes. (Laughs) We sort of eloped if truth be told. I don't know how my parents didn't just die on the spot. He had been married before which Daddy frowned upon you know. I didn't know anything about Stella or that child.

EJC: Did you ever meet his first wife Stella?

CR: (Pause) Jimmie told my father I cost him $18 for the license, the ring, and the preacher.

EJC: Where did you honeymoon?

CR: New Orleans. He got a pass from the railroad. He had all of $40 in his pocket. On the way he gave me a $20 bill and said whatever I make, you get half. But he never had a cent. Like that old saying: we had chickens one day and feathers the next. My daddy would tell him: "James, you don't play hard to get. You play hard to keep."

But at home he was sweet as the day was long. To the world he was unafraid. That's the face he kept. If he liked you, he liked you. He loved circus people. And the blues. And Coney Island. He said it was like a circus by the sea. He liked people who really worked for a living. He'd say: "Those are my folk. They will buy your record and wear it out." He had funny sayings. Like: "The most lowdown dog is just as good as me. And I'm just as good as the toppest dog." That's who he was.

EJC: He was the daring young man on the trapeze.

CR: He'd say you gotta have a big head to stay afloat. When we was in Bristol, the time he made that first record for Victor, we didn't know if it was a test or if they would actually release it. Anyway, that night James ran into some friend of his at a restaurant and told him (Note: Carrie imitates Jimmie with her shoulders back and hands on her hip): "Well, I just signed a big contract with Victor Records so we'll be moving north soon, that's where the business is." And I just looked at him. Oh, he could bull. But I guess that's what made him.

EJC: Did he yodel when you first met him?

CR: That might have come later. I don't know where he picked that up. Seems like we went to see the Marx Brothers. They came through Birmingham at the theater there. And their mother was touring with them. She was in the act. And she did a yodel in whatever song she sang. And James took note of that. Yodeled all the way home. I don't even think he'd played that much when I met him. He and Elsie (Note: Elsie McWilliams,

CR's sister, JR's writing partner) had a little band in town with somebody. They played together as a trio. Later on, he'd yodel after everything he said. "Mother, can you boil me some coffee?" Here comes the yodel. "Mother, would you help me find this or that?" And another. I didn't even notice it after a while. Like working in a bell factory.

EJC: When Jimmie became successful, how did your life change?

CR: Well, first he went all over town and paid back everybody he owed. Up to then he'd buy a guitar on payments at one place and then cross the street and sell it at a pawn shop. So, squaring all that kept him busy.

Then he wanted gentleman things. Nice shirts. Initials on his cuffs. He bought my mother a new icebox. He special ordered records from H. C. Speir's place in Jackson. Apple boxes full of 'em. Blues. That was before we moved to Texas. If he found out some police chief's wife had something we didn't, he'd have to have it straight away. When he found out Ralph designed his own house, he had to design ours. That's how he made Yodeler's Paradise. He said if your manager has a nicer house than you do then you're in trouble.

That photo there behind you. That was taken when the Peers came down to visit. That's at the old house. That was Peer's second or third wife, I don't remember which. It took him a couple to settle on one.

One time I got a letter from Maybelle (Note: Maybelle Carter of the Carter Family). She had sent a photo of her and her sister Sara wearing mink coats. We used to gab all the time. Anyway, James saw that and it 'bout drove him out of the house like a bull. "If those hillbillies got minks then you ought to have one, too. Throw your things together, kid. We're gonna score you a fur." We drove all the way to San Antonio and back. He made me drive. I'd had my license for about a week. He'd say: "Mother, it's easy. All you gotta remember is your yellow board and your red board. Yellow means slow. Red means stop. And clear means gun it." That's before they had lights.

When we got home, as soon as Anita was asleep, he made me model the coat. Wearing nothing else! (Laughs) "Walk down the stairs. Now walk back up." He'd a been happy if that's all I did. I'd ask him: "James, what if some fan drove up and saw me prancing around with nothing on but a fur?" He'd say: "You can't enjoy it until you spend it." He'd say: "Remember the good times. If you don't, every time you hear a whistle it's gonna be me, like a clown wagon on all your thoughts." He was a funny guy.

EJC: What was he like as a father?

CR: He loved his girls. He didn't have any trouble showing love like some men. I didn't know anything about children. I found out. (Laughs) I practically was one when we met. First, we had Anita. He thought I looked like Anita Stewart. So that's where that came from. And little June. That broke us, I think. It'd break anybody. Jimmie had a friend, Sammy Williams, who got killed in France. And his mother died when he was a boy. But he said losing June, that was the worst. He'd say it was the only club he never wanted to belong to.

(Note: CR pauses here. She's been holding a tissue in her hands, tearing away tiny pieces. A grandfather clock chimes in the living room.)

EJC: You said in your biography of Jimmie . . .

CR: You read that?

EJC: . . . that someone asked Jimmie to write his life story. Do you know if he ever started it?

CR: I don't know. He'd say: "They're after me to write a book." But I don't know who that was. He got very serious about it. I told him he should write it before it was too late. He'd give you this look. Those dark brown eyes. They were the only serious thing about him. He had a briefcase with him all the time, I know. I assumed that's what was in it. Funny, I never once looked. Someone, I guess Ralph's office, sent a briefcase back after he passed. But I didn't recognize it. And it was empty.

EJC: I've heard rumor that Jimmie was going to leave Victor.

CR: (Shakes her head) For Columbia? That was never serious. Who told you that?

EJC: I spoke with . . .

CR: They wanted him to do a test on "Worried Man Blues." But I don't think he ever made a record of it. I don't know how that rumor started. If he did, I never heard it. I think he told Peer that so he would hurry up and advance him money for New York.

EJC: There's a song your sister wrote for Jimmie, "My Little Lady," that mentions someone named Haydee. Do you . . . ?

CR: . . . I don't think I've told anybody this. The day he died the strangest thing happened. You won't believe it, but this is God's honest truth. I was putting gas in the Packard. I don't know how we only wound up with that one out of all those cars. But the fellow at the station was busy with someone so I just got out and was fixin' to pump the gas myself. And the fellow runs out and says: "Oh Mrs. Rodgers, I'll take care of that. Just you wait 2 minutes." And I looked at the clock and this funny feeling came over me. Something in my head said remember what time it is. And it was, I dunno what it was, quarter after two. And I rode home in such a state you know. I found out later that's what time he died that night. At the Hotel Taft, room 1909. That's where we stayed the first time he brought me to New York. When we were living at my sister's in Washington.

EJC: He's buried in Meridian?

CR: The funeral was in Meridian. Mr. Peer took care

of it. He made a lot of money from Jimmie. He's still making money to this day.

EJC: But you didn't stay there?

CR: I came back to Texas. And all that time after, I felt him right next to me. Plain as you. I just had this feeling like he was with me. And that went on for a short while. 'Til one day I was driving somewheres. And for a split second I sort of forgot, you know. Forgot he was gone. I just thought about the errands I needed to accomplish. And then I remembered, and I felt so bad that I wasn't thinking about him. Just for that second. And right then—it's like I could hear his voice in the car. He said: "I'm gonna let you go now. You're gonna be all right." And then he wasn't there.

(PAUSE)

That's all I've got to say.

(END OF RECORDING)

BLUE YODEL Nº 1

SLEEP BABY SLEEP

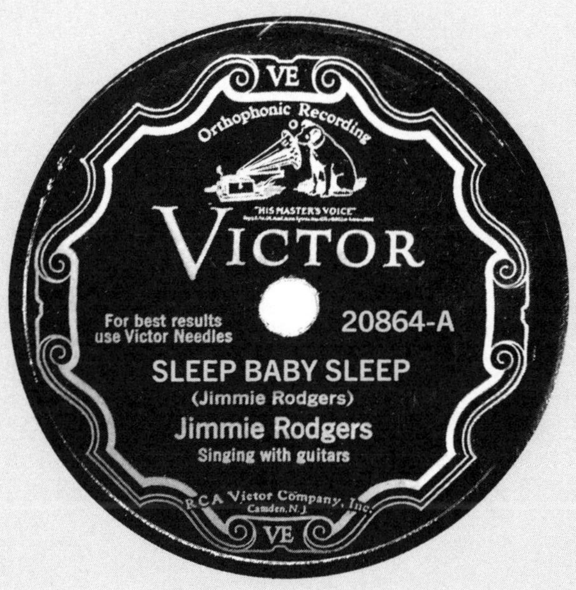

May three, 1933 heyy that rhymes!

Hi Little Boots,
Your Papa misses you. I'm just about to hop on a steamer to New York for some sessioning. By the time you get this from Granpaps and Gmaw's mailbox (tell Meridian I said hello), I'll be in Madhattan. I thought I'd better take a moment under a shady tree and peck you a little note on my trusty Remington.

Peck>peck>peck

I even took off my boots so I can air out my toes in the grass like you do.

Where have I been all these days? Well, I had to drive to Memphis to see an old friend off at the train station. While I was there, I had supper at the Arcade and had a big ole milkshake. Chocolate, of course. I told Mr. Zapatos you said hi.

Then I had to make a quick trip up to Tulsa to pick up a little something. On my way home I got up early early in the morning and went sightseeing. Drove all round that house I told you about, Villa Philbrook.

Remember that story? Last summer the owner Mr. Phillips paid me top dollar to yodel at his swank BBQ. Oil, oil, oil is all anyone talked about. Heaps of folks in pearls and furs herded together to watch a big hog turning over a fire. I was so busy shaking hands I hardly got to see the place.

The house is made of cold stone, not nice red brick like ours had. And there's a dome in the entry that goes way, way up. Doesn't feel much like a home. Feels more like a place you'd go to meet a judge. The driveway is all stone too. Can you imagine the poor fellows that had to lay those out end to end so the shades all matched? And then buff them smooth so baby Phillips won't get a blister?

All the house windows are tall with brass frames and brass hinges. Out back there's a go-forever garden laid out like a great big Thanksgiving table full of flowers every color of the rainbow. You can almost imagine you can see pumpkin pie and blueberry crumble. The hedges are frog green and fluffy like cake frosting.

Hey you! . . . you're on page 2

As pretty as it is, it don't look like a place a girl and her Pops would want to bounce a ball or play chase. If that garden could talk it would say: NO FROLICKING ALLOWED!

Mr. Phillips told me he built the joint for his wife Jen Jen (short for Genevieve, which we nearly named you). For a lady with such a pretty name, she's hard as old candy. I bet she's never cleaned a poopy bottom. No chickens in their yard. Not like yours.

I heard you asked Mama why we had to sell Yodeler's Paradise. Your Mom and I thought a big city like San Antonio might be a better place for us. I loved our old house and I know you did too. But it was far aways from town. And I've had to go to the doctors quite a bit lately. You'll like San Antonio. I sure do. It'z way easy there to pop on a train and go places. While I'm working this spring, we thought it'd be good for you to spend some time with your granfolks and make some new friends in Meridian.

Did you know that Mississippi is where I spent my summers when I was a kid your size? I played in those streams with the fishy fish and swimmy snakes. In summertime the air gets so thick you'd think you could just stuff it in a bucket and set it in the shade 'til it melts like ice cream. You'll have a heap of fun there. But your home will still be Texas.

Did I ever tell you the story of how we got to Texas? Your mama and I spent a little vacation here just the two of us and the air was so clear and the sky so blue it seemed like home.

So's we packed you up and drove you in the big black Packard so you could stretch out with your pillow and Raggedy Ann and daydream yourself into whatever house you saw along the road. That's what I used to do when I was little.

I'd hop a train and lean out the big door with my feet swinging and suck on honeysuckle trying like mad to get one of those little drops and think, "What would it be like to live there . . . or there?"

Keep reading page 3hree payge 3 . . . I mean it

Maybe—I thought—I'll take the house with the screened porch so I can eat a whole orange rhubarb pie and watch the ants and the flies and the bluebirds gather round and press their noses to the screen and say: "Oh! Look at James eating that pie! Give us some! Give us some!"

Nope, I'd say. No pie without a password!

And the BluJ'd say: "Who's got the password?"

"Not me," says the fly. "I'm just a fly."

And off they'd go back and forth while I'm in my rocking chair eating all that pie. Maybe I'd sing them a song too . . .

Hello birdies
  Hello fruity flies
 It's mighty kind of you all
To drop by and say hi
 But I know your love is not true
Why do I know oh why? Oh why?

It ain't me you love
All you want is my rhubarb pie.
 (add Yodel *here*) ///

Anywho, on my way home I played a little concert at a rail stop in Okemah. Met a short fella, a guitar picker with curly curly hair named Woodrow after Prez Woodrow Wilson I guess. I let him strum my Martin. He said: "I wasn't much of a fan of you Jimmie Rodgers but you're all right up close."

I promise I'll rest a lot when I get to New York. I'll be working with your Uncle Ralph. (He's not really your Uncle but he acts like it.) And I'll go Coney Islanding every day and take a nice nap by the ocean and eat a Nathan for you.

And just before I close my eyes, I'll think of you rolling around in the grass on your back, holdin' your toze and spinning yourself round and round like one of your Pops' records.

Last page is 4
keep reading more

Remember—if you ever get scared or feel sad like all you wanna do is sit in the dark and fold yourself up like a folding chair and invisible yourself, take a deep breath and step out in the sunshine and say hello to someone instead. Especially when I'm far away. That will always make you feel better. Maybe try to write a funny song too.

This letter is so long you should tell your mama you don't have to go to school today 'cause you learned all your lessons from your Pops.

Sweet dreams Little Boots. See you there.

Always your Pops

p.s. I drew you a map of Yodeler's Paradise so you won't forget it. Now draw me the second floor. Let's go back there someday.

Yodeler's Paradise

Kewanee Cyclops oil furnace in basement heat$ whole hou$e
Biscuit runway
Ouch stove!
Ice box
Kitchen
Knee skinn'n steps
Curvy red leather crumb catcher
4 Roses palace
Dining room Mom & Dad boxing ring
Dreaming window for the chickens
Screen porch
Texas fly & 'squito lounge
Piano Pops
Can't play
Fire place
Livin' room
RCA yodel box
Little Boots art gallery
Magnificent mirror
Expen$ive tile
Fancy book case
Potty room
C'mon in
Car port
Sneak-a-peek window
Covered alcove
Fancy entrance
Steps to paradise
Cadillac & bicycle driveway
Patio
Doll's playroom
Little Boot's dream place

1st Floor

S
E — R — W
N

BLUE YODEL No. 2

TEXAS BLUES

The way I see it, everybody's allowed one big break in life. One big idea. Sadly, most folks never know they got one coming. And even if they catch a good one, they usually let it go, just to see if it might come back. Here's why. Your average parent gnaws at their kids to be just like them, work a sorry job, live in the same sorry town, and marry someone like Mother and Daddy. One litter to the next.

Miserable.

So, when your big break flies at you fast in that comet of time just before you fall sleep or in that early morning minute when your eyes open and your head's clear and you catch your first good breath, that big idea meant for you has about as much chance of blooming as a rose in a railyard.

I still think about mine. Anytime I'm traveling—which I've been doing since I was near ten—I stop about a mile outside wherever I'm headed, find a place just like this, close my eyes, and call that feeling. See if it still remembers me. Out in this country, you don't have to go far for the horizon to open up all around you. The mountains'll haze out of the heat and in no time you're adrift in a sea of red dirt and little islands of Blackfoot daisies, bluebonnets, and red cedar. You can see your future coming at you kicking up dust miles away. And even though you know it's coming, you can't help watching it pull closer and closer 'til it's on you.

Out here I like to think the Great Turner of the Earth can find me. And when I pull over and get out my smoke bag and roll a stick, he'll say: "Well, dad-burned my hide. If Jimmie Rodgers is gonna take a rest, then so will I." Then he'll put his hands on that giant gear box, shift the world into neutrality, and step out of his engine room and into the same sun I'm staring into now. He'll wipe his neck, take a clean breath, and together, him on his plane and me on mine, we'll listen to the peaceful sound of Mother Earth as she drifts through space.

Wear your boots out here. Texas rattlers will chase you down like they're on roller skates. Iff'n they spot you and give you that look, you better haul off in the other direction. That's why I don't go too far off road. I don't need to fear for my life in any more ways than I already do. When we lived out in Kerrville, Little Boots—that's my daughter Anita—liked to roll around in the dirt. "Daddy!" she'd say, "I bet you have no idea who I am!"

"You got me, who are you?"

"I'm a jackrabbit that just rolled down the hill."

Scare me to death. That's why I keep a scrum of little dogs. My advance snake squad. The only other place that beats this country is Coney Island early in the morning. You can get a Boylan's and a Nathan as early as you like. And the windy ocean will whisper in your ear until you're ready to walk straight out into her arms, never to return. I dreamed one night I was alone on the boardwalk. I went to get a ticket for the picture show but I had to get my ticket from one of those fortune-telling machines. When I took my seat, everybody was made out of painted cardboard. And when the picture started, right up there on the screen was my grandma and grandpops leaving Ireland for America. Then the frame burned out and there was my mama, washing dishes in some café. Except she was young and happy. Just then my daddy appeared in the doorway, eating an apple. I stood and hollered at the screen: "Don't do it, Mother! Run!" But then the cardboard people picked me up out of my seat and threw me out onto the boardwalk. That's when I knew I needed a nurse.

If I ever saw Mama again, not that I believe in that sort of thing, I'd ask her if the wind used to talk to her like it talks to me. I'd like to know if she had a big break or a big idea. She used to say people like us have to smuggle our way through life. Keep our dreams to ourselves so they have time to grow. There's a lotta mean people sprinkled in with the good. They'll trip you just to see what you look like falling. She also said I'd only remember the bad days. The mean times. That's a hell of a thing to tell your kid. But that didn't turn out to be so, mostly.

Back to our subject. Now hear me out, George. (I call everybody

I like "George." So if you're gonna stick with me all the way, I'll call you "George.") Once you get your big break or your big idea, embrace that rascal. And if you don't get sick the day you meet it or bend down to tie your shoe and get clobbered by some housewife on a driving lesson, everything will all come together for you.

Now the last time the Missus and I spoke 'stead of hurling dishes, I told her someone asked me to write a book. I didn't say who of course. "Mother," I said, 'cause I made her a mother, "I don't think I'll be around long enough to scribe a whole book. You might have to finish it for me."

As usual when we spoke of serious things, she looked at the floor, patted her apron, and sat down on the edge of that $50 chair she made me buy with all the vines on it. Most uncomfortable thing you ever set your ass in. Then she'd say something like, "Well, I don't know, dear. There's just so much I don't know."

I'll say there is. God help us, George, if I don't finish this in time and it's up to her. What I'm saying is you can't ponder an opportunity too long. You gotta sniff it out like a bloodhound. And when you find it, bite it on the ass and hold on. That's why I'm writing this fast as I can. My clock is ticking. And now that I've started, all these memories are coming for me again. Sure as one pulls in, I see another come up over the hill.

I digress. We were talking about finding your big break. Say you're like me. You pick and sing and you're looking to get into show business. Now let's say you're walking down the street, minding your own pitter patter on your way to breakfast. You see a fellow dressed a little differently than you're used to seeing 'round these parts headed in your direction. So, you get curious.

Maybe you say to him something like: "Hey friend, can you spare a flint? Where you headed dressed so fine this morning?" And he answers that he manages a roadshow, perhaps the Follies. He's in town all week but his star attraction flew the coop. He's in a predicament.

You light your smoke, nod a bit, and act like you're pondering his question. Then you reply that it just so happens that you're an entertainer too. Why, I write my own songs, in fact. Yes sir, worked all over. From Portland, Maine, to sunny Tennessee. Audition? I'd love to. How about I come by tomorrow? Say, 2 p.m.? Where you settin' up? Sure, I know it. I used to pick with the gandy dancers down there.

It's that easy.

My aunt Dora, my mama's sister, always said water seeks its own level. If she ever found a man she loved as much as a book, that would be the happiest fellow in the world. She'd say, "Now, James (I know I'm in trouble if someone calls me 'James'), when you go into town, I want you to recite this poem and put it to song. That will help you learn to be creative all the time." Then she'd put a dollar in my shirt pocket with a little pat. She won't be doing that no more.

What I think she meant is you gotta be ready for your opportunity when it comes. Have a plan. Like that fellow Gavrilo Princip over in Austria. He was all set to shoot the Archduke but his pistol jammed. Got himself the anarchist's blues. So, he steps into a little shop to get a strudel and a coffee. And as he's walkin' out, who should be broken down smack in front of him but the Archduke's coal-black Gräf & Stift Double Phaeton.

Mrs. Archduke, she's in the backseat fussing. Mr. Archduke, he's trying to tame his wife. And the driver, he's got his head under the hood, pokin' around. Probably got on one of those gray caps with a black brim and lamb leather gloves. No doubt he's flooded the carburetor. Easy to do on a Double Phaeton. She's a stuck pig.

Gavrilo can't believe his luck. He drops his eats, takes out his pistol, aims, fires, boom! Goodnight Mr. & Mrs. Archduke. There goes all of Europe's hillbilly cousins too. Now if he was driving a Cadillac, maybe we wouldn't have had the Great War.

What I'm imparting here is that big breaks come good and bad. Usually, the right idea finds the right person. I'm sure my buddy Sam thought fighting in France was his big break. It was. Just the wrong kind. One man's trash is another's treasure. For every good-lookin' dove you meet, there's sure a man who's ready to let her go. Your girl might be loyal as a hound. But if she just tidy's up the same room all day long and can't tell Bessie Smith from Al Smith, tell me what kind of treasure is that?

I hear it all the time. "Jimmie, your wife sure is some kinda woman." I'll say. Every day I dream of the handsome son of a bitch that will take her off my hands. Then there's Haydee, who bedevils my mind night and day. Wrote a song for her in fact. "My Little Lady." You'll meet her later. No ass to speak of, a little brown belly she fills up with beer, a red frock of hair like a match, and a mouth that goes on and on like a sick ticker tape. But she does she make me laugh. If I knew I could spend the last day of my life with us holding hands, looking out at the water and laughing at that ole frog joke, I'd never take a drink or fire up a pick-a-tune again. I should probably quit anyway, considering. But no one likes a quitter. The show must go on. Turn those lights out, you'll never find the breaker again.

Aunt Dora loved to read me poetry when I was a kid. Seems like most of her favorite poets got their big breaks young. And once they did, they had only two, maybe three years left 'til they fell over dead. Or gave up poetry all together to sell guns or something profitable. Look it up. Our school master, Ms. Pearl Pope, was a border at Dora's house when my older brother Tal and I lived there. We'd all read poems every night after supper. (Poe was my favorite.) In fact, Ms. Pearl's the first women I ever saw naked. ("Well kid, you caught me. You might as well take a good long look at everything.") She was unshy and lit fire to my first creations. Which Tal found so inspiring he went and married her. He always was a sucker.

Back to our subject. I went hunting down my big break early, so I know of what I speak. The first time I left home, I absconded with Ms. Pearl's bedsheets, sewed myself a big top, got a bucket of house paint, and Rembrandted big letters in red: Jimmie Rodgers Presents! Then I hitchhiked to Jackson to join a medicine show. Can you imagine? All I could sing was "The Daring Young Men and the Flying Trapeze." Sang the hell out of it though on a 2-string ukulele. Pops found me. Dragged me home. Tried again at 14. And 16. Married. Let her go. Met Carrie. Married her. Made two critters. Lost one.

I've had a bed roll on my back longer than I've slept on one, all the time carrying around a song in my head I've got no words to. I'm on this Earth to do something. What? Why? That's why I went looking for it. If I had stayed in Mississippi, I wouldn't be talking to you now. Never yet met a Mississippian who can think of anything 'cept getting out of Mississippi.

My big break came watching a flicker of all things. Any other time I might have walked right past it. But that day if you were in my skin, by God, you couldn't have missed it. I was working under canvas with a group of strummers who called themselves—get this—the Southern Hawaiians. It was a hard sledding medicine show. Not Silas Green, unfortunately. A little more like a people circus. One night only! Pay 50 cents to watch a man eat fire. See the midget beat the strongman. Professor LeStrange and his 60-foot balloon plus the contortionist Zanfretta sisters. You know the type. The customers were all the same. Some fella in a mustache and a big belly and a starched shirt rolled up at the elbows would come bullin' through the crowd to hammer the bell. "Make way, make way! Watch this, darlin'!" He'd spit on his palms and imagine he was swingin' at the head of his mother-in-law. Then with gusto he'd bring that ole hammer down with all his might. And that knocker would barely rise a foot. Thanks for the dollar, fella. Don't con a carnie.

In our show we had us a little band. Couple fellas, couple gals. We was Hawaiian as chess pie. But we had one actual Hawaiian in the band, Johnny Kekuku. From Oahu. Oh-Wahoo is how you say it. He played slide guitar on his lap and a bugle to open the show. His brother Joseph hit the big time. Johnny not so much.

Picture time. That's Delphine holding the tambourine. Miss Boot Strap from Biloxi. The kind of gal who's been intimate just twice in her life. Once with the army and once with the navy. And that's Harv, next to her on the shit banjo. The sort of fellow who would cry over a nickel and die over a dime if you ever asked him for anything. Harv never drank anything harder than NuGrape. I'm in the middle with the little guitar. Next to me is Sadie, our exotic dancer, and her man Oompie. I'm pretty sure she planted a tomahawk in him. Shame, too. He kept good time. And Johnny, our band leader, is on slide guitar. Though it looks here like I'm the band leader and I sort of was.

Kekuku. Poor fellow, he spent most of his time trying to teach us fools how to play Hawaiian. I learned quite a bit from him, actually. Him and Frank Stokes in Memphis. You'll meet him later. Anyway, we'd go on stage and flail about, tell jokes, sing tired old stuff like "Why Do You Treat Me Like You Do, Do, Do." We could hardly play a lick. Kekuku held up the whole show on his own practically. That's when I first started stepping out a bit, just to fill the time. I even got some encores. And 'bout drove him over the edge.

"Jimmie!" he'd say. "You're the sorriest guitar man in the wide world."

I'd holler back at him. "Kekuku, one day I'm gonna make so much cabbage singin' and pickin' that I'll send you back to Hawaii on a first-class ticket with a hula girl on each arm and one to sit on your face to keep your lip wet." And now he's in Hawaii. With three hula girls. You see, I gave him his big break.

Anywho, one night we got chased out of Peru, Indiana, by a freak rainstorm. Flooded us out with four inches in 'bout an hour. So we hauled off and made our way down to Ohio. That's when I set up a mailbox at the Billboard office. People can't find you if they don't have your address.

We get to Akron and set up the big tent for our next show. We hammer in the last pole, and then sure enough, boom! The crack of thunder. It starts rainin' marbles. We all race under the tent. The wind winds up. The center pole is swaying back and forth like it's God's straw. Like he's gonna suck us all up in a big breath. People are cussin' and weepin'. The Strong Man. The Fat Lady. There's nothing sorrier than a sad sack of cry-baby entertainers.

Somehow in the middle of all this racket a salesman, Silverman was his name, he comes out of nowhere, wet as a rat, and says he wants to show us his new invention. Talking pictures! Now we're the suckers, right? So we assemble folding chairs and buckets and take our seats. Silverman, he sets up a crank up motion picture projector and a portable Victrola. Gather round, gather round, he says. See the sights of the world! Well, I couldn't care less. I'd been up all night. My chest hurts. I'm wheezin'. It's humid as all get-out. But this man was not to be deterred. First, he puts up a bed-sheet for a screen. And then he starts unfolding this crazy scaffold of rubber bands and gears and what-nots. They all connect together so when he cranks the camera it turns the gramophone at the same time to run along like a side car. The film starts up and wouldn't you know it, up there on the screen are three bona fide Hawaiian guitar men.

On one side there's a fella playing like Kekuku does with a slide on his lap. And the fellow on the other side is playing a ukulele. You can tell they're good just by the way they sit.

Here's what got me. The one in the middle is playing a little guitar, just like I was holding in the picture. He starts off standing with one foot on a chair. Then right in the middle of the number, all casual like, he sits down and puts one leg crossed over the other. Not a care in the world. Just pickin' away. White suit. White shoes. Striped socks. White skipper. Black tie and a lei around his neck. He looks sharp. All the while he's playing with a motion like a side rod on a driving wheel. His pickin' hand comes down near the bridge, where the strings go in the body, throwin' hard on those low strings. Then he flicks the lighter strings, strumming where the neck meets the body. That's a softer sound. His pickin' motion's like a main rod on a steam engine. Ding. Flang. Ding. Flang.

Now just for a moment, the moving picture and the music run together perfect. And right then—I kid you not—this fellow playing the guitar with one leg over the other in his sharp suit playing that fine rhythm looks right at me and smiles. And I get a feeling inside me like there's a spotlight in my chest beaming out all over the tent. All over the world. Meanwhile all around me, it's hell's revival. The storm is on top of us now. People are splittin' their britches. No one's really listening or watching. But I am. I get the message. In the middle of all this chaos I keep my eyes on that guitar player. I can still see him now. He plays in my head over and over.

The next night we're in Lexington. There's another music act on the bill. I see this brown-skinned fellow with a wool hat, white shirt, and suspenders, playing a fine little box with a slotted headstock. And wouldn't you know it, he's playing that same rhythm. But not so fast. Relaxed, like when you're lookin' at a big oak where the top branches are tossing the breeze back and forth like a couple kids baseballin'. He's singing about a Nehi Mama. I introduce myself and he says his name is Frank Stokes. We get along fast, I tell you.

After sitting with Frank a bit and scoring a friendship, he lets me try out his guitar. Up to this point I had never played a good instrument. His was made by Martin. It was no wonder I wasn't getting nowhere with the matchbox I had. Frank shows me a few runs and says: "Man, you need to work on your English. This hand here guides your cue. This one does the driving." Frank and I sang into the night and when we bugged out, he had left me a banquet of lessons I'm still feasting on today. After that, I was 100 per-sure what I was gonna do next.

The following night we play Louisville. I get a ride downtown and find my way to the Louisville Music and Radio Company. "How much for that little Martin? Oh yes sir, I live right off Market Street. Payments? Sure, I can make payments. Make the first one now if you like." I put two bits down on a $30 Martin. Head back to the troupe. Next day, goodbye Louisville. Now I'm a full-grown guitar player. I liked

Frank's getup, too. Nice suit. Gentleman's hat. An all-around entertainer for everybody.

Let's get something straight before we go any further. I do not play hillbilly. Call me a Music Man. Singing Brakeman. Blue Yodeler. All fine. Just not a hillbilly. I could go all my life—which might only take you to about Tuesday—and never hear a hillbilly fiddle again. What's the difference between a fiddle and a violin? You don't spill hootch on a violin. If you've heard that already, you're sorry I bothered. If you haven't, now you think I'm funny as hell. You're both right.

I'll tell you another story. About two years ago, shortly after I hit the big time, I was holding court at this little record shop in San Antonio. I had just played a matinee downtown to open the Majestic Theater. Seventy-five cents a head. Three thousand seats. Sold the fucker out. Standing room only.

The night before I played the San Antonio Rotary Club. 200 clams for one song. Can you believe it? I tried to tell 'em: No sir, I do not have time. But the Rotary man insisted. Then they liked me so much they voted me in. So, I added "Frankie and Johnny" for good fellowship. The next day I did the same thing for the Texas Rangers 'cept they got "In the Jailhouse Now." And they gave me a badge and a couple pearl handle pistols. Know your audience.

Anyway, San Antonio. I'm backstage at the Majestic watching a bit of comedy before I go on. The manager of the house comes up and wouldn't you know it, it's old man Silverman, the same fellow from Ohio with the cranky movie machine. "Jimmie," he says, "so good to see you. So-and-so wants you to go come down to his record shop and meet and greet the people after the show. You know, sign some autographs."

I said I'd love to. I bought some records with me, in fact. I'll take a percentage of the sales for my trouble. He said that'd be fine. I go on stage. They get me a nice wire-back chair to put my boot on. I give 'em "Waiting for a Train," "Blue Yodel," and, being in San Antone, I finish with "Texas Blues," which I hope won't be a prophecy. At the end of the show, I make a little speech. "Now folks, if you can spare a few minutes, come down to so-and-so's record shop and say hello. They got all my records. See you there."

I yodel and flip over my new custom Martin so they can see my message to humanity right there in nice big yellow letters.

THANKS

Well, don't you know it, the whole theater follows me there. The owner of the joint, a rotund little fellow with a suit that's too small and a vest that's too tight, he's quite agitated to see this big crowd. He's climbs up on the counter, all the while moving his arms up and down. His vest is riding up his shirt and his pants are droopin'. Toupee's all crooked. "Relax, people. Jimmie will sign everything. Give the man some room to breathe. We got plenty of records for everybody."

Being in Texas, naturally I'm wearin' my 10 gallon Stetson lid. That thing is like a beacon. Wherever the hat goes, the people follow. So, I go stand on a Dr Pepper box next to the owner, who's way high on the counter now with his legs splayed to the edge so his boot heels don't go through the glass top. Everybody's hollerin'. Callin' out songs. You never heard such a fracas. And the yodeling! Terrible! Finally, the proprietor hushes everybody down and says: "Let's give Jimmie a chance to say hello to y'all."

And right on cue I holler "T for Texas! T for Tennessee!" and let out a long yodel. The place gets quiet for a second and then goes all native again. You never heard such business. Meanwhile, I see this other fellow called Ford who's the local rep for RCA Victor, the company that puts out my records. He's way in the back trying to make his way through the crowd. He's been shadowing me since I got to town. Ford's all right. We've done a heap of business all over Texas thanks to him. Back in Abilene he started putting ads in the paper whenever I came town. "Shake hands with Jimmie Rodgers at our store Monday morning from so-and-so to such-and-such. Jimmie will personally autograph any of his Victor Records purchased from us at this time. You've heard his records. Now see him in person."

I sure have appreciated his efforts. Anyway, he's fightin' like a lion goin' north in a herd headed west and can't get to us. My first thought is that he's looking for his wife Louise. I happen to know Louise is running late. Mr. Ford ought to spend more time at home. Finally, he gets up to us. But he doesn't inquire about Louise, thank God. Instead, he wants to introduce me to a reporter from the *Dallas Morning News.* Exclusive interview? Tell 'em I'd be glad to. Let's we step out back. I need something to eat.

So, this reporter's in a tweed jacket and a tweed hat and sporting a rat's ass mustache. We go out back where a Mexican kid is selling tamales from a wagon, 20 cents a dozen. I get a dozen and I ask for some hot sauce and a lemon and a bottle of soda. Me and this reporter sit down to one of those round tables that's got a metal rim around it and glass in the middle. Somebody fetches me some ice. I take a sip and give my bottle a little drink from my flask. Man, oh man. I'm so hungry I can almost taste it.

Well, I proceed to deshuck those babies and right off the bat, this writer fella says his editor sent him to find out why a hillbilly singer is causing all this fuss in the middle of the day. Now, granted I was out of sorts. The sun was blazin'. And I had been very busy since I pulled in. I had spent all night tending to Louise, then the Rotary, then the Rangers, had a late breakfast with my producer Ralph Peer about our upcoming recording session in Dallas, and then played the Majestic. I still got another show to do that night. I'm short of breath as it is. And now there's a damn riot inside. I might run out of records.

But all I want at this very minute are these beautiful, lonely tamales. I couldn't think straight is what I'm trying to say. And here's this writer pestering me about my own biograph. Telling me about how I came down from the mountain and got my big break. Which is partly true. But I know he's just reciting the same bag of cats I've been selling everybody else. For some reason at that moment all of this nonsense just got to me. That's when I cut him off in mid-bite.

"New Jersey . . ."

"Come again?" the reporter says.

I wiped the corn crumbs off my lip. "I cut 'Blue Yodel' in Camden, New Jersey." I actually cut my first record in Bristol, truth be told. That was probably my big break. But the bigger break was talkin' my way into Victor's studios in Camden. That's where I made "Blue Yodel—T for Texas" which went national. And

I never looked back. Anyway, all I could think about was getting this son of a bitch to stop talking to me so I could eat my lunch. About then someone reaches over my shoulder with a record. "Sign it on the sleeve, Jimmie!" I'm not sure what happened next, whether I smashed the damn thing or it broke in the poor boy's hand. But the next thing I know I'm pointing a jagged-ass clay record in this smart aleck's face. ("Away Out on the Mountain" if you must know. That's irony.) Maybe I threatened this newsman. I don't recall exactly. At the time I thought it was all a bit funny. But then I realized this was having a calming effect on the situation. Everything got real quiet. You could hear a caterpillar fartin' on cotton.

First rule of gambling, you can't beat the house. And at that moment, I was the house. I'll tell you a story. One time in New Orleans I lost 'bout enough to buy a nice little cottage in Meridian, my hometown. But I figured everyone at the table was in on it. The dealer, who went by Jack Sheehan but his real name was Boasberg, was notaried for that sort of thing. So, I gave him an IOU to the Bank of Kerrville. "Sorry fellows, I'm light. Call my banker." Trouble for him was, there is no Bank of Kerrville. Come to find later Ole Jack was not amused. He was furious. Still is. He even tried to shake down Ralph for it, but Ralphie told me, "Fuck 'em. Just stay out of Louisiana." The lesson is: when you got a hand, play it.

So, there I was with the upper hand and my ace was this broken record. I did look rather mean I suppose. "Now what was it you wanted to ask me?" I asked very calm and quiet. This reporter kid went sheet white. It's probably the most hillbilly thing I've ever done, frankly. Just then ole Ralph walks up. More like runs if you want to know the truth. You ever hear that calliope record he made of Fats Waller? My goodness I wore that out.

"Now, son," I says. "Have you met my producer? This is Mr. Ralph Peer. From RCA Victor. Ralph, this fellow . . . uh . . . I never got your name. Harlan, is it?"

Harlan just gulps and nods.

"How do you do, Harlan," says Ralph, and shakes the kid's hand.

I gather up my lunch and excuse myself. "I better go tend to these folks in the record shop before there's a riot. Maybe Ralph can answer a few of your questions, Harlan. This is for the *Morning News*, is that right?" I put my hand lightly on Ralph's shoulder for emphasis. "Now Ralph, Harlan's editor at the *Morning News* wants to know all about the big hillbilly singer that just hit town."

All I had to say was "hillbilly" and Ralph understood the situation. Ralph didn't like "hillbilly" any more than I did. He wanted to go Pop about as much as I wanted them tamales. I give the Mexican fellow 5 bucks 'cause he's gotta clean up my mess. I autographed another record to make up for the one I broke. Sorry fella. Never skip lunch. And Ralph goes on to give Harlan his exclusive. "Oh yes," he says, "I discovered Jimmie playing live over WDAA in North Carolina." Lie. "Jimmie's about to sign a motion picture contract with Hal Roach, you know, Laurel & Hardy." Bigger lie.

Good ole Harlan. You never saw a man pencil so fast. He'll be telling that story all his life. I can see the headline now. BLUE YODELER ATTACKS REPORTER. TEXAS RANGERS ESCORT FAMED SINGER TO CITY LINE. When I got to Dallas, Fred, my voice Victographer, hands me the *Morning News*. "Jimmie, look! You made the front page." And you know what? That little shit called Ralph Peer a hillbilly talent scout. I guess that was Harlan's big break.

Around then was when I first saw him. A dark-complexioned man in a pinstripe suit and a fierce guitar picker set up on the corner outside my hotel. Red shoes. Sharp crown. Pickin' "Waiting for a Train" with a funny chord that made his box sound like a harp. I've seen him many times since. But seems like somebody always interrupts me before I can get close. No matter where I am, within a day he's there. Playing right outside my window. All last winter I was in an oxygen tent at Methodist hospital in Houston. And he was there too. I couldn't hear nuthin' else around me but his high wailin' sound, singing me my own song like it was coming from outer space. Or deep from the furnace of the Earth.

BLUE YODEL No. 3

MISSISSIPPI DELTA BLUES

<u>Transcription Note</u>

H. C. Speir, Summer 1959.

H. C. Speir has lived in Jackson, Mississippi, for most of his life. His home is just a few minutes' drive from downtown. It's a clean neighborhood with rows of two-room brick houses all about 20 years old. Nothing much happens here. The streets are wide and shaded on each side by birch and maple trees planted when the homes were built. The sidewalks bear the mark of the W.P.A. There are no second floors. Speir's mailbox is unpainted. The red flag seldom goes up. A pink aluminum awning hangs over his front room window. And on the slightly lilting brick ledge just below the window, a white planter overflowing with purple and yellow flowers is leaking. The blinds are drawn.

If you visit, you'll likely park behind his new Glade Green De Soto. The driveway next to the house is on an incline (the house is on a slight hill) and is just two strips of concrete with tended grass up the middle that turns to small brown stones as it levels off. I'm careful not to park too close to his fender.

At the top of the driveway just to the right, Speir's yard opens up to a half-acre garden. It's not quite tomato season but he's expecting them. The day is already bright and hot. I have to shade my eyes with my hand to see it all. In the far-left corner, a bundle of tall sunflowers grow wild in all directions. I want to tell him that the disc florets remind me of Victrola loudspeakers, but I'm afraid he might think me eccentric.

In the other corner of the yard is an apricot tree, still blooming thanks to the humid weather. In its shade is a foot-tall stone figure with a bow and arrow beside a stone bench for two. His backyard faces the playground of an elementary school. It is a pretty and welcoming spot. Neat, but not overly tidy. Everyone on this street (I cruised up and down before finding his number) has the same white picket fence. Speir's is a little taller than most.

He was not a hard man to find. We spoke by phone first and he was most cordial. When I got to Jackson, I found lots of folks who remembered his music store on North Farish Street.

In the library I also found articles about Speir in the *Jackson Daily News* archives. Ads with his photo announcing sales and store anniversaries, an appearance by Jimmie Rodgers in 1929, and for the store's closing just before the start of the war. After the music store, Speir tried selling furniture. But when a fire took all his inventory and the old leatherbound book in which he had written the addresses of local musicians and customers, he gave up retail for gardening.

As a young man Speir was a blues talent scout, a job he held while running his music store. (I never have found what H. C. stands for.) I've been told every working musician in the Delta came by Speir's to hear the sound of their own voice coming back at them from his recording machine. Some also came to play the guitars he had for sale or buy a set of Black Diamond strings. Speir's was a community meeting place.

Speir liked his customers. He liked the music they liked. He thought more people should hear it. Many of the records his customers came to listen to (and buy if they could afford to) were made by artists who got their first break in Speir's shop.

Upstairs, Speir kept a rehearsal room along with a primitive portable recording machine and a microphone (he thinks it was made by General Electric). If you could play, Speir wanted to hear you. If he thought you might have something, Speir would recommend you to any number of labels that relied on his ear and paid him a modest stipend to keep that ear open. Labels that sold race records like Okeh, RCA Victor, Paramount, and Columbia. Sometimes Speir would tell an aspiring singer to keep working at it. Come back when you're ready. That gave the musician something to think about. Before you can be taken seriously you must take yourself seriously. Be original. Be different. In all his handshake dealings, Speir had a reputation for fairness. He didn't become rich from his efforts, nor did the artists. They made a little if he made a little.

Most of the record men Speir worked for did become wealthy or at least comfortable. They relied on Speir to show them what to listen for. How to place the musicians in the room so the recorded sound was a not just a reflection of the performance but an idealized one. A few of those record men grew to enjoy and even respect the music. For others it was a job. One slide guitar was as good as another. Seen one, seen 'em all. Speir was their interpreter, a guide to a world that must have seemed to them to be the very bottom of the show business ladder. But a rung is a rung. And all climbs have a bottom rung. H. C. Speir loved the job he invented for himself.

H. C. Speir is a white man. Shortish and now slope shouldered. He takes small steps coming off his porch to greet me. His free hand hovers over an unpainted railing. His head is not quite round. His glasses are thick, bookish, black. Black suspenders hold up dark cotton shorts. His unbuttoned white shirt is wide at the collar. He wears brown calf socks and leather slippers. He smells of Ivory soap. He is bald with cotton like whips of hair around his ears. They make me think of how weeds might grow around a concrete sculpture left in nature. He smiles easily but does not look into my eyes for long.

A photo of Speir from long ago is a contrast to this man who now seems over 60. In the older photo—probably taken in the late 1920s or early '30s—the young man Speir stands in a fine suit with a long coat and velvet collar. There is a button on his lapel. His hands are at his sides, angled out from his body, looking like he might click his heels, spin like a dervish, and take off into the air.

That young man has a pleased, devilish smile. He looks of having just done something in the middle of the day a gentleman of Jackson, Mississippi, doesn't do. Or at least knows better than to have made a photographic record of the event. He is about to laugh or has just told a joke. There are unidentifiable shadows to his left. Behind him is a weeping willow or perhaps kudzu. Maybe he is picnicking with a guest. The photo has not been planned. He is smaller and lighter in stature than today, but his posture is formal, a habit of his stint in the Navy. Back then, his high forehead supported a hive of bushy dark hair and a face of contentment, a man who is his own door in and door out. Today, what remains of that grin is in shadow. An echo of light, perhaps only visible to me since I own this photograph. I know who took it. Up close his eyes are greenish gray and watery. But the grin is not present. The store is closed.

Speir is intelligent. He has the smooth face of a card player. When we get to talking inside after a short tour of his garden ("these moles . . . I block 'em out and they just pop out somewhere else") he will recall the store in great detail. As he does, his face will exhale as if sleeping. All the small muscles around his eyes and cheeks and chin will break from their labor of pulling and stretching as he goes into a trance of memory. He'll tap his fingers on his dining room table, pausing between sentences. He will take deep breaths. He will fold his arms when he thinks I might have misunderstood him.

When he speaks of his place on Farish Street, he is there, arriving at his front door early in the morning. Maybe his door key, attached to a gold chain looped into a buttonhole of his vest, gets stuck in the lock and for a moment he is tethered to his own front door. When he enters, a bell rings, a gift from a niece who is also his assistant. She is there, too, on time, and eager to impress him. As he talks, I am there as well. I can feel the thick red Persian rug that spreads out through the narrow main room of the store. I feel the breeze of the whirring fan on the tin ceiling. The place smells of clay and the sweet stink bug burn that hot vacuum tubes make. I ask Speir to think of me as an early morning customer. What would I see?

His first task every morning would be to go behind the counter, open the National cash register, and put the day's dollars and cents into the tray. Then he might lift the wooden drawbridge built into the counter and step to his studio to turn on the amplifier that powered his Speak-O-Phone recording machine, or perhaps it's a newer machine offered him by Ralph Peer of RCA Victor. On the way he passes audition rooms where customers can listen in private to the records he sells. Each room has a large window that looks out into the store. And inside each room is a phonograph machine and sitting chairs.

Housewives and domestic workers were often his first customers in the morning and his last at night. Speir would sometimes stay open late for them since so many working women didn't come home until after evening supper was finished and cleaned up in the white homes they worked for. The room where the recordings were made is not quite square, he explains. A heavy rug covers most of the studio to cut down on reflections and foot stomping by the musicians. The walls, he tells me, are lined with heavy floor-to-ceiling curtains. I would like to think they were the color of purple olives. He would open or close them depending on what might provide the best sound in the room. Open curtains provide a little more of a "live" sound. Close them all the way and the room becomes impervious to the outside world. The recording contraption is in the far-left on an oak table.

As he speaks of his recording machine, Speir points out the mechanisms and their peculiar sensitivity to certain frequencies. Low sounds might make the needle jump. Loud singers might overwhelm instrumentation. To accommodate the limitations of the machine he would move the square microphone, attached permanently to a metal stand, to different positions for each song depending on the volume of the performers, their abilities, and instrumentation.

Imagine, he says, two musicians have come to make a record. They listen and take his directions haltingly at first. They are shy, not sure what they've got themselves into. Sit, Speir says. Relax. As they do, Speir will suggest they slightly change the direction of their chairs to better orient themselves to the microphone. As they practice, he listens. Talking to me over his shoulder from then to now, he observes the arc of their voices. Where they go soft and where they get loud. Most who come to Speir have never recorded. So, he teaches them the art of performing for a microphone.

Today, Speir is an organic farmer. He has not recorded the blues in almost 20 years. When he heard my car pull up, he stood watching me from his back porch for a long minute, his palm on the screen as I got out of my red Skylark and walked along his car. I had to steady myself with a light hand on the De Soto as I made my way between his car and an uneven patch of gravel, all the while trying not to muss his very nice rose bushes. He did not frown on me for touching his car and I was grateful. As Speir stepped out, he held back his porch door from slamming and walked to his garden, one hand holding a pair of pruning shears. I followed. His voice makes me think of tires rolling slowly over gravel. The beginning of our conversation I recall from memory, before I turned on my recorder in the house.

EJC: Good morning. I'm sorry to interrupt your day in the garden.

H. C. Speir: That's quite all right. I picked you some flowers from over here.

EJC: Thank you.

HCS: I have to get these carrots up before all the rabbits abscond with them. (He talks as he picks, kneeling into the dry dirt.)

EJC: I was told you're an organic farmer.

HCS: Yes. That's right.

EJC: What is that exactly?

HCS: I stay away from insecticides. Just dirt and water and minerals. Phosphate rock. Ground limestone. (He talks and digs.) A fellow up the road does that for me. Bone meal. Soybean meal. Manure.

EJC: How long have you been doing this?

HCS: Oh, I guess maybe ten years now.

EJC: What do you grow?

HCS: Everything! Rutabaga. Kale. Chinese cabbage. Collards. You should stay for dinner.

Sitting in his dining room, I start my recorder. By the furniture and settings, I sense a female presence, but it also feels like she is no longer there.

EJC: Do you feel there's a connection between your love for gardening and your love for music?

HCS: I suppose there is. Music speaks to you just as the weather speaks to you. You can ask it questions. It will answer. I felt the same way about the artists I met. You can tell by listening what it is they're looking for. What you must look for. I pretty well knew how to do that. I wasn't the best. Pretty good.

EJC: You had a music store.

HCS: That's right.

EJC: On Farish Street. Right here in Jackson.

HCS: That's correct. I opened on Farish in 1925. Back then it was a hub, you understand. Lots of businesses. Traffic. Churches. Stores. Hotels. That sort of thing.

EJC: A Black business district.

HCS: That's right.

EJC: And why there?

HCS: I liked the music. And I thought I had a thumb for it. I went into the Navy out of high school. After that I was in New Orleans, working in a Victrola plant. Putting together the motors. I thought then I might open a music store and I wanted to be able to refurbish what I sold. They didn't have many salesmen that could repair them, you see. Columbia made Gramophones and the Victor label made Victrolas. Most of my customers couldn't afford electric models. The turn models went for, oh, $9.95 up to $15.

EJC: You were drawn to recording blues singers. It seems like you had a reputation for treating them as individuals.

HCS: I like to think so. I had a reputation for not crossing people. I tried to help the singers see it through. I gave them a good environment. It's a lot like gardening. I tried to find a place where their voice and their guitar and the music fused together. That's all. It was a study in human nature. Musicians are funny people.

EJC: Oh, I know.

HCS: You got introverts and extroverts. When you had a good artist there was nothing better. Some people, like Charley Patton, they just were so composed as performers. They took to the microphone like it was a collective of people. They could see through it to the other side. I didn't have the headphones that you have today. But I could listen as it was being cut and I got to where I could tell—if they went somewhere and made a master from what I made—how it might sound. Sometimes a chill would go right through me. The first machine I had was a Speak-O-Phone. Not a great sound but in some ways it did what was called for.

EJC: What was your day like there?

HCS: I'd arrive around eight. My niece would help me out. She might take over for me late in the morning. I had a friend who worked at a luggage shop across the street. And I might go there and talk. Later on, I might drive to a small town nearby and look for talent. When I started sending artists to labels, I went out looking for people sometimes. And we'd stay open until 10:00, 10:30 at night. A lot of my customers were maids, house workers. And they wouldn't get off work until maybe 6 or 7 o'clock at night. Nighttime was the only time they could shop.

EJC: What did they buy?

HCS: Blues, mostly. Many of my record customers were ladies. During the summer months we might sell hundreds of records in a day.

EJC: Musicians came too.

HCS: Musicians would come in as well. Sure. And then some of the companies like Columbia and Okeh might send someone to the store to talk about what was doing well.

EJC: What did you sell there, besides records?

HCS: Radios. Some violins. Ukuleles. Guitars. Black Diamond strings were pretty good. Stellas were a good guitar for blues. Hardly ever saw Gibsons. Martins recorded fairly good. Epiphones too. But Stella was the best of all of 'em. They had three sizes. The concert size I saw quite a bit. And the jumbo. Stellas gave you a kind of natural resonance. A reflection. Which was perfect for the singers I saw. You see a Martin or a Gibson, they were fine guitars but they wouldn't cut through to the microphone I had. Their tone was small. It wouldn't get out of the box like a Stella. I had to be careful. The diaphragm in the microphone, that's what hears the sound, was very sensitive. Sometimes if the singer was hollerin', I'd have to keep the mic maybe ten, twelve inches away and angle it just so it would catch everything and not be overwhelmed. And if you were some place recording to wax instead of metal—say I got hired to go to Memphis or some other place to manage a session—you had to be aware there too. If the temperature changed too much, you'd have all sorts of trouble if the wax was compromised. You'd lose the full sound. If the wax was exposed to a little bit of heat, it wouldn't sound true. Like two kids talking through a tin can and a string. (Laughs) The groove that needle cuts is so slender. A label like Paramount, they didn't handle their wax plates properly. If the heat comes in on that groove every record you press will be faulty.

EJC: So, you paid careful attention to the sound of what you were putting to record.

HCS: Well, you had to. Say you were recording some fellows singing to a washboard and an accordion. Now from my point of view, I could tell by the way they were sitting and the way they would be in proximity to the microphone if one player might dominate another. So, I'd move one back or forward until they were in a kind of mutual harmony together. Maybe they like to huddle close. That would be all right if they were performing on a porch somewhere. But in a recording, you wouldn't be able to appreciate the individual instruments all that well. So, I'd move them around. I knew when to turn the dial back when it come to a high sound or lean in for a quiet sound.

After they might rehearse a few times, I'd memorize any of those parts that might give me trouble. I'd stay out of their way. But I might reach for the dial and smooth the sound out at times. Otherwise, your needle wouldn't track.

EJC: Did people come and audition for you?

HCS: Sometimes. And I traveled some. There were various places where I might hear about artists. And occasionally I'd work for those companies. RCA Victor and what have you. They might send me to Memphis or Atlanta to listen to the talent.

EJC: Did you have a favorite?

HCS: Well, I don't know. There are some I remember more than others. For character. Tommy Johnson made good records.

EJC: And Charley Patton.

HCS: Patton was very good.

EJC: But you'd listen to anyone.

HCS: Sure.

EJC: And as I understand you never managed any of the artists you recorded. You wouldn't try to buy their songs.

HCS: No. No, I wouldn't. Some did. Put it this way. If a man came to me anxious to make a record because he's heard his pals made one, he's not concerned if you're dishonest or not. He wants to go all the way. And he wants you to take him there. But I never did that. I knew all those fellows at other companies. Some did pull shenanigans. A lot of 'em enjoyed the music. They enjoyed the blues but had no ear for it. They might try to pass me on talent. But then they'd come back for my help, you see. Because they didn't understand the music. Sometimes the artist might come back to me and say, well Mr. Speir, you do a better job recording me. The other fellow might try to buy them. Buy their songs. But I never did. I tried to put them at ease so they could perform freely. In character.

EJC: Did the performers drink at sessions?

HCS: Oh yes. The people I handled didn't mind a little drink. It would remove the fear of being there. It helped their emotional feeling. It was what you'd call a stimulant. It lifted them. A lot of singers, most of 'em got into drink. Dope. If they couldn't afford moonshine, they'd find something else. Sterno or antiseptic. If they went too far and the performance fell apart, well (laughs) we'd just wait 'til the next day. It didn't bother me. (Long silence)

HCS: Patton was a natural performer. You know his records?

EJC: I do. I enjoy the Mississippi Sheiks, too. Did you know them?

HCS: I did (rubs the back of his neck). They were very fine. They sold well in this part of the country.

Patton came in quite a bit. He was from around here I think but he moved south of Memphis. With his wife. But he was always an enjoyable person to spend time with. He knew everybody. They were his family, the Chatmons. His family. You know them?

EJC: I do.

HCS: I thought you might.

EJC: I heard a story that you bailed Patton out of jail once.

HCS: (Folds arms, nods, and looks at the floor in silence. Scratches his ear.) Mmm. Well, he wrote me a letter, you see. He and his wife at the time, Bertha, they went to a party. And at this particular party something happened. A woman killed a man. Someone came in while they were performing and the woman just cut a man down with an axe. Right down the middle. Patton said he kept playing. He was too afraid to stop. (Laughs) When the police came everyone had left. So, the police took them to Belzoni, Charley and Bertha, and put 'em in jail. And he was supposed to go to a recording session in New York the next day. So, he called me and asked me to write a letter to the judge, help him out, and I said sure. I drove up and met him and got him out.

EJC: You helped him.

HCS: I helped him, yes. He had records to make. (Laughs) He made good records for Paramount. I sent a lot of artists up there. Seems like I did a test for him. A gospel group. With Willie Brown. Maybe he wanted to hear a new song he made.

EJC: Do you remember Jimmie Rodgers?

HCS: Sure, I met Jimmie. He auditioned for me. A little while before he recorded for Victor. Jimmie at that time had a little Martin guitar he got from—oh what was his name? Memphis fellow. Frank Stokes. A little Martin it was. Sold it or gave it to him. And with Jimmie that worked all right. 'Cause his tone was so high. And he was playing straight rhythm. You can play one kind of song with one kind of guitar in one place and go somewhere else and the acoustics aren't right at all. But that was a good compliment to his voice.

EJC: Do you remember what he played for you?

HCS: No, I don't. Well, he might have played "Frankie and Johnny." That's an old song. You hear it a couple different ways. "Frankie and Albert." Now that I think on it, I recall he did "Early Morning Blues." That was originally made by Blind Blake. Which was unusual. And he did good. I asked if he ever wrote his own material. And he said he was fooling around with some things. And I said well, you come back sometime after you get that together.

EJC: Did he ever come back?

HCS: He came back after he made it. (Laughs) He played right in my store. He came through Jackson with some kind of traveling group. First he played at Gresset which was down by the train depot. Mostly a white clientele. But then he came here. By himself. We had a big time. This was after he had released "T for Texas" for Victor. He packed 'em in. We advertised he was coming, you see. I told him I'm ready to record you now and he said Ralph Peer would probably tie him in knots if he did such a thing. (Laughs) I knew Ralph. But the Mississippi Sheiks—the Chatmon boys I told you about—they came down to the store and they played with Jimmie that time. I hadn't recorded them yet. Some maybe. But that was before they were making records.

EJC: They played together?

HCS: That's right.

EJC: Do you remember what they played?

HCS: Sam Chatmon played a bass fiddle. I know that. Had a big ole hole in it. And two strings. But they played good together.

I don't recall what they played. A few numbers. Whatever it was called had a line: "He's a country boy and he sure don't know the town." That was the lyric Jimmie sang and it broke everybody up. Bo Chatmon later cut that. Old song.

EJC: Pleasant guy? Nice guy?

HCS: Oh yes. Jimmie was the kind of fellow you couldn't help but like. His manner was more like my customers. He was in no hurry. He liked to get along with people. He knew records, too. In fact, that's why he came into my shop. He'd carry about a dozen or so records into a listening booth. Listen all afternoon. Then come out and buy three or four.

We talked about something he liked I had made. At that time, I said I'd hear him out. That's when I told him to go write some songs. I wouldn't record anyone unless they had songs that, you know, they made up themselves. Thing about it, you could hear some skinny fellow like him—a little shy or not otherwise standing out—you could hear him sing in person and not think anything of it. But when you heard him on record, it was good. That's why I told him to make his own. He got a lot better.

EJC: Do you remember what records he liked?

HCS: I think he had a good ear for songs. I can't remember what we talked about.

EJC: So, he came more than once?

HCS: Oh yeah. We didn't get a lot of white customers. Some, sure. Jimmie, I remembered him because he came back later, you understand. I realized this fellow come in quite a few times. And he got to know the records I carried.

Now when he came back after he signed to Victor, he bought a box of records. My niece carried them out to his Cadillac. I think he asked her out but she was wise. She said no thanks. (Laughs) I remember he liked the Beale Street Sheiks. He and Frank Stokes were friends. I think they worked together. He probably liked artists on Okeh, Paramount. Black Patti. Those were the kinds of things he'd ask me about. Blind Lemon Jefferson he was a fan of.

Later he said: "Am I good enough for you now, Mr. H. C.?" He didn't need me then. He was on his way. But he'd ask what I was recording. What I liked. He liked to pick up musicians and play somewhere, a hotel or something like that with people he just met. At that time, he was hot enough he could just (snaps his fingers) get something together and invite whoever he'd like. Tommy Johnson told me Jimmie heard him on the street and said: "Come on up and play a show with me." Jimmie was playing on the roof of the King Edward Hotel. He marched Tommy right into the lobby and into the elevator. Probably the only Black man that ever walked in the front door. Jimmie didn't care. Jimmie was a lot like a jukebox nowadays. He could play about any song he ever heard.

EJC: It must have been hard work running a music store in the Depression.

HCS: I pulled through. When I think back on it, maybe it was my error not being the manager for these artists. But it was important that whoever I saw got a share. I saw to that. If I got $100 for placing some talent to Okeh or Paramount I'd be sure the artist got something. That was all right for both of us. If

Jimmie had me as his manager, I might have made us both some money.

EJC: More than he wound up with.

HCS: (Laughs) I think he did all right. He had a good deal. Spent what he made. You can't do no better than that.

EJC: Not many female artists.

HCS: I did quite a few. The blues was a woman's business. They were the best customers. It would have been good to find a female artist like Patton. But in that area anyway most of the best talent I heard was male singers. But that's just what came my way. Other places might have been different.

EJC: Why did you close?

HCS: Around 1940 it just became a different business. My expenses went up. I had clerks and rent and tax. I figured I had gathered all the daisies in the field and there were no more to pick. Paramount Records offered me the whole company for free. All I had to do was bring the factory to Jackson. Move the equipment. They said I could have it for a dollar. But I had just bought a gas mine. I lost a lot of money in that and I just couldn't find investors. Back then, for some reason, banks wouldn't loan you money to build a factory in the South. I don't know why. We could have moved the whole blues business to Jackson.

EJC: What did you think of Jimmie in hindsight? How do you compare him to all the talent you met?

HCS: He was good, certainly. He found a lot of success. I'm not sure who he was inside his head. Only he knows if he would call it success. Someone like Tommy Johnson, in comparison, was a brooder compared to someone like Jimmie. Tommy didn't work much. There was just no place for him in society, really. But he made good records. Some singers sound better on record than they do live. Others sound fine but when you turn your back to them you don't feel anything. Tommy Johnson was such a person who sounded better on record. He had a speech impediment. He made a whistling sound when he sang. But it didn't translate to record. So, it was all right. Jimmie sounded strong when you were in front of him. But he sounded even stronger on record. Some singers really are complimented by the focus of recording, trying to get it right. Jimmie was one of those.

EJC: Did you ever hear the singers complain about how other record labels took their royalties, their copyrights?

HCS: They didn't know any better. Like I didn't know any better. Sometimes I might give them $50 a side. Some of them did record for $25 a side, I know that much. I dealt with them straight. As long as I could stay clear of the business, I thought I was ok. I didn't want trouble. I just wanted to record the music. When the war came, I thought it was gone forever. Maybe I was wrong.

EJC: Well, I think I've taken up enough of your time. It's such a pleasure to have met you. I've heard so much about you from . . .

HCS: He came back, you know.

EJC: I'm sorry?

HCS: He came back. Jimmie did. That's right. He was sick as could be. He said: "Mr. Speir, would you cut a test for me? I always wanted to make a record in your store. I'll pay you $50 a side." But he wanted to do it when everyone had gone. He came back about 9, 10 o'clock that night.

EJC: When was this?

HCS: Oh, I don't remember. What year did he die?

EJC: 1933.

HCS: I think it was probably near that time. Fall maybe. He came after hours. He said: "Mr. Speir, I'm gonna cut two records." And he put a $100 bill on the counter. He did one take of each. One performance of each. He said this first one is for you, Mr. Speir. It was a blue yodel about playing on Farish Street. I wish I still had it.

EJC: You don't have it.

HCS: No. I was in the furniture business, and I had a fire there. And I lost my datebook, my notebook where

I used to keep track of everyone I recorded. And a lot of the aluminum masters I had laying about that I held on to. Those were lost too.

EJC: That's too bad.

HCS: He made one by himself. And the second one he made with a young woman.

EJC: Oh. What did she look like?

HCS: I think she was Sam Chatmon's niece, he said. Red hair. (Laughs)

EJC: (Laughs)

HCS: They were very close. Seemed to me. They did a duet. They marked well together. I got a balance and they did it once and he never asked to hear it back. He told me: "Now you keep this because sometime down the road somebody might come looking for it. Keep it somewhere safe at home." I said, ok, Jimmie. I kept that one at home. Let me see . . . (Leaves room)

(Voice becomes louder as HCS re-enters the room.)

HCS: It's lucky I did what I was told. I played it once myself. It's a pretty good record. You think he was saving this for you?

(Sound of object on table.)

(END OF RECORDING)

BLUE YODEL №. 4

EVERYBODY DOES IT IN HAWAII

When I'm driving on a long stretch of road under a full Mississippi moon, it's easy to feel like I'm the only one awake in the world. Especially if I'm wound up. I get to where I'm lookin' so hard for deer and anything else that might jump my pathway, I start to hallucinagize I see lost souls, phantoms in my beams. I see my buddy Sam, blown in two in the Argonne Forest. And my baby June, all grown up. Going my way, songboy? If I lick my knuckles, my spit smells like the bottom of her feet. Nothin's off limits when you're trying to stay awake.

Considering how shit these roads are down in the dirty britches of the USA, my Caddy was doin' all right. Hell of a car, Caddy. Even the doors say class. When you shut yourself inside, you get that sweet airsuck sarcophagus sound, like it's pullin' in a cool breeze to keep you air-o-dited. Whereas your average T-model's a tin can comin' in and goin' out. That's Ford for you: tin man, tin ear, tin car. Now just look under the Caddy hood. See for yourself. You'll see straight 8 cylinders strokin' powerful pistons of metallic delicacy. Go deeper, and you got a pumpin' air-cooled jet black v16 with a heart of iron wrapped in arteries of polished aluminum chrome. Over there, you got your ride potential-o-meter. And behind it, your carbohydrator, and some tackle-o-meters. Naturally, I got the option of a Crosley radio. I've even heard myself on XER coming out of Mexico.

But you don't have to be in the music trades to drive one. Here's what I used to do 'fore I could buy my own. On a Sunday 'round church get-out time, go saunter into a Caddy dealer dressed in your finest black threads. Find a young salesman, an eager type who rubs his hands together a lot. Don't say too much. You wait long enough, he'll do all the talkin'. Tell him you're in the market for a new carriage. Something upscale. Keep a map in your front pocket and pat it sometimes, like it's a wad of cash. Dealers love cash. Then, pick yourself out a new model that looks like an aeroplane inside. Run your fingers along the seams. Make a pondering face. Then put your arms to your side like a tea kettle and give 'em the old: "Well, doggone it, I suppose I ought to take this jalopy on a road test." That kid'll get so excited, he'll split his suit to fetch the keys, arms goin' one way and legs goin' the other. He'll take you somewhere there's no traffic. Then it'll be your turn behind the wheel. That's when you let her rip. And when you hit 99 and the dealer-man grabs his hat and asks you what you do for a living, tell 'em you manage the Blue Yodeler.

Once me and Will Rogers broke 120 in a gnat's eyelash on an army airstrip near Fort Worth. We were on a Red Cross tour, hopping over three states' worth of starving windblown families that Hoover decided were too poor to vote. I was the opening act of course and I didn't mind a bit. He even called me his lost son. Oh, we had a big time. Chorus girls galore. And so much chili. Everybody wanted to make chili for Will Rogers.

"All these goddamn beans, Jimmie," Will hollered out on a plane ride over Opelika, grippin' the wicker chair as we bobbled on a cloud. "What the Midwest needs is more Irish. Next time I'm on WLS, I'm gonna put out a call for Chicago to send down their retired policeman and teach these people to grow some damn potatoes. Mercy!"

When the dust got too thick to fly, I offered my wheels to get us around. Carrie and our housekeeper, Annie (back when I could afford her) about died when we walked in the house together. "Mother? Annie?" I said, "This here's Will. He talks for a living."

Will leaned right into it, taking Carrie's hand and rubbing her knuckles. "Hello, Mrs. Rodgers, I'm Mr. Rogers. Pleasure. This man says he's your husband. Is that true? Maybe we should switch." And gave her a hug.

Before Carrie could answer, Anita was tuggin' on the poor man's trousers. "Say, mister, does my Pops owe you money?"

"Anita! Oh, I'm sorry, Mr. Rogers!" Carrie tried to corral Anita but she just nibbled on her mama's fingers. "Ouch! Honey, stop that."

Ole Will didn't care. He was used to people makin' a fuss over him. He kept three conversations going at once. "Oh, that's all right, Mrs. Rodgers." Then he turned to Annie. "Thanks for the tea, Annie. No sugar. I keep some in my tooth." Then he turned to Anita. "Now look here, little lady, your daddy don't owe me nuthin'. In fact, we're both in the business of people owing us." Then he got down to her nose. "Just remember, when you grow up, if you want to make crime pay, become a lawyer."

After dinner we took Carrie's Packard and bronco'd in it for about a week all over Texas and Oklahoma. And when we burned her up, we moved to my Caddy and drove her full out. Will was impressed. "Son," he yelled over the motor, "this is about to turn into one of those things that's only funny when it happens to somebody else."

The Caddy came special ordered from a dealer in San Antonio. Billed to RCA, of course. I'm sure they'd want me to travel in style, being their road rep and all. Harley Earl is the fellow who designed it. He and his pops had a custom garage in Hollywood. They cut mine like they did for Douglas Fairbanks with a trimmed-down body for a cleaner line when the top's down. I added vanilla wheels and a Mandalay blue trim. Two thousand clams after I checked boxes for all the extras. Radio. Tuckaway place for my pearl-handled pistols. Hey, don't scoff. Highway robbery is no joke.

I had ulterior motives in scoring a Caddy. I knew when I lost my room at the Gunter Hotel nobody else was gonna put up with me. "Mr. Rodgers, I'm afraid management has asked us to ask you . . ."

Yeah, yeah. I knew it was coming. No fool's ever beat those TB Blues.

After a show, I'd let Henry, my driver, off at a roadside cabin while I spent the night in one of the swank new travel parks. Even Haydee stayed with me out there one night in the leather rumble. Funny how she looked in the morning, all copper red in the sunshine. Turn one way and she'd be damselin'. Turn the other and she'd look scary as hell.

"Babe, you got two profiles. Left is before Jimmie, right is after." And she'd laugh and laugh. If a woman don't tantalize you when she's all a-muss in the morning, no amount of powder is gonna make up for it. That's a sure as shit fact.

These are the things that go through my mind when I'm fighting the night. All of life's questions and hard answers come easy in the dark. Why? When? Because. I've always thought if you could gather everybody you're fussing with and put 'em in a Cadillac on an all-nighter, you'd settle all your grudges and sandstorms once and for all. And by the time you'd arrived wherever you were goin', you could live clear and smooth for all the clicks left on your timer. That's the problem with people. They don't go on enough long drives.

Musicianers like me used to find work everywhere. Now most of the rag shows have died out. I hear even Silas Green is having trouble. Fortunately, when I do get an offer, my name's hot enough I can ask for pretty much what's-ever left in the till. And these days that ain't much. Sometimes I think I'm keepin' Vaudeville goin' all by myself. One good thing about playing these little towns, I can always find a hospital that don't mind helpin' me out if I'm in a spell. I'm a card-carryin' lunger after all. And who doesn't want to give ole Jimmie a boost? I admit, it's a matter of pride I held out so long before I had to hire Cora full-time. You'll meet her soon enough.

Only thing 'bout these long drives, you gotta plan your gas stops. That stretch from east Texas to Mississippi is damn near barren. And you don't want to wind up wheezin' dry and havin' to go knockin' on somebody's door at 2 a.m., hoping you don't get a belly full of buckshot. As you might guess, this predicament has occasioned me before. First rule of hammerin' on someone's door late at night, stand far the hell back with your hands where they can see 'em. Better yet, hold your hat.

"Good evening, friend. Sorry to wake you up. Yodelay-hoo . . ." Down this way, usually the response is, "Honey, get a load of this. It's Jimmie goddamn Rodgers. And he's out of gas."

Let's back up a notch. Before we came to this drivin' part of the story we were in a bunch of silliness in San Antonio. From there, my man Peer and I took off to Dallas for some sessioning. Whether you're in a proper studio or some warehouse, a recording session takes up two rooms. One is for the engineer and the other's for the musicians. Ideally you want your recording studio in a spot that's got a high ceiling so the sound floats up nice and easy 'til it turns to mist, 'stead of bouncin' back in your ear. And you'll want to hang some heavy curtains on the walls to help diffuse all the racket. Then, lay down a nice thick carpet, get yourself some straight-back chairs, a little table for your beverage, an ashtray, a lamp, and a piano to tune to, and you're all set. The microphones all have umbilical cords that lead to the other room, where the engineer sits. I call him a Victographer or voice photographer. At RCA, they put a nice big window between the rooms so you can gawk at each other. The producer and engineer handle the recording contraption and listen for the things you're too busy to notice. I wish more ladies were in the business but so far, it's all fellows. The ladies, however, work the stampers in the factory. Keep reading.

When you're in the studio pickin', you can't hear them say nasty things about you but they can sure as hell hear everything you say 'cause of those microphones. I told you I made my first big record, "T for Texas" ("Blue Yodel" on the label) in Camden in what had been an old church. I had to lobby for it hard. Ralph hadn't ever been around a white fellow that played blues without making comedy of it, I guess. It got hot all 'round the country. Fast.

And if you ask me, I think deep down, Mr. P. was a little peeved at my success. I was a step ahead of his instincts and he wasn't used to that. The next time I came to New York, Ralph left his old lady in charge. Said he had to go somewhere and find the next

Blue Yodeler. Well, that didn't sit well with me. You can own my publishing, hoss, and take a piece of me coming and going. But don't you ever nickel and dime me when we've got work to do. I had that old bird of his runnin' out for lemons one minute and cough drops the next. I let that session drag on just for spite. I'll admit it. I get that way sometimes. Not all the time. Like Lincoln. Some of the time.

Anywho, when you're in a studio, you and your engineer communicate through a little intercom. He places a bare lamp right by your microphone. That sucker has a red bulb in it and when the red light's on, that means "go." Then the engineer gently lays a sapphire needle onto a thick disc made from beeswax that's been kept in an ice box. (Lately they're using something else. I can't keep up.) Once it's up to speed, your engineer gives you the finger and you start your tune. As that sapphire needle hears you squawk, it shivers this way and that, gently cuttin' grooves into the wax. Little sounds make little grooves. Big sounds make deeper grooves. The turntable turns by means of a series of gears powered by the steady gravity of falling weights and counterweights. As one weight goes down, another goes up, keeping the record going at a constant speed. When you render a good one, they usually ask you to try another right behind it for safety in case an intern drops the first one. Then those grooved discs go back in the Frigidaire and stay chilled until they go to the factory, where they're dipped and double dipped and emulsified in nickel, copper, and all kinds of foul chemicals 'til the disc forms a metal plate etched with those precious grooves. That metal plate becomes the "mother stamper." Your A-side and your B-side each get their own mom.

Then, all that goes to the factory, where the ladies do most of the work. They clamp each of those mothers to a giant round press, kinda like you see at a dry cleaner's. The operator places a record label and a big clump of black shellac clay that looks like taffy in the center of the press. Then she brings that clamp down with a heap of weight and a shit load of steam and presses that slab into a round record. Then she trims off the fat 'til it's a perfect circle and ta-da! You're in business. Now do that a million times and say T for Tennessee.

Prior to our get togethers, Ralph and I convene somewhere quiet to audition whatever I've written, half-remembered, procured, or been sent by my sister-in-law Elsie (who you'll meet in a minute). We get 'em in shape so they all run about 3 minutes and 30 seconds. Any longer and you run out of groove. That's when that little weight hits a little pillow and stops the turntable. If you blow one, and I've blown plenty, you can look through the glass and see the knob twiddlers put their head in their hands, loosen their tie, and say rude things you can't hear. Tough break, fellows. To know me is to love me. The artist may drive a Caddy, but art rides a bicycle.

When we were in Atlanta some time back, I brought in a little band of fellows I found on the street. They were wailin' away on "Frankie and Johnny" fierce, which just so happened to be what I wanted to cut the next day. We sounded fabulous together. I don't know why Ralph never released that version. Funny thing. If a Black band is firing behind me, Ralph always seems to be low on wax. "Not sure when we're gonna release that, Jimmie, but that was fine. Let's move on."

However, if I'm cuttin' a tune with a silly orchestra that I paid a mint for, the boys behind the glass get very ambitious. "Jimmie, try this new mic. Jimmie, try this gadget." I suppose because they think it doesn't matter. Ralph's fondest wish is to go pop. He's not content to keep on the sunny side.

Ralph's all right for a company man. He just don't get out enough. That same week in Atlanta, he cut a mess of things with Blind Willie McTell. He thought he had one up on me when he introduced us. "Aw hell," I teased. "Red Hot Willie. Why didn't you say so?" Willie went by many names then.

"Hey Blue!" Willie grinned once he heard my voice. "I knew it was you when you walked in the door. From that awful shit you wear."

I told Ralph to make sure he cut Willie's tune about cheesy eggs. But mostly what I remember about Atlanta is after we were done cuttin' and I was loading up to leave, Willie's girl Ruth held me up with a rusty old pea-shooter, aimin' at my temple with one hand and snappin' her fingers with the other, blowin' bubbles, one, two, three. "Billfold, cowboy! Hurry up!" I assumed the position, but my compliance was halfhearted.

"Go ahead and shoot. But I can't guarantee I can stand still."

She was not amused but put it away when Ralph and Willie came out the front door. "Fuck you, Jimmie-man," she hissed and put a foot to my backside. I helped Willie into their T-model and leaned in his window. I gave his shoulder a squeeze as Ruth turned over the engine.

"Hoss, you know your old lady here, she's not to be trifled with. You might think about sleeping with one eye open." Willie grunted over the sound of Ruth grinding the gear box to the nub. "Too late, Blue."

I digress. You've been so patient. So, this session in Dallas, the one I've been trying to tell you about for a couple pages, just about broke us all. I was typing up my song scripts on Fulton Hotel stationery while Ralph and his engineer were setting up the space. Carrie's sister Elsie came along with new numbers to try. Elsie and I have been scribbling together for years. Good egg, Elsie. If I say, "Sister, I need some tunes," she gets the job done. She'd suffered sessions with me before. But on this occasion, Elsie spent most of the time running from Joe Kaipo, the Hawaiian steel man I bailed out of jail, much to my eternal regret. Joe kept trying to sit on Elsie's lap, and sister was having none of it. She finally put out a cigarette on his hand ("My husband's a sheriff, you little freak"), ran into a mop closet, and slammed the door.

She was sore as hell. But the whole shebang was not a highlight for me either. These fellows I picked up to accompany me called themselves "the guitar hounds." And like most hounds, we spent the night crawlin' from joint to joint, first trying to lose Kaipo and then trying to find him. Our search seemed to radiate all over south Texas. And by the time we found him halfway to El Paso, beat up and ornery, I was already itchin' to dodge the whole aggregation and get on with it on my own. I was used to being everybody's New Year's Eve party. But this was too much for even me. Kaipo said something about Hawaii and I said I could use a hula girl 'bout now. Just then Elsie came bustin' out of the closet, stole a paper and pencil, and went off somewhere for about 20 minutes. When she came back, she tossed "Everybody Does It in Hawaii" at my feet. I read it through, makin' up a tune. "Very good, sis," I whistled. After it was all over, the least I could do for Elsie was drive her home to Meridian. And that's where this part of the story really starts.

We had just crossed into Mississippi. It was about 3 in the morning. Nobody out here but us. That's when I spied little specks of something all over the road. In my Caddy beams, it looked like little green rocks as far as I could see. Except they jumped. The road was thick with a bullfrog orchestra. I pulled over but kept the engine at a purr. Elsie came out the back door in her bare feet.

"Jimmie, why we stopped?"

I was in the road on my haunches. "Sis, come look at this. Watch your feetsies. Don't step on 'em."

She came up behind me as I crouched down, lit up by the Caddy beams. "Oh my God," Elsie was holding a little quilt Carrie had sewn for her. She leaned on my shoulder, which I always liked. We were pals, you see. There's something about a woman who's your pal leaning on you familiar like. Almost like if she had the choice, you could have been her fella. Fortunately for me, Jesus asked her to dance before I did. Son of a bitch gets more than I do. But I digress. Those bumps in the road were big ole bullfrogs stretched out for at least a mile or more. "What are they doing out here?" Elsie chewed on her nails.

"Mating season I'm supposin." I lit a smoke stick. The croakin' was loud as my ride.

"Well, what are we gonna do? The poor things." She had a good sleepy voice.

I puffed. "I don't think there's anything we can do except just drive over the little bastards."

Elsie walked up the road 'til she was almost in darkness. Now she was like my visions of the dead. I almost called her out of there, but she came back on her own. "Look at them all." And yes, she had to pick one up.

"Woman," I flicked ash on the road. "He's gonna leak on you."

The frog took up her whole palm. "He's so sweet."

I flicked away my smoke. "I can't stay out in this air anymore. I'm gonna choke." I got back in the driver's seat. Elsie coaxed the toad off her hand, got in the back, and off we moseyed. For the next two miles, I kid you not, we squashed probably thousands of those croaksters under my Goodyears. Elsie just sat quiet in the back with her hand on her hat. What is it with people holding their hats when I drive?

"Girl, it's like a frog rodeo out here," and I leaned my head out the window and yodeled into the wind. "Now if we were in my old Dodge, you'd have felt every one of those like they was under your butt."

"You're terrible." Her giggle was just like Carrie's but a bit deeper. And I liked it. "I bet you know this country cold, don't you?"

"Oh, lady, I do. The first time I left home I ran off with Billy Terrell's Entertainers. I joined him in Hattiesburg and we worked all through here."

"Where 'bouts?"

"Couldn't tell you. I was so windblown I never knew where I was really. I got off in Arizona. That's how I heard about Kerrville. Good for my cough." (The engine was purring but I still had to yell).

"Did you play guitar then? I can't recall."

"I auditioned on banjo and guitar. You know how I do."

"Yup!" Elsie looked out the window at the pitch black.

"I told him I'd been around."

"You begged him to listen, in other words."

"Hey, lean up here so I don't have to holler. The best way to get what you want is to ask for it."

"You been to New Orleans since we high-tailed out of there?"

"Hell no. And if I can help it, I'm not gonna stop anywhere in Louisiana again."

"You lost enough to buy me a nice little house."

"That's factual." I watched her in the rearview, but she was gazing in her mind and didn't see me. "But anyway, I met Billy in Meridian. I asked if I could audition and he had mercy on me.

"Did you yodel?"

"Sort of. I wasn't quite there yet. My big number then was 'Flying Trapeze.' But I'd go into a little yodel now and then. He just sat there rolling cigarettes. Then I tried one on guitar. Billy perked up and said: 'Kid, do me a favor. Don't play banjo.'"

This made Elsie laugh, which she did with some guilt, I thought, the kind religious people have when they're enjoying life. "You won him over with your savoir faire." She put her hat on the seat and looked at herself in the rearview mirror, playing with her curly brown hair.

"Like I won you over." I looked at her but she was not to be distracted.

"My sister," she said quietly. "Not me."

The frogs kept comin'. "That is correct. Your sister."

"I always liked you on guitar." She put her hand under her chin, leaned on the front seat and walked her fingers back and forth along the seams. "Banjo not so much."

"You got any more songs for me, hun?"

She acted disgusted. "I just gave you a bunch. Give a girl some air."

"I was thinking about that time you came to Washington. You were a scribe on fire."

"All expenses paid," Elsie chimed in quick.

"We got some good songs on that trip."

"Yeah, we did." Elsie then went quiet a long time which worried me. Her voice got froggy. "Jimmie, how long you think you can keep this up?"

"I'm gonna die in my boots, by George. I can tell you that."

She went silent for almost a mile. "I have to tell you something."

"It's not mine, baby." I thought I'd get a smile but I didn't.

"This is serious." Elsie pouted.

"I'm serious, too."

"I think this is my last trip."

"You quittin' on me? Aw, c'mon."

"No, not quittin' outright." She put her head to the side, like she was ready to go back to sleep. "I don't wanna go on these sessions no more." There was more coming so I waited. "You're breaking my sister's heart, you know. And I just can't be in the middle."

"Well, it's breaking my heart, too. It ain't easy being away from home all the time. Driving all night. Hacking my lungs out. Hoping I don't pop a gasket."

"That's what I'm talking about, Jimmie." She slapped the seat with her hands. "What's the point? Why are you still out here?"

"Your problem is you don't respect the hustle."

"Oh, now wait a minute." She punched my shoulder. "What does that even mean? Respect the hustle." She punched me again. "You're an idiot!"

I kept eye contact by mirror. I thought of all the frogs we were killin'. "Yes, Mrs. McWilliams, I agree with you. This is unsustainable. But what am I gonna do? I got a mortgage, three bull dogs, a wife, an ex-wife, one kid I never see, another I'm afraid to see, and a manager who's got a bigger house than I do." I kept Haydee to myself.

"You sure that kid is yours?"

"Stella's? Looks like me."

"You think they all look like you."

"That's not all."

"There's more?"

"And a revenant." The frogs were thinnin' out. So was I.

"What do you mean, a revenant?" Elise sounded more disgusted than ever.

"For the last year or so wherever I go—hotel, diner, theater—there's this fellow playing my songs. Singing the hell out of 'em, too."

"Oh c'mon! Hey, you got some gum?" She leaned up to my seat.

I handed her my Wrigleys. "Shit you not." I start drumming on the steering wheel. A nervous tic. "He plays one of those little May Belle guitars with the mother of toilet seat neck."

"James! Mother of toilet seat!"

"That's what it's called. It's got flowers and vines painted on it. I asked Mr. Martin over at Martin guitars about making me one." (I gave her my pretend German accent.) "Jimmie, uze been writing us for years about being za Martin musician. You vant a little Martin, ve'll get you a little Martin. But zose Stella guitars, zey are junk! Junk!"

Elsie threw the wrapper out the window. "So, when's the last time you seen this fellow?"

"Last month. At the Earle. In Washington. When I got out, this fellow was sitting out front of a Green Tavern burger joint 'cross the street, singing the hell out of 'T for Texas.' He was good, too. I was on my way to see him, but somebody asked for an autograph and he split."

"Maybe you ought not to wear a ten-gallon hat in Georgetown." Our eyes met in the rearview and she stuck her tongue out.

"Well, Mrs. Sunday School. I tried to find him. No luck. He played this chord that I can't get out my head. One of those—what's that you play on piano that I like?

"Diminished."

"Diminished! Well, this chord he played was un-diminished."

She giggled again. She burrowed her chin back down in the front seat, 'cept she was movin' the stick of gum back forth across her mouth. "Is this fellow who's following you makin' fun of you?" She was curious now.

"No, no. He's just plumb good. He was there in New Orleans, just after Jack turned me out."

"Oh yeah. You did tell me about him." Elsie chewed on her thumb. "Ralph say anything about that IOU to your imaginary bank?"

"Jack or Boasberg or whatever name he's going by tried to shake him down for it. But that's not gonna happen."

Elsie leaned back in her seat. "I wish I'd seen this character. Maybe you're hallucinating. It's not that Snoozer Quinn fellow that you and Louis went driving with. The one whose head's shaped like a peanut?"

"Nope. Not Snoozer. Bless his heart. Nobody's better than Snoozer. This fellow's a Black man. And he can pick. Should have heard him play 'Waiting for a Train.' Most lonesome thing I've ever heard. It'd make a better record than mine. If I produced it."

"Well, who is he?"

"He's my revenant. Don't you see? He's waiting to catch me. That's why I gotta keep moving. Stay on my feet."

We drove and drove. The toads disappeared. All was quiet, but

I knew Elsie was awake and was just going to let me talk. "Hey girl, remember that song about Haydee we started in New York?"

"'My Little Lady.' You cut it, remember?"

"I did but I want to cut a new one. Change it up a bit. I got some new lines."

Elsie made a face. "I like that name. Never heard it before. Old girlfriend?"

I didn't answer.

Elsie rolled up her blanket and put her head down. But she was up again in a minute. "Well, I think you better finish it off on your own. You don't need me." She sounded tired. The kind of tired where you're all awake about it.

Now I went at my nails. Neither of us was gonna have any digits left after this trip. I pulled the car over on a little sandy spot but kept it idling. What the hell is sand doin' on this road? The gnats were fierce. Maybe there was a dead hog around here somewhere. Elsie rolled up the window. I was suddenly chilly.

"Why'd you stop, Jimmie? Are you gonna make me get out?

"No. I gotta pee. Don't watch me."

"Not interested," she called out as I shut the door. "You better keep your lights or some truck might slam into us."

I waded into the bushes and did my piece. There's no more lonesome place than Mississippi just before dawn. Especially when you come to realize against all your better nature that you're back and you may never again have a chance to get out.

"Watch for snakes," Elsie hollered.

I finished, got back in the car, and pulled back on the road. We drove on in quiet.

"C'mon now, E. We can't stop now. What are you gonna do? You just gonna stay in Meridian all your life, married to the po-po chief?"

I could see Elsie running her finger along the metal door seam. "Oh, it's not so bad. I can break the law and he can't bring me in." She leaned forward in the seat again. "What's wrong with that?"

"Nothing. Nothing at all. Why can't I do that?"

"'Cause you're an entertainer. That's what you do. I'm gonna write you a song called 'Black Cat Crossed My Path.'"

"Something tells me you've already written it."

She smiled. "Workin' on it. Blues is not really my thing. That's your bag."

"Yes m'am. Livin' it. Singin' it."

"You're gonna have to pay the piper, Jimmie," and she poked me in the neck.

"I know it, girl. Here today. God tomorrow. Hope he likes my records."

After a bit, Elsie curled up to go to sleep. "I just wanna go home."

"Well, that's where I'm takin' you. So shush." I was frustrated now but I don't know why.

Elsie yawned. It was almost light time. I could feel her opening and closing the ashtray behind my seat. "You should just stay home. That's all I'm sayin'. You might like it." And she was out.

The last time I saw Elsie, really saw her, was last fall at her folk's 50th anniversary. I even grew a mustache. I figured there might not be much time left for that kind of frivolity. We had a picture made, standing in front of the house. Inside was a nice spread. Ham and chicken and dumplings and drop biscuits. But by then all I could think about was gettin' outta there and seeing if I might find Haydee one more time. Everything was down to one more time.

We carried on in the family room around her upright. Lotta nice memories there. We played "Mississippi Moon" and stole looks. And it was all right, you know. But something between us had broken. Right before I snuck out the kitchen door, I asked her husband, Lee, for a cigarette. She was waiting when I stepped out on the screen porch. Like she knew I was gonna skedaddle. "Hey, sis. How'd you sneak out here?"

She looked hard at me. "Jimmie? Where you goin'?"

I fiddled in my pockets. "Nowhere's." Her porch was just a stamp-sized thing with a little poker table and a dying old sewing machine. I tried to find my lighter. I couldn't keep still. I think she knew why. "I'll be back, sis. Little business I gotta take care of." I leaned on a beam and made circles on the screen, an unlit cigarette between my fingers. Elsie had her hands behind her back but she didn't look girlish anymore. That's what living with a policeman'll do to you.

"You know, I finished 'Black Cat Crossed My Path.'" She smiled and we had a lovely moment lookin' at each other. "You wanna hear it?" And she didn't wait for my answer.

Black cat crossed my path
And I cannot look away
Sure as I shoo him yonder
He'll come back to stay
I left him chicory coffee
Milk and sugar in a bowl
Now that black cat's gonna haunt me
'Til I give 'im a little more

I whistled. "Look at you. Church girl singin' the blues." A hoot owl called. "You know, we were pretty good together, sister."

Elsie pushed the screen out and held it open for me. "Yeah, Jimmie. We were pretty good." That smile, I've seen it on every Mississippi face I know. A smile of pity. How dare you dream, you silly boy. I knew she would one day regret we didn't go back inside and write another tune in front of everyone, if anything just to shut 'em up. I stepped outside the door she opened for me, flickin' that unlit cigarette under a holly bush. Time had moved on us and we didn't even feel it. Like being on an aeroplane. We were closer to remembering who we were than being who we are. And who we are wasn't gonna last near as long as who we were. Everybody in this goddamn state is in such a hurry to get old. Black and white.

I walked on, wavin' my hat. She was still holding the screen door open for me, like I might change my mind and walk back in. "Elsie . . ." I turned 'round and pointed my hat at her. "We made something holy. Remember that."

If she said something after I turned around, I didn't hear it. And that's the last I saw of her. I wished I had brought "Black Cat" to New York. Ralph might have spotted me another $250.

For many weeks after and even now, with the honkin' sounds of Time Square below, I've shut my eyes and thought of Elsie's tune. A god-fearing little lass like her, writing a good blues. It was still on my mind when I went to see Sam Chatmon after leavin' her place. And still that evening when Haydee and I snuck off to Farish Street to make a little record of our own. Haydee had written something nice for us to sing together. For us and the kid. And right in the middle of giggling and learning the damn thing I realized what Elsie was trying to tell me. Her “Black Cat” song wasn’t for me. It was for her. I was the black the cat who crossed her path.

BLUE YODEL № 5

YODELING FIDDLING BLUES

TRANSCRIPTION

Sam Chatmon, Musician. Hollandale, Mississippi, Summer 1959.

Sam Chatmon and his brothers formed the recording group the Mississippi Sheiks in the late 1920s and became one of the most popular aggregations in the Delta, of which Sam is especially proud. ("Muddy Waters once rode 20 miles to see us. If we played a town of 100 people, 80 would come out and the other 20 would be babysittin'.")

Today Sam is in his early 60s. He is more or less the same age as Jimmie would have been. He lives in Hollandale, Mississippi, a town of about 2,000 just west of Highway 12 in a small house he owns outright that looks to be standing mostly from habit. A small set of steps leads up to a sinking front porch right into his living room. Sam was waiting for me when I arrived, sitting on a free-standing section of fence outside his house holding a small black and red Gibson guitar made in the 1930s with a scrolled decal on the headstock ("they call that a sunburst finish"). A long rope of leather, one end tied to the headstock and the other to an ivory pin in the bout of the guitar, serves as a strap. Just below the sound hole is a long tortoiseshell pickguard. It's a handsome guitar, not a student model, and looks to have been well taken care of. A professional working man's instrument.

As I arrived, Sam was patting out a rhythm on a battered gray mailbox nailed to the fence. A gash in the lid looks to have been made with an axe so the mailman can slip in letters. His name is hand-painted in black. Sam's face is thin and almost always smiling. He has freckles on his cheeks. He's clean shaven but plans to grow a beard. ("Like my pops."). On his head Sam keeps a well-worn brown newsboy cap, the same color as his dress trousers. His blue-gray dress coat was unbuttoned and his clean white shirt was left open at the collar. Sam's casual blue-gray leather house shoes matched his coat and were complimented by high black socks. A small calico puppy, perhaps 3 or 4 months old, sat dutifully at his feet in the grass.

Most of our talk took place in a pine-paneled living room. Photos of children and a woman that I thought might be his wife were everywhere, but the house was quiet. The sitting room opened into a small dining room and kitchen. The refrigerator clanked. I feared it might give out while I was there. Sam rocked in a straight-back rocking chair.

EJC: Where did your people come from?

Sam Chatmon: We came from a place called Bolton. You know it? We were 20 miles from Vicksburg and near that from Jackson. My pops fought for the Union. Under Sherman. Marched all through Georgia, Alabama, and Mississippi. He said they used to haul a wagon full of dead men. And when they came to a creek bed, they'd throw 'em in like stepping stones and drive the artillery over 'em. (Shows me a picture.) That's him there. Memphis 3rd Calvary Colored Regiment. They chased down Jefferson Davis. They got him in Mexico. He said Davis' eyes were wide like this the whole time they brought him back. Probably thought they'd behead him. But they didn't.

(Plays guitar). And the ladies then, the ladies took care of the children while the men were in war. My Pops said they would get a wheelbarrow and they'd mix together oats and water and meal and whatnot and they'd feed everybody's kids at once.

> (sings)
>
> Gather 'round, children
> Gather while you can
> Come watch your daddy
> For he's marching out again
> See all the pretty ladies standin' and cryin'
> As they wave him fare thee well
> Which one of you belongs to him
> One can't never tell
> No, one can't never tell

EJC: Your father was a musician.

SC: My father was a musicianer. That's right. He learned from a fellow called Miller. I started at three. Started playing with my brothers when I was seven. I learned bass. And then guitar. I'd put a guitar on the floor and just hold it on my lap. Long before I could play.

EJC: Do you remember any of the songs your father taught you?

SC: Sure, I still play 'em today. "Little Liza Jane." Bob Wills made a record of that. (Plays and sings)

"Can't get a saddle on a old gray mule. There's a young mule there look all right to you." (Stops) You were asking about Jimmie. He liked those kinds of songs. They didn't have many changes, you see. Jimmie played a straight rhythm. A stomp. I showed him some runs. We'd sing all those songs. My whole family played. Sisters, brothers, cousins. All played.

EJC: When did you meet Jimmie?

SC: The first time I was broke down on the road between here and Vicksburg. I had a flat I was trying to patch. And it was near dark. He drove by in a brand new Buick. Black. He slowed down, you see, and almost passed me and then he backed up. And he said: "You're Sam Chatmon. I've seen you play." And we started conversing. I had a performance to make that night. And he said, "Get in." I said, what about my car? He said: "Leave that piece of shit!" (Laughs) Excuse me. He said: "I'll buy you another one." And he drove me to Vicksburg. I told him, this is a nice car. He just laughed. He said: "When I need to fill it up, I just yodel and the meter goes from E to F."

The first time I played with Jimmie was at Speir's store. On Farish Street. He was coming through with some entertainers, you see. He had a big record then, Jimmie did. He knew my brother Bo and maybe Lonnie, too, from somewhere. He saw them playing out and said: "Why don't you join me, I'm Jimmie Rodgers. I know your brother Sam." Well of course they knew who he was. He had that record. (Sings) "T for Texas." Good record. So, we went down there to the shop and just

threw in with him. Crowded! Woo! Couldn't hardly move so many folks come.

EJC: How do you think of him now? What comes to mind?

SC: Jimmie? He was a curious fellow. At the same time he didn't care for any fuss. He'd sit and cross his leg you know, like this. Sharp crease in his pants. Sharp mother . . . oh, excuse me again.

EJC: Quite all right.

SC: He'd just sit like this, guitar on his lap. And he'd sit there and be comfortable and play anything you wanted to hear. Sometimes he'd just listen to you. He knew a lot of records. A lot of old songs. (Plays)

> Don't drive a stranger from your door
> He might be your new best friend, you never know
> Would you take a feather from your pillow bed
> Come tickle your loving daddy's head.

But if you went fishing with him, he'd just be in his overalls like anybody from the country. Stay all day. He was fun to be around. He favored my niece, Haydee, you know. They'd sit and fuss together. I don't know where they met but he'd come here to see her. She teased him something awful. He didn't mind. (Puts guitar down and puts both hands on his knees and leans forward). She'd come and take off his hat and put it on her head. He was bald, you see. And the kids, all her little nieces, would get a kick out of that. She had short curly red hair. (Laughs) That's right. You know it. She was funny like he was. They were very particular together. (Leans back and picks his guitar back up.) Last time I saw him he wasn't too well.

EJC: You know Jimmie had a song where he sings "Haydee, my little lady." Was that your niece?

SC: (Long silence) Haydee was my sister's child. (Looks at the floor.) Goodness. Lovely young lady.

EJC: And she played, like y'all?

SC: We all played together around that time. Haydee, too. We played regular at the Edward Hotel in Jackson. And recorded there. One time, Jimmie came through and stopped by the house. Stole away from whoever he was traveling with and came out to the house here. Not this house, another house. We put out a pork butt on the charcoal all day. Buried some corn underneath the charcoal. In the ground, you understand. That's a good meal. I think Jimmie really just came to see Haydee. I see these things. But he was a gentleman. He had to be. On account of my brothers. They could throw.

EJC: I'm not sure I understand.

SC: They all threw knives. They'd drink a little and practice out back. Used a tree for target practice. Voom. Voom. Voom. One after the other. Like pitching baseballs. They'd cut the bark off a tree (snaps his fingers), bam!

And Jimmie, he said: "Lawd!" (Laughs) "You gentlemans are dangerous. Can you show me that?" He got pretty good. But he was respectful after seeing all her uncles throw those knives. If he came downtown, he'd call to us and we'd come play with him. You asked where we first played together. I think it was the Edward Hotel.

EJC: In Jackson?

SC: That's right. He needed some individuals to join him. He called us his Howlin' Guitars. He heard Haydee play in the backyard, knives zoomin' all around. And he said, "My goodness. That lady can drag a bow." That did it, I think.

He wanted to fill out his sound. Jimmie asked me: "Sam, what if I could get someone to bring you a bass. That's a good sound, the bass. We'll make us a big band. I'll get our sponsors to find us one so you don't have to carry it." I said to him: "Jimmie, when is your engagement?" He said it was that night. Nine o'clock. (Holds my hand.) So, I said: "Mr. Rodgers, it so happens at 9 o'clock tonight, I become a bass player." (Slaps knee) And away we went. Haydee, too. She played violin. And Walter Vinson came with us.

EJC: Walter wrote "Sitting On Top of the World."

SC: That's right. You know! Walter was an idea man. A composer. He and Jimmie would throw songs together sometimes.

EJC: So, this was Jimmie Rodgers and the Mississippi Sheiks, playing together. (Sam hums in agreement). Do you know what year this was?

SC: I couldn't tell you, no.

EJC: And Haydee . . .

SC: You see by then we were travelin' everywhere, all up through Chicago and St. Louis. New Orleans. But the fellow who put my brothers to record was from Itta Bena. Italian fellow. Lumbo. He had a grocery store there and hired them to play. Kept 'em playing all night. Walter wrote "Sitting On Top of the World" at his place at four in the morning. Lumbo sent them to Okeh. They made that record there at the Edward Hotel, I believe. Good record. You know Charley Patton?

EJC: His records, yes.

SC: Now Charley Patton was my brother. Last time I saw Jimmie, he went down to see Charley 'bout somethin'. Anyway, Charley told Lumbo about my brothers. And got them recording. We were on our way then. Lumbo had a recorder in his store but he didn't have the touch Mr. Speir had. He made the best records. And his shop was the place to be if you were a musicianer.

EJC: Do you remember any songs you played together with Jimmie?

SC: Where now?

EJC: At the King Edward Hotel.

SC: His blue yodel songs. "Frankie and Johnny."

Didn't matter. We'd shadow him. Anything he wanted to play. He'd say: "Follow me, hoss, and hang on to your britches." And when we came to play, he marched us right into the lobby and up the elevator. None of us had ever walked through the front door of that hotel. Not allowed. But no one was gonna stop him. He was a star. And he knew it. During the show at some point, he asked me confidential: "I'd like permission to pick up your niece." I had seen them talk together. Right over there by that stump. That was a pecan tree. Lightning came and cut it (gestures with his hand) straight like a hot knife on butter.

EJC: So, what did you say?

SC: I said sure! You go ahead. She knows you. I thought she'd scare him off if he meant romancin'. He saw all her uncles, understand (laughs), so I wasn't worried. She could throw a knife too. I didn't think nothing of it. Anyways, at the end of the night, I was calling the dances, you know. Jimmie was a song man but not a dance man. (Laughs) I was both. We would sing something like "Little Liza Jane" and I'd call out, "Men carry your ladies to the bar, promenade to the bar." Well, Jimmie, you wouldn't think he could lift nothin'. He put down his guitar and he picked up Haydee and carried her to the bar. She kept on playing, too. Swept her off her feet. Then some fellow came up to Jimmie, gambler-lookin' fellow, and started shakin' his finger at him. And Jimmie yelled: "Anybody for an autograph?" And turned the place out. He made a distraction and got out of there. We had a boy with us. Young fellow. Chester Burnett.

EJC: Howlin' Wolf!

SC: That's right. He was already a big fellow. 'Bout 18, 19. He'd carry around the hat, you know, for the band. My brother Charley gave Chester music lessons. He and Jimmie, I think they'd trade a guitar back and forth and sing some. Anyway, I was repairing a string, sitting by this big palm. Chester tugs on my shirt and says: "Mr. Jimmie says to tell you that he needs to make an exit. Without delay." So, we hauled out of there, all of us jammed in his touring car. I said, "Jimmie, what 'bout that bass? They gonna fuss at you for leaving it?"

He said, "George, they're making more as we speak. Leave it!" (Laughs)

EJC: Did you play on the Mississippi Sheiks song "Yodeling Fiddling Blues"?

SC: I was there when they cut it. (We listen to the record). That's a good record. No, I don't hear myself. But I watched them cut that.

EJC: Was that written about Jimmie?

SC: I don't know about that. He was sure in a hurry to get to Texas. (Laughs) You'd have to ask Walter. They might have created that together.

EJC: Is that right? I ask because of the lyrics. About a man who makes his living yodeling and has to move to Texas. That's what the lyric is about. And it was made around the time Jimmie moved to Texas.

SC: I wouldn't put it past him.

EJC: How often did Jimmie and Haydee see each other?

SC: (Adjusts himself in his seat.) I can't say. He was a welcome man 'round here. But there was another fellow who wasn't too keen on them together. So, she went to Oklahoma for a bit. And finally up to New York. She had a cousin up there. Queenie. But I know they saw each other not too long before he died. He was visiting his relatives, I think. Had a mustache. And he came over. That was the last time I saw him.

EJC: Did Haydee ever come back to Mississippi?

SC: Not that I'm aware (scratches his chest). She got out of Mississippi. Wasn't right for her here anymore. My brothers helped her up there and took care of that. Haydee died there. Shortly after Jimmie I think. She had some people up there that let us know. (Starts singing)

> I went to the water
> And all the creatures of the sea
> Say all her life's washed away
> Pity poor birdie singin' a blues for me
> If my child never knows
> Her mother and pa
> May the creatures of the sea
> Please help her along

EJC: That's a lovely song.

SC: Haydee wrote that. She was a composer. Knew almost as many songs as Jimmie. They liked the "Sugar Blues."

They sang together on that. I taught him harmony. Well, I sang harmony to him. He'd sing straight. Whenever you start to sing harmony with him, he'd lose his place and end up singing your part. He never sang in church. We used to sing one together.

He's a son of the country
Never been to town
Sold his cotton for a song
Laid his money down
Gone to seek his fortune
But it won't be long now
'Til he's back in the fields
With his hands on the plow

Music, you just can't hardly get out of it. It grows with you. And it'll take you everywhere if you let it.

EJC: You got a lot of great stories, Mr. Chatmon.

SC: I'll tell you. One time we came in from fishing, me and Jimmie. Went to a market on Farish Street. In our overalls. And we were getting a couple NuGrapes. If you were with Jimmie, he'd never let you pay. And they had a little café there with one of the early record machines. A Seeburg. Now, no one knows him there. Jimmie goes and plays his own record, "T for Texas." And when it came to the part—now this is the truth here. When it came to the part where he yodeled on the record, the whole store yodeled along. Waitresses. People in the aisle. Didn't break from what they were doing. Just (Sam yodels). Copied the record note for note. Jimmie was tickled. He was proud, you know. He knew then he'd made a good record. 'Cause that's where he found the blues. In that community. And he felt he had done right by it.

EJC: (Long silence) Do you think about them, Haydee and Jimmie?

SC: I'll tell you the truth, as sure as I breathe. I dream every night they're right here, sitting just where you are now. "Let's go, Sam. Let's hit it." And sure as you're born, I'd go. I wouldn't care where our destination may be. Look at that, that's (a) real tortoiseshell pickguard. Jimmie got me this guitar. We were in a furniture store in Jackson. They had guitars in the back. Jimmie said, "Sam, which one should I buy?" I played about a dozen and said: "This one." And he bought it and handed it to me. (Long pause.) So, I'll lay aside some strings just so I'm ready if someone knocks on my door and says, "Sam, are you ready to play? Let's kick off."

(END OF RECORDING)

BLUE YODEL No. 6

THE SAILOR'S PLEA

It seemed like my room at the Gunter Hotel. I was sitting in a coarse sofa chair the color of dried blood. The window was open. My head was killin' me. I was tracing the curly cue designs on the fabric with my finger. Big Peggy was on my lap in a nighty, trying to get my attention. My head rolled over her bosom. The radio was on, but it was playing the wrong Gene Austin song. This perturbed me. So, I took Peggy's hand and played with her fingers until they made the shape of a pistol, like kids do. And as I made "ping, ping" noises, I aimed her finger barrel at the dial. Red hots came firing out and blew the whole thing to bits. I raised my noggin'. "God damn, would you look at that. I just shot the radio."

Peggy patted my head. "Honey, you high as a lab rat. Peggy's all over here. Look this way."

And then all of a sudden, I was on this little putt-putt steamer with Gene and his wife Kathryn. And Carrie was there too. We were going down the Potomac on the 4th of July. Everybody had picnic clothes on. Now part of this trip really happened. Gene was a fan and took us out in his boat the summer of '28 when I hit. That was a good time. I drove my brother-in-law down M Street in Georgetown and we could hear "T for Texas" coming out of every other window along with Gene's "My Blue Heaven." That's what Gene called his boat. Except in my dream his boat was in a bathtub.

The water was all sudsy, like the Potomac. Gene's in a purple dress shirt and a yellow bow tie and green suspenders standing under a little blue umbrella. I can't see who's holding it. Behind him I see the stains on the tub and the soap holder. But Gene thinks he's on the river. And the engine's going putt, putt, putt. No one else seems to know we're in a bathtub but me.

Gene says: "You're never gonna get anywhere playing the tent circuit, kid." All this time, Gene's gnawing on a fried chicken leg.

In real life, I 'bout set fire to my sister-in-law's kitchen cookin' it up. After I cut my first record in Bristol, we drove to Washington and stayed at Carrie's sister's place so I could be close to Victor's studios if Peer called me back for another session. When he didn't, I went anyway. We'll talk about that later.

Anyway, in this dream, Carrie's standing next to Gene and handing him one fried chicken leg after another while he talks and chews. And I can barely hear him above the sound of the motor. Gene's speaking voice is scratchy, too, like a worn-out record. He talks for about two minutes and then he says to somebody, mouth burstin' with chicken: "My side's done, turn me over." And he stops talkin' 'til somebody flips the record, then he starts up again. All the while he's lecturing at me, pointing a half-ate chicken leg in my face. "You got a hit record now, boy. We gotta get you moving."

Meanwhile, behind him I see this young fellow, kind of an island complexion, in a white sailor's cap. He's running the motor. I keep thinking I've seen him before. All this time Gene's wife Kathryn, who was all about 20 if you wanna be generous, is in a satin dress with a long loop of pearls around her neck she keeps fiddlin' with. And she's fanning me with this ridiculous palm that's so big it's tickling her nose. She's the first in a long line of Gene's wives who would pick up a palm and fan whatever man came through the door. Everybody in this dream is pretty much real, now. Except we're in a bathtub.

So, Gene's jabbering at full speed and finally I remember where I've seen the boy who's running the motor. And I'm sure it's that same fellow, Julian somebody, who hacked up that architect's mistress in Wisconsin during a perfectly pleasant lunch just like ours. And so I keep motioning Kathryn to the railing, in case we gotta jump overboard. Meanwhile Gene's holding onto the railing with one hand and schooling me on show business with the other using that grimey chicken leg. Only time he stops is when he wants his record turned over.

"Jimmie, you need to play theaters, get off the penny circuit. I'm gonna make some calls for you." And he takes his chicken leg and puts it to his ear like it's a phone and starts talkin' into it. "Hello, room service? This is Gene Austin. Book Jimmie into the Earle. And I'm done with my bath. Get me out."

Now the Earle is in Washington, if you've never been. It was the first big theater I played after "T for Texas" hit.

You just can't beat a backstage, people running back and forth like squirrels in a coffee can. The long curtain ropes, heels clipping on the wood. Gals undressing right in front of you. "What kind of prop do you need, Mr. Rodgers?" Oh, a wire-back chair will do. When you're in a new crowd, there's nothing like that feeling that you know what they don't, that you've been doing this since you were a kid. And now you got a hit and the audience knows it but the players don't know you. They're all wrapped up in themselves. And who can blame them? But it's your moment, and you're ready. And once I hit, there wasn't a cold hand in the house. That was the last time I wore my railroad gear. Some son of a dog caught me coughin' in the alley and called me the "Singin' Undertaker." Last time I wore that fuckin' getup. That's what I was dreaming when three rotten kids woke me up, climbing on the railing in front of my deck chair.

"Hey, Mister, you're talkin' in your sleep."

"Yodelayoo, boys! Are we in New York yet?"

"Nah," they all answered.

I pulled up my flannel blanket. It was a bit chilly on deck. "Scat off then! 'Fore a wave comes up and knocks you cold. See those gulls up there? They like to swoop down on you and pick at your belly button, pull out your intestines, and wrap them clear around the boat twice while you're hollerin' for your mama." I had their attention now. "And when they're done and all your insides are cleaned out, the sea will come up and drag you down to live forevermore with all the pirate skeletons."

"Shut up, y'gibface!" said the fat one. He was the balls of the bunch. Chewing some kind of candy on a stick. All three wore identical caps, short wool pants, and suspenders.

"He's gonna get you killed, you know," I said to the other two, who were pushing each other a little too close to the rail for my liking. "Come here. All of youse. I got something for you. Gather 'round. Put out your palms. Right. Now, here's a nickel each. Now,

I want you to do me a favor. Charlie Chaplin's somewhere on this boat. Go find him and tell him Jimmie Rodgers wants to see him."

Off they went. Beside me, oblivious to my command, was Cora Bedell, my personal nurse. With a big head of curly blonde hair under a floppy hat. Quite a few gold teeth, too. A bit on the heavy side but not enough to make any man think twice. I'd say she has 10 years on me. And about the funniest broad I've ever met. She saved my ass when I was in a ditch in Carthage, Texas, last year, sick as hell. She gave me a shot, patted my bottom, and got me through a little show I had to make. I told her then if I ever could use her full-time, I'd ring her up. She always knows just when the honey's wearing off. That's why I call her Ole Pleasin'. Nothin' ruffles her feathers. She's seen it all.

"Good morning, Mr. Rodgers." Cora looked straight ahead at the sea. She had a lap full of magazines and newspapers.

"Good morning, darlin'. You know there's room for you under this here blanket, too." I turned on my side and imagined, as I often have, if I could be in love with her. And I wish I could. But I just love her instead. She laughs from her belly. I could tell she was holding back 'cause she was bitin' her tongue. I needled her some more. "Tell me. Out of all the entertainers you've oiled up and kept road worthy, am I your favorite?"

She turned a page. "Oh, absolutely."

"Glad we got that out of the way." I straightened up in my deck chair which was stickin' to my skin. "Before I dozed off, you were reading my first chapter. What did you think?"

"It needs work."

"The whole country needs work, darlin'."

"Am I gonna be in this story of yours?

"In it? You get a starring role." We were quiet for a minute. I drew my blanket back up to my chin. "Why aren't you married, anyway? You're pretty fetching in the right light." I could see now she had her April issue of *Women's World*. Ain't that the truth.

"We've had this conversation before."

"Did you like him as much as me? I mean, how could you?"

Cora looked out at the sea and closed her eyes in the sun, patting my boney leg. "I liked him all right. I've forgotten how much I liked him. He was a bit . . . ornery."

"Ornery? I like ornery."

"Not this kind. More like a poacher. Not the sort of fellow you'd get along with."

"Hmm. Ok. Children?"

"Nope," she went back to her magazine, turning pages, and took a deep breath.

"Would you like one? The Lindbergh kidnappers are in the market. They probably work for RCA Victor. They got a division for everything."

"Would I want a child, you mean? Only if it could be a girl but just like you."

"Now you're talkin'. Pleasin', let's you and me elope." At that she laughed and laughed, dropped her magazine, and put her hands to her face.

The boys came back. The leader was huffy. "We saw the Captain and he said Charlie Chaplin ain't on this boat. You owe us another nickel." All the boys looked alike but the leader was a little shorter and stubbier. The tallest was the most shy of the lot and I guessed he was the one they picked on. "Are you fellows Irish twins?"

Cora giggled out loud. I think all the world would stop fussin' if they could hear that giggle. It would make a man think everything he says is funny. The lead boy puzzled. I could tell he wanted to scrap with me. He'd probably kill me honestly but the gravitas of my age and gray pallor gave me a thin advantage. The ship was bobbing now. I thought I might be sick on them but it passed.

"Who says we're Irish?" The boy scrunched his face.

"You know what?" I rubbed my chin. "You look like me when I was way-high." I raised my hand to show them just how high way-high was. "I'm Irish. My grandparents were from Cork. Like in a bottle." They stared back at me, blank. "You boys deaf?" Kids these days. You speak right to 'em and they don't say a goddamn thing.

"No." But they all looked at each other as if to confirm they weren't deaf, just in case one of them was but the others hadn't the heart to say so.

"Well of course, the Captain's gonna tell you Chaplin isn't on board because then he'd have a riot." I lowered my voice to a whisper. "He's in disguise!"

"Oh." One elbowed the others. "Told ya."

"So, here's what you do. Look for a short fellow with little feet and no mustache who's dressed fancy. If he's funnier than me, that's Charlie Chaplin." They ran off. I called after them. "Then tell him you got an older sister."

"Jimmie!" Cora giggled at all of this back and forth and slapped her magazine on her lap as the boys scampered off. One of the sailors was telling the couple next to us we had come around the horn of Florida. "How you know so much about Mr. Chaplin's peccadillos?" She learned forward, curving her back, locked her hands 'round her knees, and closed her eyes on the sunlight.

"Aw, some time ago before I met you, I went out to Hollywood... Can I have a pick-a-tune?"

"No, you cannot have a pick-a-tune."

"Oh, for crying out loud, woman, have you looked at me lately? I'll be lucky to see Lady Liberty."

"You'll make it to New York."

"That's up to you." At that Cora laughed again. I leaned on my elbow. My energy was coming back. "I'm gonna look straight into your eyes and I want you look in right in mine. I'm even going to wipe the hair from your eyes—there—so you can get an idea of how tenderizing I can be." I tugged on her arm and gave her a squeeze. Right then I wished we were any place else. "I'm not taking this boat home. You get my drift? So how about you give me a goddamn cigarette and if I start coughing to death you take it from my mouth and throw it overboard."

"Jimmie . . ." She seemed cross but happy at the same time. "Well, I won't say it."

"I'll say it for you! Fuck you, Jimmie! That's what you want to say, right?" At this she was defenseless, reached in her pocketbook and gave me a smoke stick. That's when you know someone loves you, when they keep your brand of cigarettes even though they've swore they wouldn't let you smoke.

"Thanks, girl. You got a flint?" She did. My first puff made me warm all over. But the second I regretted. Once that smoke hit my throat, I could feel my chest close up. I hacked and threw my blanket off. Cora looked at me disgusted which only made me laugh all the harder. Then the boys came back.

"Oh, Christ, you three again. It's been five minutes!" I caught my breath. If I had died right then they'd still be waiting. "All right. I'm cuttin' your salary. Pennie each. Now if you don't bring me Charlie Chaplin I'm gonna get the Captain to throw you overboard. Now git!" Cora was back in her magazine with a shit-eating grin on her face. I took her hand which was hot. "I'm sorry, darling, people are trying to keep us apart. So, when we get to New York I want you to do something for me."

"What's that?"

"If anything happens to me on this trip, I want you to bring my briefcase to someone for safe keeping."

"You get yourself a lawyer or Ralph or somebody else to worry about that stuff."

"No, no, no. Ralph will just send it to Carrie and Carrie will set it on fire. Like she did to the bouquet I sent her. I want you to take it. But you have to give me your word."

"Ok, fair enough. What's in it?"

"My life story."

"And who am I taking it to?"

Just then the boys came back like the three demented little wise men, determined to deliver. "Oh, Jesus, you critters. Now what?"

"Charlie Chaplin's here."

I took my cigarette from my mouth, "You don't say? Where?"

"He's playing in the theater in 5 minutes."

"In *The Circus*," said the shyest boy. It was the first time he spoke and the other two looked at him, shocked.

"Oh, that's swell. I love *The Circus*. Pleasin', can we go?"

With high dramatics, she shut her magazine at last. "Yes, Jimmie we can go. Now, boys, go save us four seats in the back. (She gave them more coins. These kids were having a rich afternoon.) "We need a seat on either side of us if you can. Jimmie here is under the weather and we don't want to bother anybody. Now go. Scat!"

I was all gears with no grease trying to stand. The clouds way yonder were dark. I love the way I could feel her body against mine when she leaned in to help me up. The sun was brighter around the stern and I couldn't wait to get there.

"You were saying about Mr. Chaplin?"

"Ralph and I had lunch with Laurel & Hardy when we went to California a few years back. Did I not tell you this? They were filming *Pardon Us*, their first talkie. Their producer Hal Roach took me and Ralph to the set and they were having a hell of a time filming this blackface scene. It was all wrong. So, I was talking to Stan about how I used to do it."

"Oh, you didn't."

"Hey, I was trying to make a living. Believe me, I didn't do it long. There's nothing lower than that racket. But Stanley and I got to talking. Did you know he's English? And when he first came to America, he and Chaplin used to room together. Stan would fry pork chops and Charlie would play violin to hide the sizzle. He said . . . ," and I leaned in for emphasis, "Charlie likes green fruit."

"And you don't?"

"I like my fruit bruised, like you!" She laughed so I kept on. "I like 'em just when they're about to fall and they're just so grateful when I catch 'em. Anyway, at lunch Hal said Stan and Laurel might could use me sometime. So, when Ralph and I went to work that day phonographing, I said why don't you cut me a test record of me doing a blackface skit to show them what I sound like. 'Cause now it's all about how you sound on a microphone. I knew once they heard this voice, they'd know I could cut through brick. Ralph puts me with this awful comedian they dug up from somewhere. Put us on some script they had laying about. I think he was just humoring me. Well, just then Louis Armstrong comes by 'cause we were set to work that day."

". . . Oh I just love his records," Cora looked straight ahead as we walked to the ship's theater. It was almost like we were a couple. Sweet.

". . . And Louis, he's on the other side of the glass just shaking his head like this"—(I shook my head)—"and we when we were done cutting, this lousy script, Louis says, 'Ofay, ain't no way you're gonna put a shine to that shit.'"

"Had you met him before?"

"Louis? Hell yeah. Many times. We were gonna form a duo and call us Black and White. And so, Louis says, 'Let me produce this correctly' and he and I summoned up an old skit we knew and on the spot we cut it to wax. And it's funny as hell. He brought along some gage, you see. Mexican smoke. So it seemed funny as hell. Afterwards I'm getting my breath and Louis goes in the booth to talk to Ralph. And I can see Louis and Ralph have words about something. Louis' wife Lil was playing piano and she had been bossing him around fierce. After that, he took his cash and scrammed. On his way out, he told Lil, 'You can roll that fucking piano home by yourself.' Then he looked at me. 'Good luck, Jimmie boy. Watch out for Fatty Arbuckles.'"

All this time while I was telling this story, we were slowly making our way to a little ballroom off the deck set up with chairs. The walk made me weak, and I needed Cora's shoulder again. The ship's movie house wasn't much. But it was warm. No crowd, thank goodness. It was close to dinner time. "Pleasin' look! They got a piano up there. Why don't you go stretch out on top and I'll play you something."

Cora paid my plea no attention. "Move over, let's get this blanket on you."

"Did I tell you I wrote a new song just for you, 'Honey Britches Blues.' I'll sing it for you."

My gals got honey in her britches
And money all day long

Cora shout whispered, "Cut that out."

The fellow in front of us in a boater turned 'round. "Mister, you sound just like Jimmie Rodgers."

"Oh, thank you, friend. I wish. Wouldn't that be fine?"

Cora put her head on my shoulder and I kissed her forehead and dug my hand 'neath her hive of hair. "Lady, what are all these bumps on your head?"

"That's where I buried your women."

"Sounds about right."

Cora had put a cloth mask around her mouth as she helped me get settled.

"You better wear one of those 'round me."

We got settled in and Cora tucked on another blanket over me. "So, who am I supposed to give this novel of yours to?"

"Haydee Chatmon Brown."

"Who is Haydee Chatmon Brown?"

"A sweet little brown gal with red hair like a matchstick." I took off my shoe to itch my heel. "She's from Jackson. And she's fixin' to have my child." Cora gasped and asked me all kinds of questions. But right about then she put a stinger in my arm. And this is where I have to stop this chapter. 'Cause the last thing I remember as I snuggled next to that epic bosom of hers was watching ole Charlie put his head in the mouth of a lion.

BLUE YODEL No. 7

OLD LOVE LETTERS

He was all of 12, 13 years old. A squirt! I was only about 10. He went by James then. Dress shirt. Cloth pants. Suspenders. A rascal! Great smile. Taught me to roll dice. And he did a bit of magic, too. Coin tricks. I don't know how he wound up here. I think he was workin' some kind of circus. My father found him and took him home. That's the kind of man he was. We had a department store in West Blocton. Back then the whole town was owned by the Cahaba Coal Mining Company. My uncles put him to work blocking hats in the basement with me. "Teach James the ropes," they said. Geesh. He was hopeless. His mind wandered. He had a ukulele he took everywhere. Sometimes he didn't touch it. But he was never without it. Yeah, he was pretty bright. Crafty. Good memory. On Friday nights we would have him dim the lights at sundown. Our congregation was tiny. But we had the only dimmer in town. And you won't believe this, but our synagogue had a tennis court. Do you know who Melvin Israel is? He's my cousin. Goes by Mel Allen now. He does play by play for the Yankees. He was Lou Gehrig's favorite. Mel used to come to services here when he was a student. Brought all his friends from the university. Anyway, James! Whew. James learned by doing. He would watch us say the prayers over the candles and the bread. And he memorized them both. (Snaps) Like that! And on occasion he'd recite them, too.

Later on, he got a job with the Tuggles across the street. They ran a photography and tailor shop. Good business. I don't know how long James stayed there. I heard his father came looking for him. But he made a point to say goodbye.

We kept in touch. After he was famous, he came through here driving a Buick. Very nice car. Color? I don't remember. Yes, I do, powder gold. It looked like a bullet. He had supper with us outside at the picnic table. He did the prayer over the bread. My father was impressed. But my mother made a point to boil his dishes. She knew he was very ill. James and my father got along. My father would say to me: "You could learn something from this boy. He's very successful." James asked if we needed anything. My father said no. But as they were talking, James pretended to drop two silver dollars which he proceeded to pick up and give to me! "Jacob, I think you dropped these."

Jacob Israel, West Blocton, AL

I grew up in Phoenix. The Southern Pacific had a local that passed right by my parents' house. We lived about 10 blocks from town. I was near 15 so I guess this was around 1916, 1917. I was walking down the track on my way to town. Probably lookin' for a job. And I see this fellow coming toward me carrying a bedroll on his shoulder. He saw me and started waving like he knew me. He was wearing blue jeans and a Levi's jacket. And a gray Stetson with a pyramid crown. Back then, you didn't see kids wearing Levi's like you do today unless they were workin' in them. His whole face was streaked with grease. He got up to me and asked if I'd share a smoke and we sat down on his bedroll. He had a tin of Prince Albert. He said he had just come in from Hassayamapa. Said he was broke and hungry and asked if I thought my folks would make him a meal. I said sure.

Seems like we were friends right away. So I brought him home. We put his bedroll on the porch. I asked him to wait in the living room and I went in the kitchen and said, "Mother, I met a kid who could use a meal." And she said, "Well where is he?"

She looked him over. Jimmie seemed like he was ready to scat. But he stood up straight and looked her in the eye and said, "Hello, Ma'am. Your son invited me in and I took him up on it. I'd sure love to share some supper with you." My mother, she was from Georgia. Everybody loved her for her southern hospitality. She asked him how old he was and he said 16. And so we ate on the porch steps and waited for the rain that was coming. He could put it away. My mother gave him the third degree all through the meal. Wanted to make sure he wasn't wanted by the police.

He said his mother was dead and he and his father were estranged. He said he had worked call boards and such for the M&O and all around Oklahoma. Mother told him he could wash up and stick around until my dad came home. Now my dad, his family were German. No fuss. To the point. But once Mother said it was ok, he said that's fine by him. I offered Jimmie to share my room but he said, "I sleep better outside." I think he knew then he had TB. I'd wake in the night and hear that dry hacking cough.

I had a little 5-string banjo, Bruno & Son, and he had a uke and we'd sit on the porch and play the "Spanish Cavalier." He sang the hell out of that tune. And he'd make some railroad blues with verses of his own. Kind of like he did later with his blue yodels. I can't tell you those. They were a little bawdy. Man, he was quick, though. If he saw someone walking down the street while he was singin', he'd put them in the song right there. He was a creative soul. About a week later we both got jobs at Henry Poor's Planing Mill. That's long gone now. We made about $2, $2.25 a day. His first paycheck he offered to my mother for room and board. She said, "You just keep that and go get some fresh clothes." His eyes lit up! So he got a new pair of cheats and a jacket and a white silk neckerchief. He'd tie it around his neck in a double knot with the ends back over his shoulders. You know how I mean? He had a hell of a time untying it. But he wouldn't give up that ole hat. Later, Jim bought himself a Flying Merkel motorcycle secondhand. Bright orange. One of those eight-valve racers. At night, he'd go racin' down the street, hollerin'. All you could make out was yellow and blue flame from the exhaust. Our neighbors didn't care for him too much.

One day he went to town on his own. Came walking home. And I said what happened to your cycle? He said: "I had to part with it." Next morning, he told my parents it was time for him to hit the road. "I've got to mark off and go." We couldn't believe it. I was crushed. But he just shook my hand and said, "George, you take care." He called everybody George. I tell you what, he traveled light. In about five minutes, he was ready to go. He left me his ukulele. A Supertone. I still have it. I don't know what made him kick off like that. I was kind of hurt. I'll never forget him walking down the track with his bedroll on his back.

Sterling Weber, Phoenix, AZ

I ran a tent show, Billy Terrell's Comedians, all around the southern territory. Kentucky, Virginia, Mississippi, all those places. You won't believe this, but we carried 35 people plus an orchestra. Seated around 2,000. And 1,500 reserve. We had red, white, and blue chairs with my name on 'em. I think it was around '23, we landed in Meridian. And this kid, looked like he was all of 20, come up to me, sort of a hat-in-hand type. He was a sight 'cause his clothes was sharp. Dark suit, dark vest. Really good-lookin' shoes. I thought, who the hell is this? He said he wanted to sing on the show. I said no, son, you won't ever catch a break in your own hometown. They'll murderlize you. Well, he kept talking how he sang a blue yodel. I thought, what in God's name is that? So I said, look, I gotta shave before the show. Come up to my room. You got 'til I'm done shaving to convince me. He came up with a guitar and banjo to audition. Couldn't play banjo worth a darn. But I liked his voice. And then he tried one on guitar. That wasn't much better, but it suited him. Truth telling songs. Blues verses. I told him, you're different. So, I said I'd put him on in Hattiesburg which was where we was goin' next. I put him in the truck with me and we got mudded out on the way there. Mississippi didn't have no roads to speak of then. We were in hell and high water all the way. Snakes and frogs. I gave in about 5 miles out. We get to town finally the next morning and we're setting up for the show and the whole crew could see he was green. They was razzing him terrible. Put popcorn in his guitar. He'd tie up one post and they'd untie whatever he did and make him do it again. Finally, I had to say, "Shut up, you little bastards. Give this kid a shot or you're all fired. He's gonna shame you." I'd say stuff like that to 'em. Well, Jimmie played three numbers at intermission and got two encores. They loved him. We went on to Louisiana and Texas and up into Arizona. He went home somewhere in the Midwest. I think his daughter died.

About three, maybe four years later I'm in a music store in Norfolk and one person after another is asking for Jimmie Rodgers records. I thought, shit. It can't be! And behind the counter they have an autographed photo of him there. Man says they got 300 records on order, all sold out. I thought, dadgum! It's the same little fellow. So, time passes. Business got really rotten. I sent him a telegram at XER in Mexico. Late at night you could hear that anywhere 'cross the country. I told him things had been tough the last three years. I had lost a lot of money and I was really in a fix. I was in Paducah at the time. I had no idea how sick he was. This was early '33. I asked him if he could come do a show for me. Could we work something out? He wired right back and said, "George, I'm Cadillacin' there now. Rent the house. Charge 75 cents up front, 50 cents reserve." I got some candy and had balloons made up. I had cut a deal with this preacher who was trying to get rid of a load of popcorn. Jesus, I had so much popcorn. Jimmie said you can keep all that. We worked out a deal. Booked the theater on a Monday. That afternoon, I could have just cried. People are lined up down the sidewalk, around the bank, all over the place. I couldn't believe it. He pulls into town 30 minutes before showtime in a silver Cadillac. Sum bitch is nice. It's him, his driver, and this blonde woman, kind of buxom built, in the whitest nurse's outfit you've ever seen. They pull up in back. They go off in the dressing room. He's terribly thin. Gaunt. I think to myself: what have I done? He's gonna die on stage. He comes out the dressing room, grinning ear to ear. I thought, man! What happened to you? He says get him a wire-back chair. Ok. Walks out, puts his foot on the chair. Kills it. "Texas Blues," "Moonlight and Skies," "Frankie and Johnny," "Waiting for a Train," and one other. I think it was the blue yodel he auditioned for me. I can't remember. Three encores. Comes off dripping wet. I told him hoss, you saved my ass. He said: "It's the least I could do." I give him his cut, he gives about half of his cut back to me. Puts his hand on my shoulder and says: "Walk easy, George. It's sunset time." About a week later, I get an envelope full of popcorn and a signed picture of him: "To Billy Terrell. One of the greatest showmen I ever met." Two, three months later I heard he was dead.

Billy Terrell, Roseland, LA

Oh yeah, I met him lots of times. That cat was my friend. He come through the prairie. He knew the folks I worked for. He'd perform there. He just liked to be a part of things, you know. He'd play and I'd listen. I loved his sound. And he'd point me out. He'd say: "You care to join me?" I said yes I do. He'd yodel, you see, and I'd howl back at him. We'd go out in the woods or in the fields somewhere and just sing. When he first met me, my voice was already breaking in. We'd see one another time to time. He came back and like always, you know, after he was done, he'd call me over. "Sing for me, kid, let me hear you." And I let out a howl and he stood back. "My goodness, Chester. You are a howlin' wolf now. You're gone." He didn't give me that name. Charley Patton gave me that name. But Jimmie Rodgers, he was my friend. And he thought well of me, too. My man. A one and only.

Chester Burnett, The Howlin' Wolf, Chicago, IL

I had a little band with my brother in Bristol. We called ourselves the Teneva Ramblers. We played a show in Knoxville at the Knoxville Smokies ballfield. And we all stayed to watch the game. That's where we met Jimmie. He said he was on his way back to Asheville and he was on the radio there and getting hundreds of letters every day. And he was looking for a band. So, we said ok, and became the Jimmie Rodgers Entertainers. Of course, it turned out he didn't have any of that. No radio. Nuthin'. But then he did get us a job playing at this resort there. We got free room and board out of the deal. I don't know how he did it. He could talk the bark off a tree. We played every day and had the run of the place. This went on for a few weeks. We went off to do a date in Johnson City, I think. We had three flat tires on the way. Took us forever. When we got back to Asheville, I called my father 'cause he had a friend at a dealership in Bristol to see if I could find a trade. He said, "C'mon." So Jimmie and I drove to Bristol, about 90 miles, and traded my old heap for a used Dodge. Which wasn't much better.

Afterwards, we stopped by my mom's. She ran the boarding house there. Yes, that's right, in Bristol. And when we walked in her place, it was littered with musicians. Banjo, guitar, fiddle. You could hardly move. Jimmie said, "What in blazes is going on here?" That's when we found Victor was in town. Well straight away, Jimmie went across the street to this hat factory where they had set up. Their turntable was hooked up to this pulley system. A couple microphones. And a curtain around the performers. Big green thing. So, in between takes, Jimmie spoke with Mr. Peer and his engineer and said he'd like an audition. They said ok. We'll try Wednesday. We get back to Asheville and Jimmie says to his wife and daughter—he called her Little Boots—he says: "Time to mosey. I'm gonna wax a record." And they just put their things in a bag and they were ready to go. I'd never seen anything like it. They had nothing. They were in the car in no more than 10 minutes tops.

Well, us running off to Bristol to cut a record didn't sit well with my brother. First of all, Jimmie already acted like we were his band. So, on the way there, he and my brother quarreled over how we'd be listed on the label. Naturally Jimmie wanted to call us the Jimmie Rodgers Entertainers. Well, push came to shove finally. Everybody was overheatin'. I'm driving and watching this go down in the rearview mirror. Jimmie's next to me. Little Boots is in the middle. My brother is behind me. And Jimmie—I can just see him leaning over the passenger seat with his arm stretched out. He looked at my brother and said real quiet: "Well, George"—he called everybody George. He said: "I'll just mark off and make my own record." I think that's what he wanted to do all along. We got to Bristol and Jimmie went up and talked to Mr. Peer and said he'd have two songs ready the next day. So, he cut his songs and the next thing I knew, he was off to Washington, D.C. In my car. The one I had just traded for. I never did figure that out.

JIMMIE RODGERS
NATIONAL RADIO ARTIST
VICTOR RECORD ARTIST

ATLANTIC 2325-W
1151 3rd St., N. E.
WASHINGTON, D. C.

Mr. C. Grant, Teneva Ramblers, Bristol, TN

My daddy was a wildcatter. He lost his shirt at that and wound up as an engineer for Shell. But before that he used to go with Jimmie. They met as kids in Phoenix. Running around with their shirt tails out. Raising all kinds of hell. Jimmie came through here on some tour. I couldn't have been no more than eight. I remember because at the show my daddy put me on his shoulders and I about peed my pants I laughed so hard. The show had clowns and jugglers. But when Jimmie came out the place just exploded. When he was singin' it was dead quiet. He'd tell stories in-between. God, he was funny. I didn't understand anything he was talking about but my daddy laughed like I had never heard him laugh. So I did, too. It was so exciting. Sometimes he'd get caught in a cough and somebody would yell "Spit it out, Jimmie!" And everybody would cheer you know. Cheer him on to keep going. Afterwards Jimmie came out to the house. Drove up in this beautiful jet black Buick with silver trim and white wheels and a white top. And when he got out, he had on white cowboy boots, black suit, black vest with silver piping and a white shirt. And a white hat. He looked like the car.

I remember Jimmie had this flask. I had never seen anything like that because my daddy didn't drink. And he asked my daddy if he minded. He said no and sent my mother to fetch some ice water. We came in the house and sat in our old living room. And Jimmie just drank from the flask with an ice water chaser. All night. It got late and I was so happy because nobody was putting me to bed. He and my daddy were just talking about music and guitars. They sang some together. I remember Jimmie had this cigarette lighter that had a clock on it. And he would fidget with it. Light it and put it out while he'd talk. Jimmie saw me looking at it and while he and Daddy were talking, Jimmie scooped me up and put me on the chair next to him. And he said: "Let's give you a lesson on how these work." I remember looking over at Daddy. He said, "It's all right."

It's funny, I remember Jimmie's fingers. They were all knobby. But he was very patient with me. Taking me through all the pieces of it. How not to overwind it. How to turn the wheel to strike the flint. It took me several tries. Finally, I got it. And he kissed me on the forehead and said to my Daddy: "Well, I think she's worked hard for this don't you, Pops?" And he gave me the lighter! I still have it. My mama about died!

Someone said, "Off to bed." Daddy threw me over his shoulder. I remember waving at Jimmie like this, just with my fingers, and he waved back the same way. The last thing I heard him say was something like: "Don't fiddle with that in bed. That's a daytime toy only." He was a gentle soul. Didn't seem like the kind of person that could last too long. You know what I mean?

Genevieve Weber, Phoenix, AZ

Sure, I knew him. I sold him eight or nine cars. Buicks, Cadillacs. Special ordered one from Detroit. He had a Model A he called Thirsty the Christmas Tree. Pine green. He painted the roof red. Had pistol pockets in the door and a place to hide a pint. That feller, oh, what was his name? John somebody, who real-estated his house. They'd all pile in that and drive to Mexico, Pedraw Negras and places like that. Jimmie gave me a bottle of Four Roses once. He had a prescription. He came here one morning to the dealership driving a real nice V12, brand new. In Diana Cream. Looked like he had been up all night. The thing was, I had sold him another one the week before. In Tunis Blue. I said: "Jimmie! Where's the blue Cadillac I sold you last week?" He just waved me off and said: "Aw, hoss, I had to let her go. She had a flat." And he keeled right over. So, I put him in the back of a 16-cylinder Phaeton we had on the floor to let him sleep it off. This was the Depression and I knew nobody was gonna buy that car.

Well, come afternoon, we had opened the big windows out front 'cause it was summertime. I was helping somebody or doing something in the office. And Jimmie, that rascal. He woke up, crawled in the front seat, found the keys in the ignition, started her up, and drove it off the showroom floor onto the lot. I hear somebody say: "There goes Jimmie Rodgers!" So now he starts circlin' round the dealership, yodelin'. You could hear him all through the dealership. Son of a bitch. People are runnin' out. Getting autographs. I was trying not to laugh but I was pissed, you know? I hollered: "You gonna pay for that? He says: "Aw, George! Send the bill to David Sarnoff!" And off he went, honkin' the horn.

Joel Cavendar, Cavendar Cadillac, San Antonio, TX

I had just started working for the *Dallas Morning News*. And everyone around the newsroom teased me for wanting to interview Jimmie Rodgers. I guess he chewed up a reporter at the *San Antonio Express* a few years before. But I asked for the assignment and I got it. I found Jimmie in a tourist court a little ways out of town. Some street musicians told me where to find him. Lord knows how they knew. It was just Jimmie and his driver, Henry. Short fellow. Wore a uniform and a visor the whole time. And leather gloves which I thought was kind of funny. Jimmie had a Thessalon Green Cadillac. I had never heard of such a thing. He made me say it three times. Gray seats, green trim. His driver kept it spotless on the outside. Jimmie wasn't getting out of the car, so I got in and we drove all around Dallas, parts I didn't know existed. Jimmie stayed slunk in the back seat, me on one side and him on the other. He smelled terrible. And there were little bottles of stuff on the floor. He kept a small leather pouch tucked under his leg. He'd just pat it as he talked. We drove around and he seemed super agitated. Very polite though. Every once in a while, he'd turn his head while he was talkin' and follow somebody he saw outside, like he knew them. When was this? Spring '32. I'd just got engaged and I remember worrying my fiancé was gonna think I'd been up to no good when I got home.

Jimmie kept on talking about this new contract he had with RCA and how he was making more money than Gene Austin. But to me he seemed like he was broke. His driver kept looking at us through the rearview mirror. He'd look at Jimmie and look at me. I had a grandmother that was real touchy like Jimmie was. And my trick with her was just to relax. Take a deep breath, and don't be in a hurry. I mean, the worst they could do was throw me out of the car. After awhile, he started nodding off. Then I asked him about current records he liked and he perked up. I didn't know anything he mentioned. He asked me did I know where Blind Lemon Jefferson lived 'cause he was from Dallas. I said, no sir. I'd never heard of him.

Here's something funny he said. I asked him if he'd ever been down to Mexico and he said he'd sung on XER, the border station. But they kicked him off 'cause he was sellin' autographed photos of Jesus Christ. I didn't know if he was kidding me or not. He also said he got his yodel from watching Minnie Marx, the Marx Brothers' mom. I guess he saw them at some theater in Alabama and she had a spot in the show. That must have

been early '20s. And she would come out and sing and yodel. I didn't know if I could believe that either.

At one point I asked him if he might retire one day. He said: "Son, I'm not even here." And right then, his driver interrupted him. "Time to rest, Jimmie," and they let me off in front of the paper.

I went to the show that night. The fellow playing before him, Cliff, I can't remember his last name, was helping him out. I saw him give Jimmie a shot. I assume morphine for his TB. Jimmie looked at me as he was gettin' it and said, "Eat your vegetables, kid." It was shocking at the time. I had never seen anything like that. But what really shocked me was he popped right out of the tent and gave a hell of a show.

Now morphine don't do that. I asked Cliff: "What did you give him?" He just laughed. "Interview's over, George." That was the end of that. After the show, we all carried Jimmie back to his car. He was totally limp and drippin' sweat through his suit. He could have been dead then for all I know. They were kickin' up dust while folks were still clappin'.

Carl A., *Dallas Morning News*, Dallas, TX

The whole job of a recording engineer is to be a kind of psychiatrist. You have to trick artists into doing their best. Each one is different. Now Mr. Caruso was the easiest artist who came to the laboratory. Nothing seemed to make any difference to him. He almost always sang perfectly. With confidence. Fearless.

Back then it was an acoustical process. Are you familiar? Those are the days when you had to sing into a horn. It was terrible fidelity compared to what you can get today. But if you listen to those records, you can tell how powerful he was. Caruso would make that needle dance. We'd have people in the big studio three rows deep to watch him. He'd chat with everyone and be friendly. He liked to have a crowd to perform for. But when his hands would go up to start, he'd shut it down and get to work. You wouldn't hear a peep from the audience.

Now John Philip Sousa, he would bite his fingers and use vile language at the musicians when they made mistakes. One time we were working a long day. Lots of trial and error. And Mr. Sousa got so perturbed he actually got down from the director's stand, went over to the hat rack, found the hat of the offending musician who made the mistake, a cornet player, brought him his hat, threw it on the floor, and jumped on it. What followed was more or less a riot. We'd have comedians come in and they'd have to put on their makeup and costume otherwise they couldn't remember their bits.

Others? Well, Frieda Hempel. She was a piece of work. She sang for the Philharmonic. Half the time she was intoxicated.

Yes, I recorded Fats Waller. Very amusing gentleman. When he talked to you, he'd have one eye goin' one way and one eye goin' the other. He loved the pipe organ we had in the studio. Mr. Peer would pick him up after his nightclub shows. Fats would sleep in the car and come up just before 10 o'clock and Mr. Peer would have a thermos of coffee for him. And he'd get right up and play. I attended one of his birthday parties in Harlem. Lots of folks there. Cab Calloway, Duke Ellington. I saw Duke play guitar. I was made to feel most welcome.

Now the first time I recorded Jimmie was in '28, I think it was. Mr. Peer told me one of his hillbilly artists was coming for a session with some accompaniment. But Peer had to go off to record someplace, Memphis I think, and so he was gonna send his wife to look things over. Well, everyone arrived on time, but we had all kinds of problems. For one, I think we were already trying to cut costs by running two wax masters at once so we wouldn't have to cut a follow-up of a good take for safety. Then we started running late with rehearsals as Jimmie went looking for a fruit stand to buy some lemons for his throat. We were supposed to go, oh, I dunno, 10 a.m. to 1 p.m. Something like that. It got to be 2 o'clock and we had nothing to show for it. When he finally came back, we worked all afternoon on tests. Jimmie had not worked with the musicians that Mr. Peer had hired, you see. They were still learning how to play together, which with Jimmie wasn't easy. His timing was more like you'd hear from a Black artist. These fellows didn't know what was happening. Irregular intervals and such. Mrs. Peer was fit to be tied. I suppose she just thought a hillbilly artist would play three songs one time and leave. Not Jimmie.

Finally, we started in earnest and Jimmie kept ruining one disc after the other. He'd stop right in the middle to change the arrangement and ruin the take. Or he'd yodel in a different place. The fellows trying to keep up with him were having a hell of a time.

No, Jimmie wasn't bothered by this at all. He'd just laugh and say: "Well, you just put one of them platters out the window and call the bees to work. They'll make you all the discs you want." We cut to wax then. (Laughs) You could not hurry that man. But I admired that. He was patient. Chain smoked, one after the other. You knew he was ready when he'd cross one leg over the other. He'd say: "Ok, George. Now I'm ready." And I'd be thinking, well what the hell have we been doing? But then he'd pretty much have it in a couple takes.

Jimmie wanted to hear what he'd done. A reference cut. Playback, in other words, which we couldn't do in those days. So we'd run Jimmie's little portable home cutter alongside the master so he could listen back to what he did. 'Cause before tape, we didn't have playbacks. If you play back a wax master, you might ruin it. When he'd listen down to the reference we made off his cutter, he was all business. Yes, he and Peer were usually in agreement on the best take. When they had a good cut, they'd just look at each other and smile. And Jimmie would buckle his knees if it was good. Jitter like crazy. He'd put his head down and fold his arms and jiggle his legs if he liked it. If he heard a mistake in the reference, he'd stop jiggling for a minute. If he started again, then you knew it'd be all right. He'd say: "I feel it." Little mistakes didn't bother him. If it was way off, he'd say: "I don't sound like myself." Once we got a good one Jimmie would look at me and say: "Fred, you're a very fine engraver of my voice." I still have a photo he signed for me. "To Fred, my recreator. Thanks for all the trouble I gave you."

One night, Jimmie stayed after Mr. Peer left. This was when Eli Oberstein had come along as A&R man. He was a real pain in Mr. Peer's neck. He put the word out that Peer was wastin' the company's time cutting these hillbilly artists. Maybe even accused him of financial mischief. No, I never got that impression. Peer was on the square, seemed like. I think, frankly, Oberstein was jealous of Peer. Because at that time, Sarnoff had to sell Peer's own publishing company back to him. They made Peer sell it when he joined the company.

But Sarnoff was smart, you see. There was a lot of talk about anti-trust laws. And so RCA got out of the publishing business and they just gave Peer's company back to him. Mr. Peer was doing very well at that point and was essentially his own operator. RCA paid all the costs and Peer took the profit.

Oberstein didn't like that arrangement. At all. He wanted Peer's job and was gunnin' for it. I don't know what was said between them but there was some bad blood from the get-go. And it started spilling over into the sessions. On top of that, Oberstein was paying disc jockeys for airplay. Peer hated that. He made it so Oberstein couldn't work southern DJs. They just took his money and put it in their pocket and played whatever the hell they liked. (Laughs) He didn't know that territory like Peer did.

Oberstein one time tried to disrupt a Rodgers session. Maybe Peer couldn't be there, I can't recall. He threw out the Black fellow who was playing bass. Jimmie was fit to be tied. He came charging into the booth and got right in Oberstein's face. "Don't derange my music." When was this? I couldn't say. Maybe a year before he died.

Anyways, I'm in the middle, just waiting to see if the session was gonna kick off again. Oberstein had said something about the balance not being right and Jimmie, boy, he let him have it. Got right in his face. "I'm the reason RCA's quarterly earnings went up 20 percent last year. Don't you dare tell my man here how to do his work. I ain't yet seen a record with your name on it." And Jimmie puts his hand on my shoulder and just stares down Oberstein. I don't think anyone had ever spoken to Eli like that. Jimmie's eyes, man. Whew! If he fixed on you, that was it. To most everybody he was kind in every way. But if he looked at you hard, I dunno. Something else was goin' on in there. No backing down.

Later when things got quiet, Jimmie asked me if I'd cut him some test recordings to take home, new songs he was working on. I was so bunched up at that point. My nerves were shot. No way I was gonna get to sleep. So we cut maybe two, three tunes. We were experimenting with some new kind of acetates by then. One take each. Flawless. I asked him, why couldn't you do this when the clock was ticking? He just laughed.

When we were done, I asked if he'd seen the tunnels that ran underneath the studio. He said no. They went under the old church studios. Mess of tunnels down there. So we go down and on the way, he pours me something from a little flask. "You don't want to drink after me, kid." We go down there and we start hearing laughter. A lady's laugh and all this carrying on. So we keep goin'. We're in almost total darkness now. There's like one bare light bulb every 10 feet. And we find these executives having a party with some ladies at a wide part of the tunnel where it meets with other buildings. Like a foyer. Kind of hard to tell what was going on. They had a dinner table and a couch and candles set up. They were deep into something. They had made a very nice environment for themselves. (Laughs) Jimmie says: "Wait right here." I keep back and he follows the racket. Turns out it was Mr. Oberstein and several other big shots and these two ladies. Jimmie just watches them for a minute at the edge of the light with his hands in his pockets. What time was this? Oh, midnight. Late. Then Jimmie lights a cigarette just as cool as can be. They hear his lighter flick and see the flame coming out of the darkness and the ladies scatter. Eli's just standing there. He can't really see who's there. And the ladies, everybody, they all slide back in the dark. And Eli's left by himself.

So, Jimmie takes a step and says: "Now Mr. Oberstein, what are you doing working on the Sabbath?" And then Jimmie walks over to the candles they had set up on the table. And he put his hand over the flame and he makes the Jewish prayer over the candles. I'd just been to a Passover dinner at my boss's. I was in shock you know. I'm sure Oberstein was. When he was done, Jimmie says: "Now Mr. Oberstein, since tomorrow is Saturday, why don't you just let me and Fred handle the session. You enjoy your day of rest." And Jimmie touches his hat like this, you know. Like in the movies and salutes him. And on his way out, he calls back, "You got rats in this building, Eli. Mind your ass on the way out." Oberstein never came to another Jimmie Rodgers session, I'll tell you that. No, those studios are gone. They put a subway through there I believe.

Last time Jimmie came to record we cut him at the New York studio. Yes, that's still there today. Elvis Presley . . . what's that record he did on Milton Berle? "Hound Dog." He cut that there. No, I retired in '49. But I heard about it.

Anyway, Jimmie had a tremendously difficult time. He had this nurse with him, kind of a big gal with gold teeth. She'd cool him off in between takes. He'd say: "Hang in there, George. I gotta pitch some rubies," and he'd cough up these big ole jewels of blood. They just jumped out of him. And she'd go hover over him for a minute or take him aside and then after a bit he'd be ready to go again. It was sad.

We had set up a cot for him in a rehearsal room so he could rest. The rehearsal room had a big window like you see between the control room and studio. That last day, I could see them having a very animated conversation about something, Jimmie and the nurse. I mean heated. No, I couldn't hear them. We had a cot for him in the studio as well. She propped him up with pillows and hung a microphone down over him to make it easy as possible. When he came out for the last song, I don't know what it was, he stood up for it. He put the fellows that was with him aside and played by himself. And after he was done, he got real quiet. I hit the intercom and asked him: "You all right, Jimmie?" He said: "Yeah. I always loved that sound." But there was no sound.

And that was on a Wednesday, I think. I came in to work on Saturday so we could listen down to the references we made and choose a master, 'cause he was set to take a train to Washington. And somebody said he was gone. He'd died.

Fred M., RCA Victor, Martinsville, NJ

TEST PRESSING

B-SIDE

Let Me Be Your Sidetrack

TEST PRESSING

"HIS MASTER'S VOICE"

SER. No. 06-VB-2105-1a

CAT. No.

ARTIST Jimmie Rodgers
acc. C. Gibson

TITLE Let Me be Your Sidetrack

COMPOSER

RCA VICTOR DIV. OF RADIO CORPORATION OF AMERICA CAMDEN, N.J., U.S.A.

We met in Louisville. Nineteen and thirty-one. That was the only time. Victor set up on Main Street in an empty furniture store. Mr. Peer and his engineer were in one room, like an office, and we were in the show room. They put curtains on wheels around us. Then they put towels over the doors. They wouldn't shut all the way 'cause of the wires. Talk about hot. It was rough. They couldn't keep the wax cool to cut the records properly. The grooves weren't right.

I had worked with Peer in Charlotte. Roosevelt Sykes put him onto me. Sykes had a little place along the river here. What you might call a mobile operation. (Laughs) Fried fish in the front, booze in the back. The police would tip him if he was gonna get raided. And Sykes would just move the whole joint down river. He was a middleman. But there wasn't nothin' middle about him. I played there Friday, Saturday nights. Yes, lot of gamblin' goin' on. Dice. Poker. There was one fellow who ran a game there, went by Jack, Snake Eyes Jack. He asked me about Jimmie once. Said he knew him from New Orleans.

Sykes told Peer: "You should make a record with this boy." So Peer wrote me a postcard. Said he was coming to Louisville. Why don't you two work together? We were supposed to cut a whole week, but Sykes vanished after the first day. No, he never said. I never asked. (Lights cigarette)

You wanna know about Jimmie. So, that first day, we're rehearsing, and I see this fellow in a white suit, smokin' one cigarette after another, pacing. Peer would come out or the engineer would make an adjustment. Meanwhile this fellow's pacing all around while we're recording. Jus' watching. I'm thinking, who's this cat in a suit? He's gotta be sweatin' his ass off. I sure was. I thought he might be the law. But then he introduced himself. No, I didn't recognize him. I knew his records. Jimmie'd hang out in the hall and listen to everybody. He had a briefcase full of lyrics. He'd write a line on one sheet and then go to another.

He said he appreciated my sound and offered to pay my hotel and board if I'd stay 'til the following week. All the white performers cut the second week. The tune we did together was called "Let Me Be Your Sidetrack." I put a yodel on my guitar. He liked that. Yes, very nice fellow. He was in bad shape though. Right in the middle of a take, this wad of blood come shooting out of him. It was like that (puts thumb and index finger together), the size of a strawberry. All over his notes. That guitar player from the Carter Family, Maybelle, was there. That woman could pick. She was like a goat in a horse pen. The impression I got was she was there to keep him calm. She was very complimentary. "That's a nice phrase there, keep that." Very encouraging. But when Jimmie coughed that up, I saw her hand go up to her mouth. (Laughs) Oh man! She ran out of that room so fast her perfume had to catch up to her. But he just took a drink and kept on. I used a Spanish tuning on that tune. Open chord. That confused him, so we just cut with my guitar. No, I don't think it ever came out. He also cut with Clifford Hayes' band that week. That came out on *Bluebird*. You can't hear me but I'm on there. Jimmie asked me to sit in so I could earn a little bread. He felt bad Sykes had run out on me. He was most unusual, like you said. Cutting with Clifford and myself. But it was no big deal, you know what I'm saying? He was just himself.

I want to show you a picture. The last day, we all went out together. Jimmie and the Carters and myself. They worked all morning on a record where they had to read from a script. Like a play. Maybelle and the married lady (Sara) and her husband. Strange dude. Jimmie got prickly towards them 'cause it was taking forever. Jimmie, he was like an actor. He'd charm the devil's birds out of a tree. But the Carter's, they were so stiff, like three Frankensteins. You could tell he was frustrated. Finally, they called it a day. By this time, we were all moody. We hadn't eaten. And it was 3 o'clock. Nothing was open. We walked over to Fourth to Cunningham's. But the sign out front said

"CLOSED." Jimmie said: "Wait here, I'll get 'em to fry us some frog legs." That was their specialty. Couple minutes later, I hear the bell on the door and Jimmie came out, walking backwards, cussin', pointin' his hat. Evidently the proprietor was not a music fan. He didn't give a shit who Jimmie Rodgers was. (Laughs) Still closed! I was a shutterbug back then, so I told them to stand still. For my scrapbook. Don't they look like a bunch of gangsters? We were just hungry, that's all.

—Clifford Gibson, East St. Louis

BLUE YODEL Nº 8

MY TIME AIN'T LONG

I was a little boy again last night. Twelve, I think. Ragged denim overalls with red bandana patches on my knees. Sewn by my auntie of course. I was like a railway kid in an Edith Nesbit story. Lost but not looking to be anywhere. It was a lovely day. Sunny. A kid's day. I was walking along a dry, deep-crevassed road that cut through a field of high alfalfa. The sky was all blue. Pitched just off the road to my right by a stone well with a swinging wooden bucket, I came upon a large show tent. The opening faced the road. I knew I was welcome, so I ducked under canvas. Once inside, I was like Ulysses setting foot on land after his long quest at sea.

Ah! The smell of sweat and toads and dust and hay and snakes and piss and homebrew! A true mud show. I gulped it all in, big deep breaths. No cough! And it smogged all through my ribs and organs. I found a king pole and put my cheek to the pine. An old pal too long unseen. Around me, in-between-show chaos! I saw Professor Eph Williams, owner of the Silas Green traveling show from New Orleans, standing resplendent in a long purple coat with brass buttons, a white frilly shirt, purple velvet stock tie, red and cream striped slacks, and dress shoes of deep blue covered in embroidered gold flowers. Eph gave me a glancing eye when I entered but then went right back to his conversation, which was more like a lecture pointed squarely at the Tutt Brothers, grand scribers of the stage. Eph lorded over them by more than a foot, dispensing advice, hands on his lapels. ("I cleared $12,000 last season and I have an income that will keep me comfortable for the balance of my days. What have you done?") The Tutts could do little else but nod to his majesty's billowing, their faces masks of grave understanding.

A few steps away, DeWayman Niles, the contortionist, juggled baseballs around his back while dispensing his own sage advice to two ballplayers in ragged cloth uniforms with dark green stripes and red buttons, hand mended (and poorly at that) many times over. ("You all'll wind up bathing in a bucket if you keep workin' that tired route of yours.")

Over there, Peg Lightfoot, the one-legged dancer, was skipping through every hoop Pear Moppin' could throw at him, giggling at his prowess. "King" Bennie Nawahi sat in one corner on a wooden chair, playing the "Hula Blues" in deep concentration, practicing an especially acrobatic trill over the strings with a silver bar. A gaggle of kids sat cross legged in the dirt listening. Lionel the Lion Face and Zbyszko the Strongman walked across my path, each talking excitedly over the other. ("What you need to do, Strongman, is invest. I invest in my mouth. Got eight inlays in there, take a look. Hands off, you sorry ket! I said look!")

W. C. Handy, the father of the blues, in a handsome long bright orange coat with purple velvet lapels, walked 'round the tent in a wide circle, gently leading a young boy whose eyes were hidden by thick sunglasses. The boy, a little older than me, was all got up in a tan suit, white shirt, and a silk tie with orange flowers. The boy's face was snow white, like he'd hardly ever seen the sun. Handy led the boy by the elbow and spoke in his ear in a soft voice, always smiling, encouraging the young man to find his way. Handy's walking stick had a phonograph needle at the tip. And as they made their way across the far side of the tent and back again, Handy's stick would emit the sound of music as it tapped the ground, causing the boy, whose vision was all but cut out by the dark glasses, to turn, head cocked, eyebrows up, looking for the source. Then, Handy would raise the stick and the music vanished as quickly as it was heard. Handy smiled at these moments but gave the boy no further assistance, only encouragement. Handy sometimes tapped on either side of their path, which would lead the boy to search desperately in both directions, sometimes down on his knees, searching for the phantom band in the dirt. ("C'mon now, child. Don't muff those trousers. We'll find it again.")

In one corner, a short distinguished looking fellow of undeterminable age with long straight silver hair, a whisp of a silver goatee, and dressed in a perfectly pressed mid-cut yellow coat, matching trousers, and silver boots, sat alone at a small table covered in a blue cloth knitted with stars and planets. The man shuffled cards and muttered to himself as his dachshund, who he called Pfeffernusse, waited for a treat. The card man kept looking over at the kids listening to Bennie. I walked towards him to play a hand. But then in a blink I was outside in an unending railyard that stretched to the horizon in every direction. Though I could see no place beyond it, I knew I was in my hometown. There were no people but for one.

A tall brown-skinned man in a denim rail suit wielding a mighty hammer straddled a short snag of rail, striking it hard at a steady but unforgiving pace. He paid my sudden appearance no attention. I walked closer. The strip on which he hammered emerged from the dirt behind him, revealing about 5 feet of rail. With each stroke, the patch of track would inch forward like an iron ticker tape, only to be swallowed up by dirt a few steps ahead. As he swung, the hammering man lifted his steel-toed boots slightly to make way for the short patch of rail advancing under his feet. At each stroke he called out in falsetto, raising his hammer above his shoulders where it paused for a moment before hurtling downward, splitting the air at such a velocity that it seemed to whistle before it struck. At its highest point, the hammer blocked the sun from where I stood. He followed each hit with a deep hum that came from his gut. Sparks from his work fell lazily around the patch of track and his boots. A stray brushed my cheek and I touched the spot to see if I had been burned. My fingernails were long and dirty. A grouping of four or five crows circled above, sometimes landing on the dirt for a moment before scattering in all directions as the hammer found its mark. All but for one, who came to perch on my shoulder. He seemed as curious as I was at these surroundings. And unlike his fellows, had summoned the courage to stay, shuffling from one claw to the other, pinching my overall straps for support. Together we resolved to keep one another brave.

Scattered around the yard in all directions was the detritus of the railroad life, cars of every kind; freight, passenger, and even giant toy trains, some missing wheels, others with crayon graffiti, all thrown askew as if by giant playmates just called to dinner. The sound of the hammer striking echoed back on us three, the man and me and the black crow. As the hammering man called out his high note, I labored to echo him with a note of my own that was equal in pitch. After many tries, I succeeded. I then worked to echo the hum that followed each hammer strike. When I produced one of my own, the hammering man seemed to nod (as his head otherwise did hardly move). But he did not look at me.

I wished for a peach tree, and one appeared, growing out of a patch of ballpark green grass. I tiptoed towards it, treading carefully around the dirt lawn of worn cars, rubber tires, cans, iron nails, brass steam gauges, and Johnson bars that were thrown about or insanely embedded in the ground at all angles. I did not want to cut my feet as my threadbare shoes were too large. I could feel holes in the soles. A large dogwood, splitburned down the middle from lightning, was in my path and I side stepped it. Once in the shade of the healthy tree, I sat with my back against it, my head bowed, and listened. With knees up, I raked at the short spring grass with my shoes while pulling at patches of grass with my fists. The air was clean here, too. I thought the grass to be the hair on the head of the Earth. I put a reed to my mouth and chewed on the stem, wishing it were honeysuckle.

Yonder I saw a small farmhouse with a broken fence on the edge of the railyard. An old milk cow, munching grass and shooing flies with her tail, watched me and the hammering man, her head visible over the top of a weather-rotted fence. The milk cow moaned in answer to the hammering man's call. After some listening, I found a place in the wink of time between them. I thought of the sound my mother would make when she would whip a sheet off the clothesline. I did the same with my throat and found the pitch. I called to the hammering man as he swung-to. I then called back to the cow when she moaned. I then came back to catch the deep moan of the hammering man. The cycle began again and on we went. With me in the middle, I spun us into a rhythm, and became the moon to their tide.

After I was sure I had mastered their calls, I stood stretching my body taught. Bending my knees, I jumped and sailed into the air, arms wide, spinning 'round and 'round, rising. High up, I was met by my crow who beat his wings easily, hovering with me. I leveled and together we flew on, swooping low and climbing high over all of Meridian, her Grand Opera House and the Metros ballfield, one Carnegie library and then another. I laughed at my power (how come I never tried before?) and from my mouth burst magnolia petals. The wind whooshed 'round my ears. I was neither hungry nor thirsty. By turning my palms I could govern my way through the wind and clouds. To move faster I kicked my legs. After finding my childhood house I looked intensely for a person who—in the dream—I struggled with much distress to remember. But soon I resumed my flying for I was happy and knew such feelings were fleeting.

After some more calculations and tests, I was satisfied at my journey and flew back to the railyard. I circled above the hammering man and even swooped down to fly through the tuck of space he made between his bent knees and the pitching of his hammer (he would pause there briefly, gathering strength). As I flew by him, my arms fast to my side to maintain my path, the sparks he made tickled my knuckles. I looked back to admire my daredevilment and blew him petal kisses. But he paid me no mind as my breath of flowers lingered in a cloud 'round his head before settling on his never-ending patch of ticker-tape track. I then flew to my milk cow and rehearsed our moaning. But she paid me no mind either, chewing and uncaring of my circular flight above her. In gratitude for her lesson, I sucked in my cheeks and blew out just-born monarchs and daisies around her head.

Our voices twined together one more time, now sounding like a new creature, part man, part animal. Back and forth I flew to each of my voice teachers, and back and forth we called. My crow kept a cold eye on my progress. I laughed and laughed and out came more petals and monarchs from the bottom of my belly, tickling my throat. And soon every rotting thing in the yard, the milk cow and the hammering man too, and the whole field of rusty iron cars were covered with monarchs and petals of pink and white.

"Jimmie, wake up!" My skipper had fallen over my eyes. Cora and I were the only ones left in the movie room. A stampede of feet scrambled on the decks above and below us. "We're in New York?" I rubbed the heavy sleep in my eyes with my knuckles, scratching my eyelid with my Mason's ring.

"Almost. Come see the Stature of Liberty!" Cora pinched and shook me. She was thrilled. Once on deck, I buttoned my coat in the breeze, putting my foot on the bottom rail and holding fast to the top. I found a stick of Wrigley's in my pocket—not a clue how that got there—and balled it up with my teeth and tongue.

"Where'd your family come from, P?"

Cora was preoccupied watching the little foamy waves in the sea that appeared and disappeared much like the patch of rail in my dream. I made some notes on a little pad I found in my pocket. Hammer. Track. Cow. Moan. Flowers. Flying. Cora had her hands on the rail, standing straight. The breeze teased at her blonde curls peaking out from her hat and the rising sun on her skin reminded me of the flesh of a peach. "We came from Texas."

"Before that." I sounded terse but I didn't mean to. I wished I were still flying.

"Germany, I think. Whenever I asked my father where we were from, he'd snap his newspaper and bark, 'Meadowbrook Lane.' That was our street. He was not a look-back kinda guy. How about you?"

My throat was salty. "Ireland."

"No kiddin'?"

I felt reasonably balanced considering my condition and the pitch of the boat. We seemed to be going faster. "Every song I know about Ireland, the girls all have curly hair. I don't know if I've ever kissed a German girl." My gum had turned salty too. I spit it overboard. I kicked at the deck. Tingly leg.

Cora turned, grinning, and the sun caught some of the gold in her mouth. "Never? I always thought of you as so democratic."

There were a dozen conversations going on around us on deck, couples and kids. But mercifully the sea kept me from hearing much. Manhattan island was a beautiful sight to behold. I asked a fellow passenger for a cigarette and was obliged. But it was too windy to light. I tried under my coat but no dice. A trash barge puttered past followed by a couple tugboats, our chaperones into

New York Harbor. Within the hour the SS *Mohawk* docked and was laced up with long ropes. A wooden walkway maneuvered to an exit door just above the water line. After whistles and calls from bow to stern, we were ushered off. With guitar in hand and my leather bag, I went down the gangplank, wobbly, Cora beside me with a small bag of her own. I suppose I was easy to spot. A Spanish-looking fellow, about my height in a chauffeur suit, waited at the end of the walkway, standing off to one side in stiff posture, his hand on the end knob of the rail.

"Mr. Rodgers, Ms. Bedell." he put a hand to his cap. "I am Carlos. Mr. Peer sent me to fetch you." He leaned in toward my guitar. "Let me take that."

"Gracias, Carlos. I'll let you." Carlos was Ralph's new attaché and his entrée into the music world of Central and South America. All financed by yours truly, thank you very much. I had told Ralph as long as he was breaking bread with the Carter Family, the publishers in New York would always look down on him for his muddy shoes. He should take over the rest of the world instead. Ralph said he were fixin' to go to Cuba soon. At heart we were both adventurers in sound. Maybe he'd find his fortune there.

Carlos gingerly put my Martin guitar in the trunk, careful not to put anything heavy on top. Smart fella. Once the top of your guitar is crushed, even the finest instrument might as well be firewood. For this trip I brought along my trusty 00-18. I've made darn every record with it. I left my fancy model, the 000-45 with abalone inlay, at home. That's the one that C. F. Martin presented me at the factory in Pennsylvania. After, of course, I presented him a check for 250 clams.

Now if you don't know anything about guitars, a Martin is the best you can get. They're loud, balanced, tuneful, and tough. What I play is a singer's guitar. Fits right in your belly with a nice big butt. That's called the bout. They're a good weather barometer too. If the pressure's droppin', your box will tell you. I liked my fancy model but for all the expense, it didn't have the tone of my old 00-18 which was near the same size but without all the glitz. A good luthier can tap a piece of mahogany or Adirondack or rosewood, tonewoods they call 'em, and tell you if it's green, dry, or a dud. Every guitar has its own voice. My old 00-18 box can blow a match out at 20 feet. I never could figure out why my fancy guitar wasn't the stronger of the two. But then the unplanned child will often beat the planned child in a knife fight, if only for the hunger of love lost.

For tone quality alone, I rarely took the fancy model out for sessioning. I suppose I figured I ought to leave Carrie something at home that's worth a damn in case I expired on the road. The old one always delivered. I had a Weymouth too. They named one after me. I'm sure Mr. Martin thought it nothing but a cigar box. I left that one in Jackson. Maybe if the kid gets a hold of that record I made at Speir's, she'll find it. I don't know how, but I know it's gonna be a girl. I'm 100 per-sure.

Anywho, that day I came to pick up my custom Martin, Mr. C. F. offered to throw a big party for the unveiling. He ordered all his wood workers, all German and Dutch, out of the factory right in the middle of the workday. A wonder they didn't start their own war. Out they came in their oily smocks and leather aprons, looking less than spirited as their boss hustled them into precise places in the grass around the front door. I opened the case, all lined in cushy emerald green and held up the new girl for all to see. She was a real beaut, like goddamn Excalibur, with heaps of sparkly abalone inlay plus my name on the fingerboard. The sun reflected off the abalone and light was dashing everyplace. Someone played "T for Texas" on accordion and there was cheering and handshakes and confetti all around.

"Jimmie boy!" C. F. hollered in some kind of English over all the noise. "All of us have known you since the beginning, my friend. You're a real success story." And that was true. I was penciling letters to the factory from the minute I hit Bristol. And C. F. answered every one of them personally. Over the years, they'd repair any ole thing I sent 'em. Even the Weymouth box after I had to crown some fella in self-defense. (Note: if you're gonna crown somebody with your guitar, use the back.)

As sweet as that day was, I'm not sure I'd be welcome in Nazareth now. C. F. wasn't too pleased when I came back to visit a few months later to show him I had "THANKS" painted in bright yellow ink on the back of that precious music box. To be truthful,

I got the idea from Frank Stokes, a true salesman if there ever was one, who had done the same to his.

C. F. was awfully concerned when I asked to see him in his office. I suppose he thought something had gone foul with the workmanship. Not at all, I assured him. Then I opened the case and turned her over, just like I do after a show. His lower lip started to bobble.

"Dummkopf," he whispered, hands to his cheeks. "What have you done?"

"Well," I explained as C. F.'s hands reached for the guitar, "you see a lot of the establishments I play don't have a microphone. Or, there's so much hollerin' after my performance, no one can hear a thing I say. So, I figured, why not write how I feel? A picture's worth a thousand words, right?"

C. F. was a bit perturbed, I must say. His face went ugly red. "You painted over Brazilian rosewood." Now he was fixing to have a fit. He'd start cussin' in German and finish in English. "That wood came through the Amazon (he was storytelling with his hands now) on a barge for 30 miles." C. F.'s cheeks got puffy as his fingers touched the beautifully polished rosewood back, now adorned with a salutation in foot tall letters. "Men died for this wood. Logs would roll off the barges and drag men to the bottom of the Amazon. You could hear their cries in the jungle." C. F. was silent for a minute. "It cost a fortune."

"Nah," I said, poppin' a Wrigley's. "The lady who painted it hardly charged me a thing, really." I tried to explain that flipping my guitar around to say "thanks" at the conclusion of a show to hundreds of people at once was good for both our business. Not to mention saving my ass from standing for a long shake and howdy after ovationing. No tellin' how many hard-boiled ex-boyfriends and legal husbands plannin' to teach me a thing or two about country fidelity got hog-tied by a thankful crowd just long enough for me to Cadillac off the premises. It ain't easy killin' a man when he's telling you "thanks." C. F turned away, holding on to his desk. Aw, well. You can't tell a German nothin'.

Really, C. F. should have admired the paint job for the design acumen alone. I thought the long-haired gal at Hatch Show Print in Nashville did a fine job rendering it. She didn't even use a stencil. And not a drop on her overalls, neither. I watched her the whole time, sitting on her boss's desk. The wall behind her was floor to ceiling wooden planks, all carved posters. I pulled one out to take a peek. "DeLa Mano. Illusionist. Looks like a spirited fellow." In between brush strokes she filled me in.

"Oh yeah. DeLa Mano. We used to do a lot for that fellow," she said. "Before my time. Means 'of the hand.' I looked it up." We shot the breeze all afternoon. I amused myself firing rubber bands at a plank with a big ole circus dame on it. After a bit, I asked her where she was from. She never once looked away from her brush. "Well, my mama was from Barcelona and my daddy's from Woodbury, Tennessee. You know where that is?"

"I'm afraid I do." Ole Hatch made posters for everybody. Rabbits Foot Minstrels. Bessie Smith. Silas Green. My whole universe. "Whew! Y'all sure gotta lotta wood and paper in this place. I don't suppose y'all allow smokin' in here." I took out a Prince Albert can.

Hatch lady looked up from her work, very serious. "We're not allowed to say the word 'fire' in here." Amen to that. Once my box dried, it took just a few small touch-ups, and it was ready to go. "You sure about this, Mr. Rodgers?" she asked stepping back. "I dunno. Seems kinda . . . expensive."

"It's all expensive, kid," I offered her some sunflower seeds. She declined. "The trick is to pay it off over time."

All that was a lifetime ago. Funny how it came back to me just handing Carlos my box. I suppose it's all part of the final encore. Carlos and Cora made small talk as he loaded the luggage in the trunk. She gently stopped him from reaching for her black bag, the one with the goodies. "No, no. I'll keep this bag with me, thank you, Carlos. Jimmie's medicine."

Cora never has told me her recipe. "I take care of show people" is how she introduced herself when she came to my rescue in Carthage. Did I tell you this already? I was sure about plum ready to die with a curtain call 15 minutes away when she appeared out of nowhere and gave me something that perked me right up. And I think I knew what it was. I had always been petrified of the stuff up to then. When she came to my rescue again in Houston last winter, I asked Ralph to secure me enough cabbage to keep her on the payroll. Comes to $18 a day plus materials. Truth be told, we've been fast pals ever since. I have no doubt that when it comes time for me to get in front of a microphone, Pleasin' will use everything in that sweet leather bag to see me through. Carlos kicked in gear, and we drove off into Manhattan. I was feeling sentimental all of a sudden.

"P, I really appreciate you. I mean it." And I did. "Without you I wouldn't be here. I'd'a wound up some kind of addict."

We locked eyes. "Honey," she patted my bony knee, "you're there."

"No, no, sister. Not me. Dependent is what I am."

"Ok, you're dependent."

"The difference is, I don't want it. I need it."

She put my bag on her lap and rolled down the window a smidge. "They all say that. You never work up here too much, do you?"

"Nah. I'm not keen for the winters. And there's too many damn people all bunched together. If you drop sick up here, they'll just throw a newspaper over you. At least down in Texas they know me. And if I need to, I can just pull over and rest. There's no gettin' away from nobody up here. This city does fire me up though." There was all kinda fussin' on the street.

Once we got on our way, I couldn't help but admire Peer's new Packard out loud. "Hoagy Carmichael, this sumbitch is nice." Coal black outside, red and cream leather seats inside. We had a nice long, slow drive ahead of us to get acquainted. I told Cora that Ralph had recently relocated his publishing company to the Brill Building on Broadway, not terribly far from the hotel. Cora and I gabbed on in small talk. And a downtown Manhattan drive is all about talkin' 'bout nuthin'. With cars and horses and carriages and motorcycles and people walkin' every which way, it's a wonder anybody gets anywhere. A mad house wherever you look. Every block or so you'll see a lonely white-gloved cop directing traffic but there's no coordination between one or the other. I might still be there by the time you read this, nothing left of me but bones. Long drives with Carrie were always painfully quiet. Maybe our cosmic loneliness was just too alike.

Carlos was hitting every crater he could find. How could he not? New York was folding in on itself, swallowing its brick past and erupting up again in steel. I found the cigarette I was given on the boat in my pocket and put it to my mouth. But it was near busted. Cora made a smirk. Lowering my window, I wished I had another stick of gum. "Hoo wee! This town smells worse than I do." I stank. Honey will do that to you.

For quite a few blocks we stayed quiet as we made our way along Broadway. Some small talk was made when we got to Times Square but I don't remember any of it. The car seat was warm from the sun. Carlos must have been parked for a bit with the doors closed and I was thankful for the pent-up heat. Cora held onto her black bag with both hands, like a mother-in-law waiting for a train. The city whizzed past, heaving construction. Looking out at all these impossibly big buildings I felt like a man straddling two trains on two tracks, a boot on one and a boot on the other, both about to get switched, one east, one west. I couldn't go back to yesterday and there were not many tomorrows. I sang out the window, "Halleluiah, I'm a bum." No one but New York heard me.

I brought my head in and wrapped on the half-drawn-down window with my knuckles tapping the offbeats in time with my boot on the carpeted floor. I fell easy into hummin' Patton's "High Water Everywhere." Ole Charley. The only fellow other than me I ever met who could sing in meter while his guitar jumped time. If there's any pickers readin' this, all you gotta do to keep time with me or Charley is just start tapping your foot on note 1. Keep that foot goin' steady no matter what the voice or guitar does. And they'll all meet up again at the end right in time.

Patton's a hell of a ballplayer, too. The womens loved him. Sharp dresser. Curly hair. Almost red. Light skin. Looked more like an Indian than a Black man. Unfortunately for Charley, all those women raising their skirts in front of him were usually spoken for. Rumor says the razor cut on his neck he kept covered with a kerchief was the result of such misunderstandings. Having escaped with my life, such as it is, a few times myself, I never bothered to ask him the details. Anyway, last fall he summoned me to the Hill Country. Said it was important. He must have played for three hours on and off. You could hear the scuffling feet on the floor of the people dancing, me included. Charley was keeping a young fellow around him, a boy I knew from the Prairie called Chester. Back when I met him, he was all of 14 or 15, already taller than me. Big-ass feet. He could holler too. Wanted to yodel. "Sure, kid. Let's get you yodeling." He might have been my first admirer come to think of it. Every time I'd come back through, I'd look for Chester. And every time I found him, he was singin' fine. I gathered Charley was puttin' him on music lessons. And would probably break the kid's heart just to keep him from followin' too far. Charley's coat tails were short.

All night long Patton was throwin' his guitar in the air and catching it dead on. Never once looked up. That was until some woman blurred out of the crowd and axe'd another man in half right in front of him. She didn't care for his date. That brought the proceedings to a rapid end. Charley's eyes and mine met for a split second. The look that says, *glad it wasn't me.*

After the show, we all sat outside eating fish sandwiches and drinking NuGrapes, waiting for the sun to come up. Charley and Chester broke into song. Charley sang the hell out of my records. At the first light of dawn, he started preachin'. It was Sunday, after all.

"Charley," I had my hands on my belly. "I have a sincere favor to ask you." I stretched out straight and my boots dug into the crackly mud. A hoot owl hooted. "I'd like to you to preach my funeral." Chester gave us both a look as if a truth of life had just come to him.

Charley hummed, stared at the ground, and began to nod in affirmation. "Sure, I would. I'm a deacon after all." He made a noise like a giggle. We discussed some particulars including that my corpse would lie in repose holding a Bible. My little joke. I affirmed he could make that a pre-condition, but it was a book I didn't read.

"Understand, Charley, I won't know either way."

Chester looked confused for a moment, as if I had made an insulting remark. But then my words sunk in, and he laughed from his belly as he sipped. Charley's deep chuckle and Chester's howling giggle were so alike it was getting so I'd mistake one for the other. We naturally were quiet for a moment, each of us sipping or scuffling. I imagined Charley presiding over my funeral with Elsie and Carrie and my Little Boots and all those stinkin' Meridians on one side and Ralph and Cora and, who knows? Maybe Haydee and our critter on the other.

Charley slapped my knee and a bubble went through my nose. "Jimmie Rodgers, I will preach for you and I will pronounce your arrival to the heavens."

I raised my arm and proclaimed: "Ladies and gentleman, I give you Elder J. J. Hadley!"

"What now?" Chester asked, confused.

"Boy, that's me," Charley scolded, thumbs in his vest which I saw now had streaks of blood. Seeing Chester's frown, he put his hand on his shoulder. "All right, now." Charley turned back to me. "Here's what I will say to you, Mr. Jimmie Rodgers. Now then. Is your name James?"

I replied it certainly is.

"All right then," Charley cleared his throat, shifted foot to foot, stood still facing us. A near full moon was still bright behind his shoulder, shining around his head. "Ladies and Gentleman, today we honor the late great Jimmie Rodgers. This morning I take my text from Corinthians . . . uh . . . Verse 41."

Charley reached into his pocket and took out a tiny piece of paper, made a face like he had just been hit by a stink bug ("Oh that's right . . . hmm") and put it back in his pocket. "Now then. Where was I? Verse 41. There is one glory of the sun, and another glory of the moon, and another glory of the stars: for one star shall not differeth from another star in glory. And though there are stars on Earth they shall not be greater than the stars in heaven."

Chester said Amen. And so did I. Charley began to pace, and his verse turned into song. "Singers of the earth are tuning forks, struck by God, and their vibrations are heard throughout eternity." (Amen, we replied.) "And on their day of glory at the right time at the right hour at the right minute, at the right second, they will board their train to heaven above or hell below." Now, Charley became even more animated. He walked behind Chester, put both hands on his shoulders, and leaned in like he was a pulpit, sometimes placing a palm on Chester's head, who followed the movement with his eyes. Charley's voice became one of an excited auctioneer.

All aboard the Black Iron Express!
Your bags are packed and your dark suit is buttoned high
Your shoes are shined, your face is clean, and your manner contrite
The door opens
You have no luggage
You take your seat
Your engineer is unknown
The train pulls out of the station
Only then do you know your final destination
If it be Jesus driving the Black Iron Express
Then you're riding the honeymoon express to salvation
("Amen!" I raised my bottle of pop)
The Holy Spirit is your porter
The bluebird's song your whistle
Your engine is righteousness
Grace be your piston
Faith be your coal
And courage is your ticket
You train has no stops to heaven!

Charley stopped for a moment. "Uh . . . Jimmie, can you give me a ride to Memphis this morning?"

I was down to the backwash of my NuGrape. "Charley, you're preaching my funeral!"

"I gotta see a judge. Otherwise, I won't make my session in New York." Charley confided. "Paperwork is all it is. I can't miss it."

I shrugged and adjusted my skipper. "Sure, I will."

Charley raised an eyebrow. "Oh, that would be a lovely thing. Can you do that?"

I put down my bottle. "Consider me your personal driver. We better finish up now so we can scat." Charley nodded, adjusted his stance, and commenced to screamin' and hollerin', occasionally pounding on Chester's shoulders.

> On tracks of clouds
> Held fast by truth
> Made straight by deeds
> Up goes your train
> You feel no wind, no heat
> It may rain but you are dry
> It may snow but your toes are warm
> The wind may howl but you need no collar
> Winter may blow but you need no coat
> Summer may swelter but you need no fan
> Belief is your wine
> Trust is your bread

Charley held back a belch, patted his chest, and set his eyes on me. Chester looked up at Charley and back at me, unsure what was comin' next.

"Preach, Elder!" I called. Charley set his eyes on me, spinning like mad roulette wheels.

> But if you have taken from those who had little to give
> Claimed ownership of what was not yours . . .

Charley walked from beside Chester, pointing a finger at me, his coat blowing behind him madly.

> If selfishness is your song and mendacity your melody
> If you look into the river of love and see only your reflection
> If truth came to your door and you offered the chair of deceit
> If your brother came to you thirsty
> And you offered water fouled by beasts
> Then you have boarded the Black Iron Express Train to Hell
> The devil is your engineer
> Fear is your coal
> Sin your headlight
> Your train stops are Liarstown
> Gamblersville
> Deceitful Junction
> Murderers Row

All aboard
Outlaws and Connivers
Cowards and Thieves
Your cabin is a jungle of mosquitos
Copperheads, rattlers, toads, and crocodiles
Panthers and pythons
Jackals and Grizzlies
You may wish to mend your clothes but you'll find no thread
Bandage your wounds but they will not heal
Wash yourself but never come clean

Patton turned to a spot on the ground, seeing my body.

Jimmie Rodgers lies here! Who knew this man?
Did he walk in love and brotherhood?
Or did he claim invention for what he did not make?
Did he take in his brother and share his house?
Build a fire so he would not be chilled, shoe his bare feet?
Or did he run him off the road of life into the ditch of misery
Does he ride on a current of an electrified harp that hums with goodness?
Or a clanky coal dust train that howls like a hellhound

I could see the cosmos in Charley's eyes as he turned to me at last.

Two trains are pulling out of the station, Jimmie Rodgers.
What train are you on?

All was quiet. The wind blew down. I could hear the gurgle in what was left of my last good lung. "Well, Elder," I emptied the last drops from my bottle into the dirt and dusted them over with my boots. "That was mighty fine."

"Yes sir," Charley was pleased with himself and slapped hands with Chester.

"I was thinking of something a little shorter." I took off my hat, put it to my heart, and stood, staring up at the sunrise.

Bumble Bee, Bumble Bee
I am comin' home to thee.
You got the sharpest little stinger
That I ever did see.

And we laughed and laughed until the dirt swirled around us and we were erased from the earth.

Peer's car popped another hole and I jerked awake. Carlos looked back at me. "Mr. Rodgers, I'm sorry for the traffic."

"De nada, Carlos. I got a driver and a nurse if things get worse." Carlos smiled and I gave him a two-finger salute off my brim. Traffic is just not something worth fightin' about.

"Pleasin', did I ever tell you the time I first came to New York?"

"I don't think you ever did." Her voice seemed like it was around a corner. Carlos got stuck behind a horse cart.

"Don't let him shit on Mr. Peer's car, Carlos," I called from the rear. Carlos beat on the steering wheel and cursed in Spanish.

Cement dust was blowing in so I eased up the window a bit. "I came here for the first time about, oh, four or five years ago. We were livin' in D.C. at the time at my sister-in-law's . . ."

"Elsie?" Cora was always trying to catch up and I loved her for that.

"Annie. The one who can't stand me for some reason."

"I can't imagine." Cora looked out each window. She wanted out.

"Anyway, my first record had just come out. And every day I was buggin' the Victor dealer in D.C. something awful. How many I sold? I tried Ralph but we kept missing each other. Anyway, after Thanksgiving, I just thought to hell with it, I'm gonna go to NY and force the issue. So, I drove up here . . ." I looked out the front window, as if the past was right there and I could jump back to it. "I went right to this same hotel here. Except it was called the Manger." I held the back of the front seat with both hands. "Carlos, we can get out wherever you wanna drop us." Carlos pulled to the curb and negotiated with the bell hop. I leaned back into the cushy seats. "I parked over there by the Roxy. Walked in with my record and said: 'I record for Victor. Gimme a room!'" I laughed and coughed and laughed again.

"Of course you did." Cora giggled.

"Called Ralph collect. Bless his heart. Paid for my room and bought me a ticket to Camden. A couple days later cut 'T for Texas.' Ralph wasn't too keen for it. He didn't think a white man singing blues would sell. I told him, 'White, hell!'" Cora recoiled from my breath.

The lobby hadn't changed a bit. Green and white patterned tile. The entryway felt like a station until you went through the first arch, then the whole place opened into a long hallway with a coffee café to the left and a sitting room with plush plum couches nestled close in the shadow of tall palms. On your right you got your Western Union cage. A pretty brunette with impossibly long eyelashes in a yellow cap and coat with orange buttons sat bored waiting for her train to come. Some other lifetime, sweetie. Straight ahead you got your fine polished check-in desk under a marble arch. Next to that on the right you got your government P.O. Above it all a little balcony with an iron frame fence overlooked the whole shebang with a precious little thing playing piano all day long.

"Nice to have you back, Mr. Rodgers, Room 1909." I must not look well. The desk man looked green as he handed me keys. I signed the book and flipped it back around. "You see, P?" Cora leaned in beside me. "I told you. New York is an entertainer's town."

The deskman interrupted us again. "Oh, Mr. Rodgers, this came for you." He handed me a package postmarked Chicago. The envelope was from Columbia Records but the return address was handwritten: Delmore. It was covered in all kinds of stamps. Looked like somebody had taken up a collection to get it airborne.

Cora looked over my shoulder. "Who is it?"

I opened the envelope with my Barlow knife. It was an aluminum record with a handwritten label. "Blue Railroad Train. The Delmore Bros. I like it already." It came with a letter. I recognized the salutation. "Oh, I know these boys. Alton and Rabon. I met 'em in Memphis. I got them away from Columbia. They're on Victor now." Cora put her finger on the grooves. "I didn't know they made metal records."

"Aluminum. You can make these at home. I bet Ralph's got something that will play it. He's got all the gadgets." We exchanged room numbers and I asked her when we needed to take more medicine.

Cora balanced her bags and mine, took an audible breath, and blew the hair out of her eyes. "I'm right across the hall. I'll come find you. Rest."

Once in my room, I couldn't stand the stuffiness, so I opened the window and sat on the lip looking out on Broadway. Cora had put some postcards in my pocket and I scribed one to Carrie quick.

> "Mother,
> Arrived safe. Busting to get started. But you know how Ralph can be. Slow! We'll see what he thinks about the Columbia offer. Won't take it if Victor meets it. They've been fine to me. But I gotta have more money. Doctors, nurses, hospitals, Doggone. They cost a lot, don't they?"

When I went to the lobby to mail it (I don't want to die with an unsent postcard in my hand) I saw a brown-skinned fellow sitting in the shoeshine seat. He was there when we arrived too. Even with a newspaper in front him, he didn't seem like the proprietor. He was dressed more like a shamus. Pin striped suit. Blue patterned socks. Spat shoes. Looks like he could hold himself in a fight. Meaning, the sort of fellow I try to stay high and dry from. Rarely are they music lovers. Something about the way he tried not to look at us when we came in bugged me. And he was still there. The lobby was quiet and my heels made all the noise in the joint as I walked toward him.

"Hey bub. Have we met before?"

He peeked from behind his paper briefly, and then ducked back behind it. His voice was higher than I thought it would be. "I don't believe we have." He turned a page and then folded the paper on his lap. I can't say for sure but he looked like the fellow I saw in Houston and Carthage and Jackson and Memphis and every other place over the last year. Why here? It just didn't make any sense. Nothing did. I was light-headed. I offered a shake.

"Jimmie Rodgers. My friends call me James."

His grip was strong. I felt callouses on his fingertips. "Mr. James. Ira Cooper."

"Ira! You from New York? Cigarette?" I offered, reaching into my coat. He waved me off.

"St. Louis."

"St. Louis. I have a friend in St. Louis. Clifford Gibson. Guitar player."

"Don't know him."

I tugged at my ear lobe. "Well, that's too bad. By your fingertips I figured you were in the business." We were both quiet for another minute.

"What business would that be?" He didn't blink. I hate it when people don't blink.

"Well, either you chew the ends of your fingers when you're nervous or you play guitar."

He looked at me expressionless, like a mug shot. He made a finger snap. "Say . . . I know. 'Waiting for a Train!'"

My backbone shook. Liar. You know exactly who I am. "The one and only," I said, but I didn't smile.

Ira leaned forward a bit and tucked his paper at his side. "What are you doing in New York?"

"I'm here on show business. You?"

"Detective work." Ira folded his fingers together, like he was in prayer.

I held up my hands. "Never met her!" I laughed but Ira did not return the gesture. "You're a long way from home for a private dick."

"So are you." He opened his coat, showing a shiny police badge, and a pistol, courtesy of the Rome of the West.

I pointed my finger at him. "You wouldn't be working for my first wife? If you are, you're too late. The judge settled for $125 a month and she's gonna get it whether she likes it or not." I put my hands in my pockets. Ira stared straight. The lobby was filling up again. People walked in front of us. Somebody waiting for a shine gave up. We eyed each other forever it seemed like. Then Pleasin' came out of nowhere, her hand on her hat, holding a little red wool coat. I couldn't tell what she was saying to me. Something about meeting Ralph at his office.

"Sorry, kid. I didn't hear a word you said. I was just talkin' to this fellow and . . ."

"What fellow?"

I motioned behind me but Cooper was gone. The chair was empty. "Well, you saw him. He was right here. Big fellow. Dark man. Suit. A shamus, he says."

Cora dug into her purse. "I didn't notice. I thought you were waiting for a shoeshine. Ralph left me a message, he wants us to come over now." We stood there with the bustling all around us while she dug out whatever the hell it is women find in there. Oh, my head hurt.

I took her hand. "When you find whatever the hell you're looking for, why don't we get us a cab." We walked out together. A bell hop whistled for a car. Where was Carlos, I wondered. I reached in my coat aiming to find the cigarette I'd been carrying all this time. Instead, I found a red poker chip: Jung Hotel, New Orleans. How the hell? I stared at it while Cora tried to hustle me into the cab. As we inched forward into traffic, I looked out the back window at Ira Cooper, standing dead center in my view behind us. He was pointing his finger at the car as if it were a gun, made a face that said "Pow," then brought up his finger as if to blow the smoke from his killin' shot.

BLUE YODEL No. 9

GAMBLING POLKA DOT BLUES

April 2, 1959

TRANSCRIPTION

R. S. Peer (producer and publisher). Los Angeles, California.

Note: This interview takes place in RP's office in Los Angeles in the late afternoon. I found his office immaculate. The scent of fresh flowers drifts in and out during our conversation. Scattered about were several oriental pots with pink, red, and lavender flowers ("Camellias. They're called the queen of the winter flowers. I probably know more about them then anybody you'll meet.")

One wall has a tall rectangular multi-pane window that overlooks a cluster of orange and black walnut trees. Other walls have professionally framed illustrations of even more camellias. The prints appear to be made on fine paper with hand-painted black Japanese script. The room, square and spacious, has floral patterned wallpaper of pale yellow and purple with hints of silver. There are no artist photos.

RP sits at an oak desk stained dark brown that takes up nearly the whole width of the back wall. On it he has a Montblanc pen, a long-sharpened yellow pencil, a tall glass of water, a small stack of 45 singles in blank white sleeves (they appear to be test pressings), a blank lined white pad, a framed photo of a woman who I imagine is Mrs. Peer, and two telephones. The black phone has a light that alternately blinks, goes dark, and blinks again but RP pays no attention to it. A second phone, green, has no lights or dial and occasionally buzzes softly. RP always answers this phone. His cream suit is pressed. He wears a red silk tie. ("It's called the Genie. It's a Wembley. See?") The tie has a Dali illustration of a golden "Genie" pot, out of which curvy lines of smoke emerge with a woman's face, her neck outline adorned in pearls. A dark red silk handkerchief is folded neatly in his breast pocket.

He shows me every courtesy and after shaking my hand, he stands for a moment, supporting himself with some unease, both arms on the desk, sometimes with his palms spread wide, other times making quiet rhythmic taps on his knuckles. This goes on several minutes before we finally sit down. He seems to be in some discomfort, but it does not come up in conversation. Peer sits with very good posture. He has all the air of a businessman who has done well and knows it. After we've exchanged more pleasantries and I've asked his permission to tape record our conversation, we begin.

EJC: You're a hard man to see.

RP: Well, you're (looks me over, curious) persistent.

EJC: I thank you for your time. How are you, today? You seem a bit distracted. I hope I'm not keeping you.

RP: No, no. I've got this old lady whose been pestering me about camellias. I'm a bit of an expert on them, you see. She wants to know whether . . . Hold on, it's my gardener.

EJC: How did you . . . ?

RP: (Cups hand over phone) . . . By the ring. Yes . . . (speaks into phone) No, I don't want to see her. Tell her to try tomorrow. No. Tell her I've gone. Yes, that's plenty. Goodbye. (He hangs up the phone, smiles, and gestures with his hands.) What can I say? I've spent my life helping people along. You were asking how I met Jimmie. Is that recorder on?

EJC: Yes, it is. I might take some notes as well. Don't mind me.

RP: You know you're the second interview I've had in the last few weeks. Now that they're going to break ground on a country music museum in Nashville, people are coming out of the woodwork.

EJC: Before I turned on the recorder, you started telling me about . . .

RP: . . . field recordings. Field recording was all about finding talent. It was sort of my invention.

EJC: How did you get into the business?

RP: My father was a record dealer. In Independence. I used to go on his road trips to pick up records, sales meetings. He helped me get a job at Columbia which was one of the biggies even then. I started out as most young men do. Shipping clerk, mail room, that sort of thing. Learning from the ground up. I had a great memory for the catalog. And eventually I got a job with the company in Chicago as an assistant manager. In fact, when W. C. Handy and his band came through, I had the job of looking out for him. Helping him get from one train to the next you know. He couldn't see too well. My old boss started Okeh. Or helped start it. That's what got me to New York. I was transferred there. I got them into the race market when I made Mamie Smith's "Crazy Blues." That sold 75,000 the first month. I was pretty busy after that.

EJC: Why did you leave Okeh?

RP: I was young and thought I knew the workings of the world. I got a hot head and quit. After a while, I realized I had put myself in a tough position. I was making as much or more than most executives. I knew Victor wanted a piece of the southern market. But when they found out how much I was making at Okeh they said: "We can't afford you." They could, of course, but they couldn't pay me a base salary like I had at Okeh. So, I thought about it awhile and I wrote them a letter and I said I'd work for nothing if I could have the copyrights on anything I found that they put out. They didn't see the value in hillbilly and race music. A couple weeks later they wrote me and said, ok. They knew I had the touch for finding talent.

You see, I figured out before they did that this new business, the record business, was about publishing new songs. That meant developing writers. I knew Victor wanted the rural market. And I figured if I could do it with the race market I could do it in the hillbilly market.

EJC: And you paid the artists and also helped them get royalties as songwriters.

RP: That got them invested. If they wrote the song, then I offered them a royalty. We established a relationship together. Now Victor, this was before they merged with RCA, they quibbled for a while on what to pay the artists. I could have paid them nothing. Just a bottle. But I didn't want to do that. I suggested $20 per song. Word came down $20 was too cheap. They said: "We can't do that. We're a big deal! What if people in the industry started talking?" (Laughs) So then we settled on $50 per side. And that became the standard. (RP leans back. Puts shoes on desk.) Jimmie got up to $200 a side eventually.

EJC: And did he owe back his advance to RCA or to you?

RP: (Not answering) It took a little time to make them see they didn't need the same recording quality as a Caruso. I think for the Bristol trip, which also brought out the Carter Family, I had a budget well over fifty or sixty thousand to work Bristol, Atlanta, and maybe somewhere else. Memphis.

EJC: . . . with H. C. Speir.

RP: . . . and that was peanuts to them. I'd set up for three weeks in one place. Record five, six acts a day. Tear down and move on. Meanwhile I was making a quarter of a million every three or four months from the copyrights at that point. 'Cause they were all assigned to me. There was a big demand for music from the southern territory. That's why I formed Southern Music and all this (gestures around the room). To put it somewhere.

EJC: And around the time you went to Bristol, you helped put together Louis Armstrong's Hot Five and Hot Seven sessions.

RP: That was in Chicago. I put those musicians together. It was a phantom band. I hired those guys to back him. Louis was my creation.

EJC: Those are considered some of the greatest records ever made.

RP: Funny thing is, I didn't even bother going to the sessions. I sent somebody . . . what was her name?

EJC: You didn't bother going?

RP: I didn't need to be there. Louis needed money to get out of Chicago. He was being chased out of there by some mobsters. That's how he wound up in California. These days Louis acts like he doesn't remember me. Smoking all those Mexican cigarettes. California is where I got him together with Jimmie.

EJC: Why did you bring Jimmie to Hollywood? Was he hoping to break into the movies?

RP: Jimmie was bait to get RCA Victor into the picture business. Once sound pictures started, Hal Roach, who made the Laurel & Hardy films, Our Gang, Will Rogers, that sort of thing, he came looking to make a deal for the sound technology and for music to go along with it. We came out and Roach, as a courtesy, took us out to a Laurel & Hardy set there. They were making their first full-length picture and having all kinds of technical problems. So I made a deal where Hal Roach Pictures got RCA equipment and access to use Southern Music. Which at the time RCA owned, but eventually they sold it back to me. That was a good deal.

EJC: Did Jimmie ever make a movie out there?

RP: Never would have happened. Not in the shape he was in. We had lunch with Laurel & Hardy. They liked Jimmie fine. He was like them. Came up through show business the hard way. They told him to come back if he ever got his health back. I think he made a voice test out there. An old Vaudeville skit. We did make a picture with Jimmie at the studio in Camden. 'Don't know if you've seen that. They put a lot of makeup on him.

EJC: How did he wind up recording with Louis Armstrong?

RP: Louis did that record with Jimmie as a session man. He was hiding out, as I said, from somebody and didn't want to tip them off he was in California. So we kept him off the label. Jimmie ran into him out there playing cards at the Somerville Hotel. It's called the Dunbar now.

EJC: Yes, I know it. Did Jimmie ever have those kinds of problems?

RP: . . . but getting back to meeting Jimmie. By '27 we had electrical equipment. You had an actual microphone rather than a horn. Which was perfect for Jimmie. His phrasing was so subtle. Intimate. A horn never would have picked that up. The apparatus was a heavy turntable. And on that you'd set a wax blank. How big? Oh, about an inch, maybe an inch and a half thick on the platter. And these machines were all handmade in house. In a lot of the places I went, electricity was so intermittent, we ran the turntable on weights. We used gravity to keep the speed consistent.

First you built a tower, say, maybe seven feet off the ground, of plywood and what not. Built so you could fold it up and haul it in a truck. And when you got to where you were going, you'd unfold this contraption and set it up with the weights and pullies inside, you see. It ran like a grandfather clock. The weights would drop and turn the platter at a constant speed for just under four minutes. Gravity would govern the machines (coughing). But the microphone and the amplifiers were electric. The boards were simple. You could use two, three microphones at once. Add a little bit of tone control. Not much. Western Electric developed all this. Most of the acts I cut were like Jimmie, one man and a couple instruments. You wouldn't have to work too hard to get a balance.

We'd arrive someplace like Bristol and I'd be shown around places we might set up. In Bristol we picked out an old hat factory. We put up some curtains on wheels like you see in a department store. And then we'd surround the artist in these heavy curtains while the engineer would listen from the other side. It made for fairly good sound really. Someone like Jimmie, his voice cut. Other people might struggle a bit. But Jimmie did well in those situations.

EJC: Why Bristol?

RP: I think Ernest Stoneman suggested it. Bright guy, Ernest. Bristol was central. You could get folks from Virginia, Carolinas, Tennessee. At first hardly anybody came out. (Peer uses his hand to straighten his pants cuff). So, in exchange for a feature, I tipped the editor at the newspaper there that Victor and RCA were probably going to go into business together in the next year. That little tip probably made him a fortune. After he published the story—"Victor talent scout in town"—and all that, anybody that could sing a hymn came out. Every which way. Horse. Car. I think A. P. Carter fixed two, three flats coming from wherever they came from. Clinch Mountain.

EJC: What was your impression of Jimmie?

RP: He wasn't really like anybody. He'd sit and cross his leg in a funny way when he sang. And his jaw kind of swung out when he'd talk. His mannerisms were more like a Black man. He was, as you say now, cool. He was a glider. Not in a hurry. He'd tilt his head while you were talking, like he was leaning on one ear. And right before you got to the end of a sentence he'd smile, like he had been waiting for you to say whatever it was you were gonna say. For all that I could see, he was desperate. I was all he had. I liked him. And I felt for him. You got the feeling everybody must like him. And you didn't want to be left out. The musicians he came with were not a good fit. Not sure they liked him so much.

EJC: And after Jimmie made that first record . . . I never have quite understood this. He tried to get in touch with you. Is that right? And when he couldn't, Carrie, his wife, said he drove to New York to see you. But you were in Camden.

RP: Carrie . . . I hardly ever did see her, really. I don't think they got along.

EJC: Is that right? Well, here's a photo of you and the Rodgers family. Is that your wife? At their home in Texas?

RP: Let me see . . . Oh, well. She didn't ever have anything to do with the music, I mean. Not that I could see. I know what you're talking about. I had been trying to find him. Sure. 'Cause his sales were all right. Nobody knew where he was. Maybe he was in Washington at that time. I don't remember. But sure, I was thrilled to hear from him. Had I tried to reach

him? Well, somehow, I found out he was in Washington. Yes, that's right. We had an office there and I think someone had tipped me this fellow was pestering them about his sales.

EJC: You said in Bristol it was clear he didn't belong with the fellows he tried out with. How so?

RP: He was singing ni— (coughs, pauses)

EJC: Yes . . .

RP: Blues. And they were straight hillbilly. You can't mix the two.

EJC: Jimmie made quite a few records with Black artists.

RP: (coughs, sips water) He did, that's right.

EJC: I read a letter where Jimmie wrote Carrie about recording a version of "Frankie and Johnny" with a Black band in Atlanta. Very early on. But you wouldn't release it.

RP: Jimmie would bring me near anybody he met on the street. And some of those just didn't fly. He couldn't play with just anybody. He was too unconventional. He didn't change when most musicians did. It was a matter of timing. You see most white singers treat the blues like comedy. Jimmie was serious on it. Hold on a minute . . . (answers the green phone). No, don't bother. I thought you left? Ok. (Coughs, hangs up.) I like to think I'll give a listen to the person who anybody else would just holler off. Jimmie was like that. I was in effect his manager. Which meant turning out my pockets anytime we spoke. If I heard his song somewhere, I could feel the coins dance in my pocket. (Laughs)

EJC: You always have seemed to be in the right place in the right time.

RP: Jimmie would say I've survived more lightning strikes than any man alive. My feeling is if it's not God awful, then you might as well try, you know. You never know what will hit with the public. But let me get back to Jimmie coming to New York the first time.

I knew I had his life in my hands at that moment. He knew it. But just that morning somebody in the office had make a crack about some artist I had cut on. And this fellow made me so sore I thought, I'm gonna just bring in the next person who calls me, no matter what. I had a great belief in the right person walking through the door. So, in that sense, Jimmie got lucky.

EJC: So Jimmie comes to New York and he calls you.

RP: He called and said he was just passing through and would I pay for his hotel. He had checked into the Manger which later became the Taft. That's where he died. Now this was midtown, fairly high dollar. Who knows what he said to get in there in the first place.

EJC: Had you invited him?

RP: I had probably said at one time you ought to come up to New York if he was ever around. With Jimmie, that's all you needed to do. You give him a sliver of daylight and he'd run for it. So I took care of his hotel for the night and wired him a ticket to Philadelphia. I think he said he drove to New York but he wasn't sure if his car could make it back. He had a cousin up there. He always had a backup.

EJC: So he took a train to Camden . . .

RP: . . . and I got him at 30th Street station downtown. All he had was a little leather railroad bag and his instrument. I put him up at the Walt Whitman hotel which was right across the street from the studio. Checked him in. Sprightly guy. Good common sense. He got clever as time went on. He'd been on the circuit a long time. Not a guy you'd fool twice.

He wore this terrible stuff, Black Narcissus perfume, I think it was. Supposed to hide the smell of the coal dust. It got to where the whole staff at the Whitman would come down and greet him. They knew he was coming from the moment he stepped in the lobby. Big tipper. I don't know how the hell any woman could stand it but he never seemed to have any trouble there. Did you know, tuberculosis is an incredible stimulant to the sex drive?

EJC: Is that a fact?

RP: That's what he told me. Brought him a lotta trouble.

EJC: I bet you got him out of a lot of trouble.

RP: (Peer looks off in the distance and makes a face.) I encouraged him to take care of himself. (Rubs his knee.) I told him there was only one of him.

EJC: You sound like you admired him.

RP: If I could have sung a lick, I would have been just like him. He was an ideal artist. In my opinion. "T for Texas," that was the big one from that session you're talking about. It was my idea to call them blue yodels. Or maybe he called them that but the title came from me. When I first showed him around Victor, he was asking me about other artists. Every record he had was one I had supervised. Fats Waller came in one time. This (cough), this is a good story in fact. The first or second time Jimmie came to the Church—the studios were in an old church—he and Fats got together. This must have been the spring after "T for Texas" hit, 'cause Waller knew it. He and Jimmie played around a bit and had a conversation while I was in the cutting room. Fats had come to get a check, I guess. If we had had tape in those days, I might have recorded them.

Now what were they talking about I couldn't tell you. But Jimmie must have told a good joke because Fats was all giggles. And Jimmie was rubbing the back of his neck like he was winding up for another one. They were leaning on each other and whispering. Fats' eyes would look every which way when he told a story, like he was waiting for a policeman to grab him. They must have played four, five tunes together. Just off that one meeting.

EJC: What kind of music did Jimmie like?

RP: Blues. Blues over everything. Whenever he sang blues, he really hit it with gusto. He did the other songs for balance. If he found something he liked, he made it his own. He was a natural that way. But blues is what he liked most.

I didn't really find anything he couldn't sing. Now as a player, he was limited. If he was learning a tune, he'd come to a chord he couldn't play and just skip over it. But that was good for me because that way we might find an old number and make it new. I might suggest a number to him and he'd say: "Oh, I know that song." But he wouldn't know how it was supposed to go, you see. So he'd change this and change that and add a few words of his own. And then, you see, we had a new arrangement. A new copyright. "Waiting for a Train" was an old song. But the way Jimmie did it, it was completely new. 'Cause he changed the words and played the chords he knew how to play.

EJC: I'm sure you both learned a lot from each other.

RP: He wasn't at ease with orchestrated arrangements.

EJC: And they were expensive. He knew he'd be paying for them.

RP: They weren't as natural to him. But they sold too. We didn't have any rules about it. Say a tune like "Moonlight and Skies." That swept in the south. He had such a feel for what he liked that even if he did a tune badly it would still be a big seller.

EJC: That means he must have made good royalties.

RP: Well, they weren't really royalties, you see. I told him he was making royalties but it was really an advance. He'd assigned his copyrights to me. I'm not sure he understood that basically he was my employee. I took the risk. But I looked after him. Which meant advancing him all the money he wanted. He built a big house in Texas.

EJC: His will said he owed you $5,000. Was that for the down payment?

RP: I'd just warn him if he got in too deep. For about two, three years, a Rodgers record would sell over a million.

EJC: What did he do with the money?

RP: A lot of cars, for one thing. And he liked to gamble. There was this one fellow out of Louisiana, a Jewish fellow, Mark Boasberg, who went by Jack Sheehan. Jimmie got in deep with him. He owned all the joints in New Orleans and all up the Mississippi. Jack got a big head and went up to New York to put on a fix. And he took this one fellow for his whole roll. What he didn't realize, Jack I mean, was he'd scammed the right-hand man for Queenie St. Clair. She ran all the numbers in Harlem and all of Manhattan. She was tough, mind you. Even the syndicate, the mob, left her alone. I had heard she even had some dealings with RCA. But I was out of there by then.

Well, Jack was out of his league with Queenie. She sent someone down to get her money back. Trouble for Jack was, he'd lost it. Now Jack knew Jimmie was an easy play. Jimmie just wanted to be one of the boys, you know. So Jack pulled some favors and put a big game together just for Jimmie.

EJC: To pay back Queenie.

RP: Uh huh. Jimmie was coming down to New Orleans to make some records. Jack fed him some bull how these were all the best players in the territory. The card game of his life. All that. But it was a set-up.

Now this game went all night. It was stacked with Jack's boys. They got Jimmie in for ten, twenty grand or something like that. But Jimmie sussed it out. Jimmie wasn't so innocent, if you get my drift. Later on, I heard all this. Jimmie figured out it was a fix. So, at the end of the night, he gave Jack an IOU to the Bank of Kerrville. That's where his house was. The Yodeler's Paradise. Which I bankrolled.

EJC: The $5,000 house loan . . .

RP: . . . except it wasn't a real bank, you see. Jimmie's IOU to Jack was worthless. Jimmie told me what happened, so we folded up the session. He and his co-writer . . . what was her name? . . . Elsie! She got out of there in the middle of the night. When Jack found out Jimmie had turned the tables on him, he was hot. 'Cause now he was in the hole to all his guys at the table and Queenie too. Jack tried to get me to cover it. Threatened me. My lawyer looked it all over and assured me it had no legal basis since it was on the take. He told us both, me and Jimmie, to stay clear of Louisiana. Which we did. (Laughs)

Then not long after, this St. Clair and some lady friend, her assistant, red hair if you can believe it, never seen that again 'til now, came to me at my office in New York looking for Jimmie.

She said, "I like that Jimmie Rodgers. My girl here plays his records all the time." But I told them to lay off him. He was about gone by then anyway. I think Queenie was impressed by Jimmie's guts and what he put over on Jack. Otherwise, she'd have chased him down for it.

EJC: I was speaking with Carrie. She alluded to some difficulties in her dealings with Peer Music.

RP: I think you're referring (the green phone buzzes, Peer ignores it), she's referring to the renewals for Jimmie's copyrights. I don't know who's advising her. She has some fantasy she can hold out for more money.

EJC: Are you suggesting you will cut her out of the renewals if she doesn't take your offer? Perhaps by claiming she still owes you for Jimmie's advances?

RP: No, no, no. I don't want to do that. We've gone back and forth for a number of years. I just need to find someone in my organization who will work with her. I think the last offer we made was something like $25,000. I'll spread it out over 25 years or so. In the end, it's nothing. She'll come around to taking that. We can't give her everything all at once, otherwise she'd have no incentive. She's a one-man band for Jimmie.

EJC: How do you mean?

RP: That's her cause, you see. She a propagandist. A spinner.

EJC: What sort of spin?

RP: Oh, that she supported Jimmie Rodgers. That she's owed. It's a myth. To tell you the truth, my bookkeeper wishes I'd just give her everything all at once.

EJC: Well, she was his wife. He does have heirs.

RP: I don't know where she suddenly got all this knowledge. All these ideas about copyrights.

EJC: From me, I think.

RP: (Silence) From you?

EJC: You could say I have a vested interest.

(END OF TAPE)

BLUE YODEL No. 10

THE WONDERFUL CITY

The taxi let us off at 50th and Broadway and with Cora on my arm, I managed the walk to the Brill Building without feeling too winded. The weather was warm. Perfect for a suit. Not hot enough to sweat. In fact, I had the chills. Carlos offered to come too, but I told him to stay behind to rest. He and Cora had to fuss over me all night. I assured them I wasn't ready to go just yet. "You coming up?" I asked. The street seemed awfully loud today.

"No, I don't think so." Cora seemed distracted. But then so was I. "You gonna be long?"

"Naw. I'm just paying my respects. Ralph is working out a new contract. Would you hold onto my briefcase? I don't even know why I brought the darn thing. I'm awfully forgetful these days. Last thing I want to do is leave it in his office." I gave her my letter to Little Boots which I had plum forgot was still in my jacket. "Mail this, would you?"

"Ok, Mr. Rodgers." She waved the letter back at me. "You owe me 3 cents."

The Brill's lobby perked me right up. All trimmed in gold metal that mirrored reflections every which way. I waited for an empty elevator and thought I had one to myself finally when a rather splendidly dressed dark-skinned man in a flawless black wool topcoat, silver and black striped tie, blue pinstriped suit underneath, and gray leather gloves stepped in with me, smelling of gardenias.

"Pardon me," he said in a most melodious voice. "Have we met before? Are you from the District of Columbia?" He pronounced it Coal-Lum-BeeAh and rounded his t's like a diplomat.

I leaned into the corner of the elevator, feeling weak. "For a short spell, yes."

The man had an air of both formality and kindness. He kept his hands behind his back. "You're a singer, I think. Am I correct?"

I perked up and stood straight. "Yes, that's right."

"Ah!" said the man. "I believe I saw you at the Earle Theatre." He smiled, looking at the floor. "Something like: 'Got my name sewed on the tail of my shirt. I'm a hustler by trade, mama's daddy don't need to work.' Very nice. Paints a picture."

"Much obliged." Now I, too, stood with my hands behind my back.

"Are you here in this splendid building on business?" he inquired.

I tucked at my hat. I didn't know what else to do. "I'm on my way to see my publisher, in fact."

He smiled in return. His cheeks had small freckles up close. "Well, so am I."

"Let's hope we both have a check waiting for us." At this he gave the look of a fine engraving of a Cheshire cat. I extended my hand. "Jimmie. My friends call me James."

The elevator opened and he touched his gray felt hat while taking my hand with the other. "My friends"—he emphasized the "my"—"call me Duke."

Duke went left to the frosted door that said Irving Mills. I went right to Southern Music. Inside, a small battalion of women, all with the same nut-color hair doos, tweed skirts, and white blouses were typing and filing, sitting down, standing up, and bending over cabinets like so many valves on a trumpet. Another fellow who looked about twelve ran around their desks, acting like a boss, touching his tie as he spoke, trying to catch up to the gals, who showed no time for him.

Ralph's personal receptionist had an office that overlooked the street corner. With my hands in my pockets, I gandered out. There was Cora, getting ready to cross. That was a funny direction. Peer's phone gal watched me gaze out the window. She was a bit put off by my pallor and tried to stay upwind from me. Can't blame her really. Finally, Ralph came out. He didn't care much for my look either. He swallowed. "Oh, Jimmie. Come in. Always a pleasure."

I had been looking forward to just idling time with the two of us. But we had company. Sitting in a big puffy red leather chair facing Ralph's very nice desk was Eli Oberstein, an RCA company man and all that implies. Ambitious, short, round glasses, fidgety, greased black hair, and dressed perfectly but all wrong in comparison to the fellow I just ran into on the elevator. And as unmusical as could be. The music business is full of 'em.

Eli was not the kind to be caught watching a Silas Green show. Though maybe I'm not giving him enough credit. Last summer after I threw him out of my session for disrupting my peace, my engineer took me down to the tunnels underneath the studio to get some cool air. And who should we come upon but Eli and some other heeled fellow shootin' craps by candlelight with a couple ladies. That's what it looked like anyway. I never did see the ladies. They stayed in the dark. But they smelled awfully nice. Whatever they were up to, it wasn't something they could do in the light of day together.

Running into Eli again was not welcome. But it turned out to be a little big break of its own. Eli had been gunning to squeeze Ralph out of the blues and hillbilly business. Jealousy, mostly. Ralph was about to get RCA to extend my contract. And Eli was more or less powerless to stop him. Though my unexpected arrival and death's door look probably didn't help my position much.

Peer stood behind his desk leaning on his knuckles. "Jimmie, take a seat my friend." I took the other red chair next to Eli. "Jimmie, we're gonna move you over to the Bluebird label starting June 1. They sell for less but we can keep you at the same royalty rate. And you're gonna sell more records." Ralph went on to talk more blah, blah, blah about the economy and tough times. It was a demotion of sorts, but I can't say it was unexpected. Still, these cracker-salts wouldn't even have an office without me.

"You're still an RCA artist," nodded Ralph.

"And lucky to be so," chimed Eli.

Bastard.

There was silence for a bit. And I gathered it was mine to break. "Eli, you cut any hit records lately?" I rubbed the fine leather seat which made a squeak under my fingers.

Ralph sighed. "Jimmie, this isn't the right time to litigate old grievances."

I shook my head. "No sir. You're right," I slapped my bony knee. "I have none to litter." We talked some more. I got both of them to laugh a bit. Ralph introduced me to a couple fellows who were hangin' about the office, lookin' for a break. Guitar pickers who were gonna help keep me upright in next week's sessions. I asked them to come to my room later and pick a little. On my way out, by instinct I picked up the leather briefcase between our chairs. Just then Eli asked Ralph some question and they both got distracted. At the door I waved at Ralph. "See you tomorrow, Mr. Peer. We're gonna make that Bluebird soar over the Manhattan skyline."

"Uh, Jimmie, hold on!" Ralph called, moving out from behind his desk. We went out in the hallway and he closed the door behind us. "Just so you know . . ." and he lowered his voice. "I likely won't make that session. But Fred will be there. You'll be in good hands. You know what to do."

"Well, where you gonna be?" I must have sounded hurt.

"Eli and I are settling this business with Southern Music. They're selling me back my publishing. It's a formality, that's all. And I'm not sure if I mentioned this but I'm getting out of managing artists, except you and the Carter Family. So I want to be there to make sure all the language is right. You know they've been throwing out some of my masters and I want to make sure that doesn't happen to you."

I stepped back though his arm was around me. "Throw away a master? What the fuck . . ."

"Jimmie, keep your voice down."

So I mad-whispered. "Are you so desperate to wipe the Midwest off your shoes you'll just barter away everything you've done? Well, that shit is not coming off your shoes. You'll never be one of them. That's why we're here. You see the letters I get. I got widows and kids and barrel drivers and prisoners and hobos and hitchhikers and God knows who else givin' their last nickel to buy our records. Our records! That's an investment. No one's gonna go hungry for a John Philip Sousa march."

Peer tried to calm me down. "I know that. I know that."

"I'm not sure you do. This is my work. Our work. Your work. What the hell are you doing with these people, Ralph? What kind of company they got here where you gotta get on your knees and beg them to hold on to the fruits of your labor? You think any of those, those . . . curs in there are gonna still have their jobs in two years? You will. I would. If I could." Ralph tried to protest but I was on a tear, though trying to keep in a whisper. "That's just bad fuckin' business. I tell you what. (And I shook a finger at him.) I know my $2,500 is coming out of your pocket. And I know you'll get it back. You always do. But when this is done and I'm dust you make sure Carrie gets my big fat fuckin' check. Every fuckin' penny. No commission. No cut for expenses. Every penny. That's what she's expecting. And you don't let thimble dick in there get a fuckin' finger of a dime of it. You owe me that."

"Of course I will. You ever had reason to doubt me?" Ralph fussed with my kerchief and put some money in my pocket. I told you he was like an uncle. He gave my arm a pat. "Am I missing something we have to straighten out?"

"No," I touched my hat. "No, doggone it. You better get back in there. He's probably looking through your desk."

Ralph grinned and tucked both hands in his pockets. "I locked it."

"Heh. I'm sure you fuckin' did." I pointed my hat back at the door 'cause I knew Eli was listening. "I'm an earner. Tell that pip squeaky little shit I'm an earner. Bluebird or Montgomery Ward or wherever the fuck you send me. Southern Music artists earn. And I am Southern Music. To the fuckin' T."

"That's right, you're an earner. Hey," Ralph smiled. "Now what do they say about Missourians?"

I played along but I didn't want to. "It's the show-me state," I mumbled.

"That's right," he grinned some more and poked my tie. "You go wax some hits. And we'll show this bastard what we do."

"All right. You call me and let me know if there's any trouble."

"The board is just a formality," Ralph gestured with his hand, like all this was no big deal. "I'm not even on it. That's why I have to work it all out ahead of time." I had no reason not to believe him. But it all seemed sorry as a fish market on Monday morning. I was pissed at myself for losing my temper. But they don't call 'em emotions for nothin'.

I took the Delmores' record out of my coat pocket. "One more thing. Do they have the right apparatus at the studio whereas I can audition this? I promised these Delmore boys I'd listen." Something about seeing that record hit us both at the same moment. I don't know why, but right then I knew I'd never see Ralph again. And I think he did too. What a puddin' headed funny looking fellow. One of those guys who'll look like a baby all his life.

Ralph gave me a long look. "That's a good song, right there, pal."

"A blue railroad train. That's what we're on, right? Making all stops."

Ralph gave my shoulder a pinch. "Making all stops. So long, pal."

So long, Ralph. I made my way to the elevators. And don't you know it, that Duke fellow was going down with me, stepping in at the last minute. He didn't look any happier 'bout his meeting than I did for mine. We stayed to our corners. My hands in my pockets and him clutching his hat.

"Wonderful city, New York," he said, looking down at the floor.

"Can be," I hummed a tune. "If you're like Jack Horner and stay in your corner and don't try to go nowhere."

At this Duke looked up and smiled. I doubt he expected to hear a fella like me make up a new Fats Waller lyric in a New York elevator. The doors opened.

"After you," Duke gestured with his hand.

"Everyone is." I grinned. Cora was out front of the Brill, gazing at the traffic. She also had a funny look on her face. What's going on with everybody? This city gets to you right away. "Why you lookin' at me that way? Is there something on my lip?"

She pointed at the briefcase I was holding. "What's that?"

"What's what? It's my brief . . ."

"I got your briefcase," she lifted mine up high for me to see and patted it. "You think I'd lose your best seller, Hemingway?"

My case was nearly identical to what I was holding, except for the initials, E.O., on the flap. A jolt when up my spine. I broke out in a big grin which only confused Cora more. "Hail us a cab, kid. Pronto."

"Are you ill, honey? The hotel is just right there."

"Over there," I pointed to a taxi, "that one." If Eli wasn't behind us, he soon would be. I needed to get us off the street and fast. The cabdriver gave us a double take. But it wasn't fame he was lookin' at.

"You don't look so hot, bub."

"Rudolph Wurlitzer's." It was the closest place I knew to go. The driver weaved through traffic. "Sit yonder, Pleasin'. Now listen, I got a task for you." I looked in Eli's case. There was a folder with some papers, just charts and figures. But there was also a little book that had other numbers and other charts that were definitely not from the music business. I put the contents of Eli's case into mine. Then I gave Eli's now-empty case to Cora. "When we get to Wurlitzer's, I'm gonna get out and I want you to take Eli's case back to the hotel and put it in your room. And if Ralph calls and asks about it, just act like you don't know what he's talking about."

Cora seemed to follow me, but she still looked puzzled. "Jimmie, what did you just do?"

"I dunno. Maybe nothing. Maybe everything." The taxi pulled up to Wurlitzer's and I got out. I threw some of Ralph's dollars at the driver. "Take her from here to there," and Cora went on her way back to the Taft. At least I hoped that's where she was going. Once in Wurlitzer's, a little man in suspenders and a bow tie came up to me, a little nervous. I took the first record I found and waved it around. "Yes sir, can you show me to an audition room where I might listen to this selection?"

I'm dog sure he knew I was no Caruso fan, but he had mercy on me and set me up in a nice little room with a green carpet, a comfy chair, and a Victrola. I shut the door and started making my way through the contents of Eli's bag. Funny thing about a big break. When you get one, it stares at you wide-eyed, like it's just as thankful to find you as you are to find it.

Three in the morning is my pee time. That's when the honey haze wears off. I usually don't get much sleep after that. Did I tell you my brother Tal is now a policeman in Meridian? Good man to know. We once had an idea to start a café that opened at 3:30 in the a.m. and closed at 4:30. Open one hour only so every fella in Lauderdale County could come over in their pajamas, have a pee and a smoke, converse with the fellows, and then head home. And since we're all probably gonna die in the middle of the night, why not die over a plate of eggs? Or better yet, pie. Call it Jimmie's Pee and Pie Café. No resuscitatin'. Keep a nurse on duty with a gurney. If you go, that's the breaks. Carrie and I ran a café once, did I tell you? What a racket. Mother cooked and I waited tables. I had a surefire way to shut down the joint if it got crowded. If a customer asked: "What's your ice cream flavor of the day?" I'd answer: "Duck." We didn't get a lot of repeat customers.

How in the world you ever gonna satisfy anybody who doesn't have sense enough to stay home and make a sandwich 'stead of paying triple for it? I've never met so many experts on a scrambled egg. The only reason worth having a café is if you could get one of those record spitters and stack it with some good records. Like Nolan Welsh's "Bridwell Blues." Now that's the job for me.

I really wanted to play this Delmore Brothers tune but it would have to wait until I got to the studio. They wrote me a nice note, those boys.

> Dear Jimmie,
> We hope you'll enjoy this tune that Rabon and I wrote for you. "Blue Railroad Train". Lyrics are enclosed. We hope you'll consider it at your next recording session. Stay well.
>
> Best wishes,
> Alton Delmore
> c/o Athens, Alabama PO

A blue railroad train coming down the line. Right up my alley. I had the desk man send up a portable machine for me. And for the last hour, quiet as I can, I've been playing a record I picked up at Wurlitzer's by Mississippi John Hurt, "Louis Collins." A miracle of sorts it got there. But Okeh has offices in New York. Or used to. I don't even know if they're in business anymore.

This fellow Hurt, he sings one lyric over and over again. The angels laid him away. I wonder what Mr. Hurt looks like. I imagine he's a slight fellow, like me. For all I know I could have passed him on the street. He's a country boy and he sure don't know the town.

By the way, I've been typing all this on my trusty little travel Remington 3. It's been about the most reliable thing in my life. You can talk to it when you've got nothing to say and it'll talk back. I always keep some paper in the feeder. I trust that one morning I'll find it's left me a message.

`The End. You are dead.`

I opened the window. Even at this hour the street's so loud I don't know how anybody can sleep. I bet if I fell out right now listening to Mr. Hurt, maybe I'd find out I really can fly. I wonder if Hurt's the kind of guy you could shoot pool with all afternoon in a little backroom somewhere, waiting for life to find you. I wonder if he calls himself Mississippi because he can't ever leave or because he's never goin' back.

Man, what I wouldn't give to be shootin' pool in some dank little hall right now. I lived above one after I left Dora's. I can still smell the chalk and grubby carpet and wet tobacco. You can learn a lot in a pool hall. Patience, for one. Reading a man by his silences. How eager he is to say the same thing twice. Paying attention will get you farther ahead than a buck. That was the problem with Meridian. The people who were paying attention to me weren't paying attention to anything else. I was their hobby. They were using my apparent diminishings to occupy their time so they didn't have to pay attention to their own sorry selves. "Git along, music man." It's no accident you can see the Opera House and Winner & Klein's fine department store from every creep joint and pool hall.

I don't know how long Pleasin' was knockin' before I finally heard her. I opened the door to a vision with gold teeth and beehive curls in a fuzzy blue night frock. "I knew someday I'd see you at this hour. Come on in, damsel." I turned my back so she could her close the door herself. I knew she wouldn't have her feelings hurt.

Cora seemed like she was in a good mood. She was keyed up. I wondered on what. "I thought I'd find you up."

"I've been waiting for you, naturally." I gave her some distance. The last thing I wanted to do was make her ill, too. I sat on the windowsill. "I'm just pondering my future. And trying to light a cigarette with my good looks." Cora sat on my still-made bed, showing me a little leg as she flicked over her robe. I tossed her the chip from the Hotel Jung. "You ever see one of these?" She turned it over in her hand. Instantly she made a crinkly face, like she wanted to drop it. "It's a little souvenir from a fellow called Boasberg. Mark Boasberg. A gambler. Know him?" She shook her head but I wasn't sure I believed her. I kept on babbling, watching her face. "He goes by Jack Sheehan. Snake Eyes Jack. He's a right son of a bitch, he is. Got every judge in New Orleans on his card. He set me up to lose a high stakes card game at the Jung Hotel. Had the whole table rigged. I was his easy fix."

Cora tossed back the chip. "No shit." Something in her manner told me she had heard my story before. I hate knowing what everyone's thinkin' all the time. Especially since they often don't. She yawned and I got a whiff of her breath even over by the window. Cora had snuck a drink and I wanted one too.

"I figured out the whole table was taking me, but I was too far in. So I told him I'd pay him when I got home. I signed an IOU to the Bank of Kerrville. Except there is no Bank of Kerrville."

Cora nodded her head and looked at the wall. "Well played, Mr. Rodgers."

"That's what I thought. But then I come to find out it was a little more complicated than that." I walked toward her and sat down on the edge of the bed. "You see right before he had his game with me, ole Jack came up to New York and tried the same deal. Except the pigeon he fleeced belonged to Queenie St. Clair."

Cora seemed to recognize that name too, but if I was right, she was playing it cool. "Who's Queenie St. Clair?"

"She runs numbers all over Manhattan. And as soon as she found out her boy was set up, she tracked down Jack. Told him to pay up or go down. Trouble for Jack was, he already spent all her dough. Word was, Queenie put a razor to Jack's throat and was just about to swipe when he said, 'I can get you your money. I got an easy score.'"

"And that was you." Cora shimmied in her seat. She was uncomfortable. Why?

"Correct! That's where I came in. Jack found out I was coming to New Orleans. So, he told Queenie that he could play me to pay her off. And he nearly had me, too. Pleasin', you should have seen it. I don't even know where it came from. Right in front of all his bad boys, I looked him straight in the eye and said: 'Bank of Kerrville.' Elsie was there, too, which probably saved my life." I got up and paced between the window and the bed.

Cora adjusted her robe. "When did he find out?"

"Didn't take him long."

"I'm sure he wasn't happy." Cora looked at her toes, anywhere but me.

"You remember yesterday I told you about that fellow . . ."

"The one I didn't see . . ." One of her puffy slippers fell on the carpet.

"Yeah, that one. At the shoeshine. He put that chip in my pocket to jog my memory just before you got there. I think he's the fellow who's been chasing me all over creation, singin' my tunes. I betcha Jack hired him to collect.

Cora mused on this. "How much you in for?"

"About five grand."

Cora whistled and scratched behind her ear.

I flipped the chip in the air. "Kid, my premier talent is getting under people's skin. I'm sure after taking a good look at me yesterday he could see he's not going to collect. Not in this life."

"Does that mean he'll leave you alone?" Cora picked at a vein on her ankle.

"Not a chance. He's probably been sent to shoot me. Then he'll go after Ralph."

"Well, he'd be doing you a favor."

"You're not even the least bit sentimental?"

She closed her eyes and sighed. "Jimmie, you forget that I've been working with fellows like you . . ."

"Honey, there's no one like me . . ."

"True," she waved a finger at me. Blood red nail polish. "But I haven't yet been with a musicianer, as you call them, that didn't have somebody on their tail." Her blue nighty had opened again just enough to show her ample chest.

"Well, for once I think I found a way to please everybody." I waved the little account book I found in Eli's bag and tossed it on her lap. Bullseye. "Now, remember when I told you I accidently walked in on Eli in the tunnel 'neath the studio in Camden? Take a look at page 2. Look at that address. That's Queenie's address in Harlem. Now go to page 5."

Cora thumbed through the book. "Who are all these people?"

"They work for Victor." I rolled up my sleeves. It seemed hot all of a sudden. "Board members. I've heard Ralph talk about some of them before." I pulled up the desk chair across from the bed and turned it backwards, facing her.

Cora buzzed through the pages. "Well, I see a Q in one column . . ." she took her finger and lined things up. "Whew . . . if I'm reading this right, she's got these fellas in for something fierce."

"That's what I thought. My guess is Eli was her go-between to get some action in the record business."

Cora kept flippin'. She furrowed her brow at something.

"What is it?"

She shook her head. "Nothing. Lotta folks in here."

"Here's what I want you to do. I want you to get in touch with this Queenie lady and tell her what we got. Tell her she can have it. No tricks. But in return I want her to make this shamus go away." (And I snapped my fingers.)

Cora shook her head. "No, no, no. I don't think that's a good idea."

"Why not? I don't owe her anything. And I'll lead her to Jack. Tell her the truth. I just want this fellow off my back. I got work to do. C'mon! What do you say? You're not scared, are ya?" Cora just stared back at me trying to keep a blank face. Ain't a chick on planet Earth that ever looked at you blank that didn't have a lot to say. I yammered on. "Queenie won't bother you. I'm sure she despises Eli as much as I do. And without him, she can cut out the middleman. I doubt he's been a fair partner."

Cora kept silent for a minute which is a long time when you're with someone in a hotel room. "How we gonna get this to her?"

I patted her knee. "Shit, she can just come and get it. But first! Before we do, I want you to look at something." I took back the book, ruffled the pages, and found the spot. "Look there."

Cora read the name. “Screder. What the hell kind of name is that?”

“He’s the chairman of RCA’s board. They’re meeting over my contract in a few days. So, I want you to go down to the drug store first thing in the morning and get you a little book that looks just like this. And you copy just enough to make it look legit. Then you call Mr. Screder and you tell him if he wants his book, he’ll make a very healthy deposit at the New York Reserve.”

Cora looked up. “Deposit to who?”

“Not who. What. Meridian Rising Inc.”

“He’s not gonna do that.”

“Oh yes, he will. I’ll open the account tomorrow. I’m president. You’re a co-signer. They can’t touch me ’cause I won’t be here for long. And this Screder fellow don’t know you. Soon as he makes the deposit, you withdraw the money. I’ll follow him and make sure he puts it in. Soon as the coast is clear, I’ll holler. You keep half. I think that’s fair. As for the rest, find Haydee.”

“What if I can’t find her?” Cora looked at me and then back again at the book.

“I think you already have.”

She looked up wide-eyed. I thought she might smack me. Not sure I could’ve taken it if she did. “You’re a wily bastard,” she laughed and ran her finger over my Mason’s ring. “Jimmie, did it ever occur to you that this kid might not be yours? Wouldn’t be the first time.”

I stood straight, hands on my hips. “Sure. It’s possible. But my gut says she’s telling the truth. Haydee’s never asked anything of me. One of the few, I might add. This way she gets something, you get something. And Ralph will give Carrie and Anita whatever I can make over the next two weeks.”

The sun was starting to break and already the horns were blowing wild, every note of the world. And I was an American not in Paris. I sat at the open window. “You know, when my mother was dying we dragged her bed to the only part of the house that had a window. We lived at the bottom of a hill. White people, Black people, right on top of each other. If one couple was fightin’ it would make all the couples start fighting. And if they were cooing you’d get that too. Fightin' and cooing. And just when you thought you'd never hear the end of one, somebody would break the spell and it would start all over again. The day she died I walked out of the house and there was a stream of blood goin' right by our door. And up the hill there was a crowd of kids, just like you see today, all dungarees and newsboy caps. The had gathered 'round something I couldn't see. So I followed the stream of blood uphill. And when I got up there, they were all lookin' at this little black dog. Must have got hit by a truck that knocked him to the curb. You wouldn't believe a little thing like that could bleed so much. It seemed like there would never be an end to the blood."

Cora broke the spell of quiet. "It's about time for you to have some medicine."

I came to the bed and rolled up my sleeve. Cora moved around me, standing up on her knees. She had the pouch in her pocket and started her work. "You know, Mr. Rodgers, for all the risk I'm taking in this, there's something else I want even more than the money. But I'll certainly take the money."

I was dizzy already. "Oh yeah, what's that?"

BLUE YODEL Nº. 11

FRANKIE AND JOHNNY

Aunt Dora tried to make up for Mother being gone. She taught me all kinds of stuff. How to make drop biscuits. How to tie a tie. How to change the flint in a lighter. How to pack a suit in your luggage and keep out the wrinkles. (Set your dress shirts buttoned up inside your jacket, fold that whole business in half, then fold the arms over.) She also educated me on how to math my expenses and earnings. Numbers don't lie. Memory will. And if you ever do this for a living (by God), you'll burn out quick if you don't take note of what's comin' in and what's goin' out. I put everything down in one of those SE Ledger Books. (I figure it stands for Singer's Entry). It's all right there in heavy pencil. If you could gander at my book, you'd see. In January, I was out with the J. D. Morgan show. Made $192.35 over two nights in Cleveland and $135.55 over two nights in Huntsville. My hotel in Cleveland run me $3 and my gas $1.85. This is a penny business. That's how I knew old Eli might have a little book just like mine in his bag. And he did.

As much as I despised the little bastard, I knew right away he was every bit of the conniving opportunist I was. The difference is I have a heart. And as fast as mine was turning black, it still pumped red.

By the way, I've been fighting like a lion to keep up with all that's goin' on in this story but living it is 'bout killin' me. I resolved long ago to keep you out of the gory details. There's heaps of 'em. My main worry lately, besides heavin' up what's left of my lung onto my lap, was finding more typing paper. I solved that. Down in the lobby at the Western Union cage, the little gal with the bottle blonde flapper cut and skinny chicken gams found me a blank roll of white paper like the wire services use. Now I just feed that through my Remington like a ticker tape and peck away 'til

I can roll out, oh, about the length of my arm. Then I tear it out, reel it up, lipstick today's date on the side, hairpin it together, and throw it to my nurse and scribe. ("Jimmie, where the hell are the page numbers?") I figure I've got about 5 or 6 arms worth easy by now. Plus all the earlier ones on proper pages when I was trying to be neat.

We've digressed. After about a week of recording and still another to go, I've hardly had time to write a word. But it's all gone fine enough. I've had a few episodes of hurlin' up rubies. That's expected when you're singing as hard as I do. Pleasin' had the bright idea of bringin' a sofa into the studio she found in the ladies room to prop me up in front of the mic. And we set up another cot in the rehearsal room next door so I'm hardly ever on my feet. She and I've scrapped a bit over the honey dosage. ("Jimmie, I can't. It'll kill you.") Too late is what I say. A man's gotta work. Why do women have so much trouble with that concept? As for those pickers Ralph hired, they're as ragged as me. Poor critters. They had no idea what they were in for. One of 'em can shadow my guitar English so darn close I think it's me. We cut a number today I've been pickin' on since Louisville when I nearly 'bout cussed out the Carters. OH, THE WOMEN SURE DO MAKE A FOOL OUT OF ME. I tried it back then, but we called the session off after I hacked a big red jewel square onto my lead sheet. "Mercy, Jesus!" Maybelle cried on her way to the window 'fore she 'bout puked on a passing cop. That will make 13 blue yodels. Perfect.

Ralph's been in touch as we progress. When he heard I was gonna break a few days, he called to offer his house in Cape Cod for the weekend. I don't remember much else of the session, or even how it ended. To tell you the truth, I've been nodding off quite a lot. Pleasin's been a peach, though. I don't think I'd be on track to finish without her. She claims this Queenie broad was quite amenable to getting the shamus off my back. As for our embezzlement, it's proceeding as planned. The RCA dogs were eager to get back what they think is Eli's shameful notebook. But I get the funny feeling it's not gonna be that easy for me.

Here's the part of the story I do remember. We took off on a

Saturday. Or maybe it was a Friday. Anywho, my engineer gave me the weekend off. ("Hoss, you need to rest. This is ridiculous.") As I said, I thought we were heading to Ralph's cabin in Cape Cod. Why we'd bother to go to another beach instead of Coney Island made no sense. It does now. I do remember having a cup of coffee with Cora in the lobby of the Taft, waiting for a car. I don't recall getting in the car. Or much else, 'til I woke up in the back seat. Felt like we were driving over a rock farm. I was so crusty, I didn't know who I was. I beat back a hiccup and leaned over the seat. "I don't believe I've ever seen you drive, Pleasin'. Where are we?"

"Westerlo. That's what the signs says."

"Where's the ocean?" I alerted Cora that her gas dial was near empty, but she was already pullin' in to a fillin' station. "What are we drivin'?"

"How'd you sleep?" Cora watched me in her review mirror.

"Like I was catnipped." I rubbed my neck. My head didn't feel so good either. Outside it seemed like the sort of misty green wet time of the afternoon when the air's so hot you could see it drift. I wonder where my watch is. Behind the screen door of the fillin' station was a hand-painted sign, red with gold trim. Frank and Thelma's Ice Cream. By the Cone. I opened the backseat door and moseyed over to gander in the window, shading my eyes to see in. Not a soul. Nice little place though. Candy. Pop. Baseball cards. Maybe I should've opened one of these. I called back to Cora. "Frank and Thelma aren't home." I took off my jacket and cat scratched at the screen door. "Shame. Ice cream sure sounds good about now."

I walked back to the passenger side, opened the door, and dove into the glove box.

"Jimmie, what are you lookin' for?" Cora sounded cranky. They must mold 'em that way in nursing school.

A map was what I was looking for. And I was 'bout to say so when my eyes caught the registration card on the side of the steering wheel shaft. "What the . . . 'Stephanie St. Clair. 409 Edgecombe Avenue, New York.'" I stepped out and took a hard look at our carriage. I'm sure I must have whistled for all the breath I could find. "Well, I'll be archduked." I put my hands on the door frame and ducked my head back in the cab. For a minute I thought I might hurl but it went away. "You mind telling me why we're driving the Queen of Manhattan's fire engine red Duesenberg?"

Cora scratched behind her ear. The engine was still purrin'. "You don't remember anything, do you?"

"I guess not. Is Ms. Queenie our partner now?

Cora scrunched up her shoulders. "I told you. I make friends easy."

Sure was quiet for a Saturday. I kicked dirt. "Now when I went to sleep, nurse lady, we were goin' to the beach."

"Yeah," said Cora, sighing. "I got a little lost."

"Lost." Hmm. I took the map from the glove box and unfolded it on the hood. I found Westerlo. The coast was way the other way. Somethin' funny's goin' on. Like I was marked for a surprise party. You know when they're trying to get you to show up somewhere at a certain time and behave just so and you don't wanna. "Shut her off, would ya? I'm gonna feed her some petrol." Miraculously the pumps were on. I nozzled in a dollar's worth and left the station owners some cabbage under the door crack.

A rain cloud came over us. I could feel my tired old heart beating in my neck. Whatever Westerlo was or wasn't, I was ready to go. I got in the back seat to fuss out a rock in my boot.

"What are you laughing about?" Cora looked back at me in the mirror and rolled up her window. The rain moved in. She seemed nervous as hell. In the process of trying to get this pebble out, my little pistol fell on the carpet behind her seat. Cora saw it and let out a holler. I was in no mood.

"Oh, for fiddlin' sake woman. Like you've never seen a little hot rod!"

"I don't think you should be trusted with a gun in your condition."

"You're carrying heavier than I am, I bet." I finally got the rock out. "One time I was playing on this boat goin' down the Cumberland past Nashville. Me and this banjo fellow, Dave Macon. Funny old goat. Used to spin his banjo 'round like a pin wheel. He and I had doused ourselves pretty hard all day. Somehow, I managed to get on stage that night. I do my show and start to peel off. I say,

'Ladies and gents, Uncle Dave Macon.' But no Dave. So I do another encore. Still no Dave." I put my face to the backdoor window and ran my finger along the metal frame. The way the rain drops ran down the window every which way made me think of a palm reader and a very bad night in Juarez. I don't know how long Cora was calling me.

"Hello . . . Uncle Dave Macon?"

"Oh yeah. So, the MC for that radio show they got up there, the Grand Ole Opry, he's runnin' our show. Calls himself the Solemn Ole Judge. I come off stage and find him in our state room pouring water on Uncle Dave. Finally, we get his ass up. He's got these gaudy-ass cowboy boots he won off me playing rummy. He's mumblin' and slobberin'. The old judge is scoldin' him. 'You'll never work on my stage again, you old coot!'"

"So, we start puttin' on his britches and his sorry-ass boots. We get one on and Dave starts hollerin': 'Suspenders!' We tell 'im, 'Dave, we don't have time to find your suspenders.' We get his other boot on. He starts hollerin': 'Wallet!' We look all over. 'Dave, we don't see no wallet. Find it later.' We throw him out there. He twirls his banjo, does his show. Comes off after 'bout 15 minutes. Huffin' and swearin'. Takes off his boots. He's got his wallet in one and suspenders in the other." I was on my back now, kickin' at the passenger door, dyin' from laughin'. You can't say that too often. "Oh, man. We had fun."

Cora got a cigarette from her purse. "Buncha sorry drunks."

"Oh hell, P. What's the matter?" I got up behind her and roughed up her curly head ("Ouch!"). "Loosen up, you frigid old witch. Let's go find us an ice cream."

I got out of the car and rattled the doorknob again. Still no Frank and Thelma. We seemed to be on the corner of the town's main drag. There was something spellboundy about the place. Big oaks and willows. Kind of like Mississippi. New York is full of hillbillies once you get out of Manhattan. Don't let 'em tell you otherwise. I took off my lid and scratched what little hair I had left. Overall, I felt pretty good, considering. I don't know why, but I thought it would be a good idea to take a little walk. "P, you stay here. I'm gonna go explore."

“You want company?” Cora half stepped out of the car. I waved back without looking and kept walking.

I hadn’t gone more than two railroad cars when I saw a big ole peacock struttin’ all by itself, coming towards me from the other direction. Off road to one side was a post office. On the other was a little grocery. A perfect little place to bide your time. Still not a soul. No dogs, no kitty cats, nuthin’. Just me and this peacock. He was a heffin’ thing, too. Looked like a black and green and blue turkey with a shave brush crown. If you’ve ever been to Mobile Bay in Alabama, that’s what this big bird looked like. All blue and green. I paused and let him pass. Instead he turned round to follow me. A woman’s voice called out.

“Peafowl.”

I felt a chill and put my jacket back on. A little lady I couldn’t quite make out was sitting on the porch of a big ole Victorian house just off a patch of sandy road that veered to the right. “Ma’am?”

Her whole self was in the shade of a big weeping willow in her front yard. I could see she was fanning herself. “That’s what they’re called. Your bird. Pavo cristatus.” I thought I heard a bit of Texas, like she put curly cues on all her vowels.

Up close I could make out a shag of black hair, a smallish stout little frame, a pouty, rosey cute face like you’d see on a wine bottle and a purply shawl around her shoulders. Just rockin’ easy. Underneath it all, her black dress gave her pale skin a moon glow. Her house was sort of a funeral type with a spindle on top and all kinda curvy windows. When I was a kid, we called them D.O.A. houses. Ghost barns. The kind you didn’t throw pepples at.

I nodded towards the bird as it passed me, stepping towards the house. “That peafowl yours?”

She tapped her hands on the rocker’s arm rest. “Local resident. Like me. You travelin’?”

“I am.”

“You haven’t much time.”

That was a funny-ass thing to say. I put my boot on the first step of her porch.

“Pardon?”

“I said you got the time?”

"Sorry. I seem to have lost my watch. You gotta be somewhere?"

"I'm where I need to be." She rocked on. "I'm Lena."

I found a handkerchief in my coat pocket, thank God, and wiped my neck. Hot again. I felt another belch and hoped it wasn't blood. "Howdy, Lena," I nodded back. "I'm James. Or Jimmie. Up to you."

"Hello, James. Are you an entertainer? You look like one. You know, my husband was an entertainer."

"Well, I'm sort of retired now. You a mind reader, too?" I took off my skipper and fanned myself. She didn't answer. She seemed familiar but I couldn't place her. "Funny weather for May."

"You'll see June soon." When she said that I thought my mind was gonna crack open.

"Pardon again?"

"I said you'll see June soon. It'll get hot overnight."

"Lady, it's hot now."

Lena said something else but I couldn't hear what. She got up from the rocker and went into the house and motioned I should follow.

Her screen door was creaky and I clipped my boots on the dash so she knew I had come in. I didn't go further than the entry which was a little sitting room set up with a dark green, furry soft couch underneath a window that looked out on the road I just walked in on. Directly across from my seat was a broadside over the radiator. I read it out loud.

"Professor DeLa Mano. The Wizard of the East. Enchanted wedding rings. The witches knot. Good music in attendance." I've seen this before.

Lena returned with a silver tray of coffee, cups, and milk and sugar, which she placed on a glass table in front of the couch. She was shortish. Curvy. Not bad lookin' for an old broad. Maybe 60. Who can tell? Her eyes were champagne brown, sugar cube added. She fixed on me a little longer than I was comfortable. She had a pink, pouty lower lip and barely any upper lip at all, like her face came from two different people. Milky brown skin. Maybe Mexico. Mobile too, come to think of it. Hard to say. Lotta folks 'round Texas look like her. When I was a kid, I remember walkin' by a big ole house on the 4th of July—I was all of 12 or 13—and comin' on an older girl swingin' from her legs on the branch of a pawpaw tree, back and forth. I watched her all afternoon, listening to her laugh and sing to herself. I could tell she didn't live in Meridian. I don't know how I knew. Sure enough, she was there one day, gone the next. If honeysuckle had a sound, I'd say she sounded like honeysuckle. Like Lena. I pointed to the poster. "You know, I know where these were printed. This DeLa Mano. This your husband?"

She took a seat in a matching green chair with a round back and kicked off her slip-on shoes. "My wasband. Coffee?"

"Please," I answered, and she poured. The pot was strong and slightly sweet. I read down the poster. "'The Chinese Paradox.' I don't know what that is, but I think I'm living it." She giggled. "I'd like to know this DeLa Mano."

"Me too." Lena sipped her cup.

"He leave you for a show girl?" I grinned but I didn't get one in return. and I instantly regretted being a smart ass. A common thing for me. As was apologizing. "Sorry. It's my sense of humor. I'm a natural icebreaker. It's a gift."

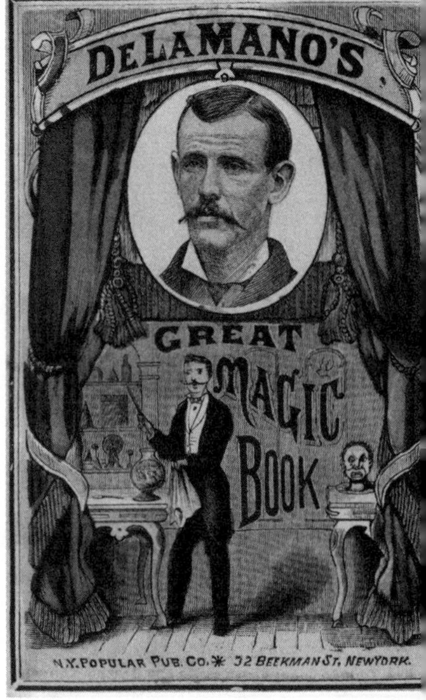

"I know you're just being funny, James. DeLa Mano was what they used to call an illusionist." Lena tightened her shawl with a free hand, holding her cup with the other and looked to the poster, as if she hadn't read it in a long time. She saw much more in it than me. "Illusion. Magic. Mentalism. He was a natural. I was his trusted assistant. One of those love at first sight sort of things. We married. And then about a year later, DeLa Mano became very sick. A doctor thought it was TB. We were never quite sure. He didn't trust doctors too much. He knew he was dying. And he didn't want to."

"No one does." I looked out through the screen door at the peacock now in the front yard, eyeing the porch steps.

"All his life he had heard of mediums who could open doors to the spirit world." She smiled. "This state is full of 'em. Legend of Sleepy Hollow. That sort of thing. I suppose it's been that way since before the revolution. DeLa Mano was a skeptic, but those stories struck his fancy. We talked about it the first time we met, actually. The story that DeLa Mano was chasing was a very old yarn. It went something like: if you were an old soul, there were other old souls who would seek you out. Welcome you. Fellow messengers. Conduits who could rescue your soul to live again in someone else. Not every soul lives on, you know. Lots do. Lots don't. DeLa Mano had come from Europe." Lena put down her cup and rubbed her fingers. "He used to say Europe was a place of dark souls. And America was a place of light souls. He was really a lovely man. But . . ." She warmed up my cup and then her own. "He was stubborn. A romantic. Lots of older men who fall for younger women are. He also didn't defer to stupid people. We shared that trait."

"Did you believe him?" I was, against my own will, becoming quite enthralled. Even now in her age, an age I'd never know myself, I could see what any fella might fall for.

"I adored him. I didn't see any reason not to believe that what he was seeking existed. After all, he and I had a sense of people they didn't have a sense of themselves. And he believed in me. No one ever had, I guess. I told him I'd stick with him. As long as he wasn't going to be left beat up at the side of the road, he should follow his heart. That's all anyone wants." She warmed her hands on her cup. "He became insatiable in his quest. Outing every faker he could. Like Houdini did. 'Mendacity' was a word I heard a lot. He was quite funny about it at home. But I could also see he was disappointed. So was I. I thought if there was any man that deserved the affirmation that he was something special, it was DeLa Mano. Then he heard about this place." She rolled her eyes around the room. "The place fakers feared. So naturally, he wanted to come." She put down her cup and leaned back. "Someone summoned him here on—what do writers like to say?—a dark and stormy night."

I snapped my fingers. "Paul Clifford. My aunt read me that book. An orphan boy discovers his father is a judge. The same judge who sentences him to death."

Lena had brought us cookies too, and she nibbled on one, crossing her legs, swinging her feet. "The story I was told is he came to this house which was owned by a group of women . . ."

I raised my eyebrows but she didn't rattle.

"Not his thing, really. No, a group of women claimed lodgers were disappearing without a trace, whispering strange incantations, and all that stuff. So, DeLa Mano came and locked himself in a room upstairs to see what would happen . . ."

". . . on a dark and stormy night," I finished her sentence. The air in the house smelled like lilacs. Yuck.

"This was a boarding house then. And when the women who owned the house came to fetch him for breakfast, they unlocked the door and . . ."

I had to interrupt. "Let me guess. They were greeted by a brand new butterfly." I put my cup down. "I don't mean to be rude. But I've worked the circus all my life, Ms. Lena. And a part of me has always wanted to meet the real thing. But no one just disappears."

"Well, it might seem like that if you're looking in the wrong place." Lena picked up her cup with both hands, pinky out. I hadn't noticed how long her lashes were. At another time she might have found work out in Hollywood. A grandfather clock chimed. A cat, calico I think you call it, scooted over her feet and then moved on. Funny how these spirit people never have a goddamn golden retriever. Or a bulldog. An animal who tells it like it is.

"So how long ago did DeLa Mano disappear?"

"Over thirty years now. I keep the room he disappeared from closed so that when I go in, I might find his breath still floating through somewhere."

"I wouldn't take that in if I were you. And you never saw him again?"

"When I got here, his trunk with all his broadsides was here. He traveled with those. It was a kind of mark between us. He promised he'd always leave those somewhere so I'd know where he'd been."

"Ms. DeLa Mano . . ." I clinked my coffee cup on the saucer and made a mess. "Did it ever occur to you that maybe these mediums he went to see were just a bunch of good ole American thieves? Maybe he told them off in such a way that they just got sore at him and chopped him up for firewood."

"You don't believe in other worlds, James?"

"Oh, believe you me. I'd be the first to hail a car, a spaceship—anything to get out of the body I'm in. Maybe he just didn't want you to see him die. Did you ever consider that?"

She didn't meet my eyes but tucked at her shawl. "I got a letter, telling me DeLa Mano had disappeared and to come at once. When I arrived all the people in the house were gone. The sheriff was waiting for me. I went to the guest room upstairs. It locked from the outside. And when I opened the door, one of his cards was still there on the floor—that was a sign between us, too. Right before he left, we joked if this ever happened, if he ever found the real thing, he would leave me a sign so I wouldn't worry. The sheriff had been told by the ladies that I was coming. But they were gone. He took me around to a lawyer who proceeded to give me a deed to this house with my name on it." Lena rested her elbows on her knees. "The deed was signed by the women who owned the house. Dated the day I arrived." We got quiet. I ran my finger around the rim of my cup.

"Nice house."

Lena blinked and daydreamed. "It is a nice house."

We got quiet again and I stared at the floor, where the past is written plain. "I started traveling when I was a kid. I saw a lot of DeLa Mano's. I always thought, there's got to be somebody out there who is the real thing. I mean for all those hacks, I figure the whole reason they're out there is because there's somebody, somewhere, who's the real McCoy. Maybe your DeLa Mano was one of those all along. And he found the door."

We both sipped our coffees. I realized then I hadn't coughed the whole time. What a fuckin' relief.

"Are you a seeker, James?"

"Am I a seeker? Hmm." I put down my coffee and saucer and put a leg 'cross my knee, tracing the leather carving of a rose on my boot. "I've spent so much trying to break in, it never occurred to me to look for a way out." Lena giggled. She seemed to relax a little. I kept on. "You know, just the other day, I went for a walk, in New York." I leaned back with my arms across the couch. "I'm a musicianer, if I didn't say. I make records for RCA Victor. The nipper. Maybe you've heard of it."

She looked at me funny over her coffee cup. "I've heard of it."

"The other day I came up to this newsstand and they had this—what do you call it—science fiction magazine, *Amazing Stories*. So I got a copy. Far-out stuff. I got to reading this story about . . ."

". . . the lava women from Venus." She winked. Anyway, I'm pretty sure she did.

"You know it?"

"I wrote it."

"Well!" I was light-headed. "Ain't this a coincidence." I picked up my coffee and her tiny stirring spoon but there was hardly anything in the cup. God damn, what is going on?

Lena stood and took my cup and put it back on the tray. "No coincidences, James." She walked through a darkened dining room to her kitchen. I followed. The kitchen was all windows, white and bright with light. She went about opening and closing cabinets, like it was perfectly normal for me to be in her house. I don't know what she was making but she seemed to think I planned to stick around. "The Lava Women from Venus . . ."

I caught her sentence and took it for my own. ". . . take the souls of selected mortals before their bodies give out. That was you? That's where I heard your name. Lena DeLa Mano. So, are you a lava woman from Venus?

Lena took a wooden spoon from a drawer made a pouty face. "Maybe I am," she answered coy-like, hip-bumping the drawer closed.

I leaned on the kitchen door frame. "You know, I used to think everybody had a break coming their way. Everybody had one lucky strike. Like you're born with a purpose." I was suddenly famished.

There was a wooden bowl filled with apples and oranges on a round, polished table. "Hey, can I have an apple?" Lena washed it and handed it over. "But I dunno." I kicked at the floorboard and felt sorry for myself. "Seems kinda cruel that all the lucky people have to check out as soon as they get lucky. I mean, what good is it to have something special to offer if you can't stick around?"

Lena struck a match and lit her stove top. She peeled carrots and potatoes and put them in a pot of water. She didn't answer.

"Was DeLa Mano his real name?" I bit into my apple. Right then, it was the most delicious thing I'd ever had.

"His real name was Zell. But I called him June." Lena started chopping an onion. "Is this going to bother you?" She waved her knife around and looked at me wide-eyed. Ok. She's beautiful.

I shook my head. "Don't mind me, food lady. I cry easy."

Lena went back to chopping. "June was the month we met. Part of his name translated to that. His middle name. He told me if he ever disappeared, he would come to check on me. He also said he might try to come back as a child, the one we never got to have. And if that body didn't work, he'd just . . ." She gestured with her knife. ". . . fly into someone else."

"I don't think we get to choose." I churned apple bites in my cheeks.

"Probably not. He was funny, like you." She shook her head, smiling. "He was born with a veil over him. Such babies are anointed, you know? They are a soul that's been allowed to continue. Do you ever feel like you're someone else?"

I didn't answer directly. "You know, you got me back there. My wife and I lost our little girl. Her name was June."

"I'm sorry to hear that."

"She was just an itty-bitty thing. Barely six months old." I rubbed my eyes. Just then it came to me, and I knocked my knuckle on the door frame. "I'm about to have another here."

Lena seemed impressed. "Congratulations. What are you gonna call it?"

I dug into my apple. "Quits."

Lena laughed and got quiet again. I threw my apple core in her trash.

"You know I left a friend of mine back there. I think I better move on, Mrs. DeLa Mano. My fate awaits me."

"I could make you some food if you like," she wiped her hands on a red checkered towel and put a hand on the counter, the other on her hip.

"No, no. But I appreciate it. Big train coming into my station." We gave each other a nice long look.

"I got a room upstairs you can stay." She stirred her concoction. I liked the twinkle in her eye. "I could lock you in and we could see if you're still there in the morning. Supposed to rain tonight. Maybe you'll get lucky."

I gently reached out and brushed the hair out of her eye and patted her cheek. "You're all right, Ms. DeLa Mano. But you know what? I will finish your story tonight. The first part was a bit slow but it's pickin' up."

"You mean you haven't finished it?" She pretended to be fussed but I knew she wasn't. "Make sure you read it on a dark and stormy night."

"I will at that. Maybe your younger self will come see me in my dreams and . . . (I fluttered my fingers) . . . fly me away somewheres." Lena had an awfully nice laugh. I was becoming fond of it. Halfway out of her house, I had a thought and turned around. She was waiting in her kitchen doorway, all in shadow but her face. "What kind of name is Zell?"

She moved towards me into the light, still fiddling with a hand towel. "Swiss. He yodeled, you know. All over the house. Do you yodel in your act, James?"

"As a matter of fact, I do. I tell you what, when I walk out this door, I'm gonna yodel all the way up the street. In fact, come over here." She met me halfway and I took her by the elbow and out the door until we were standing on the porch. The peacock turned to listen. Just us and that big ole silly bird. "You see that red automobile up there?"

"It's very nice." She took hold of my arm, to steady herself I suppose.

"Now I'm gonna walk right up to that car and when I get there, I'm gonna turn around and yodel just for you and I bet you'll be able to hear me."

I gave a little yodel as I walked down the stairs. When she laughed again, I called back. "Oh, that's nothin', you just give me a minute and I'll really let it rip." I looked up to a cloudless sky, waved to her wave, and moseyed back to the car. The peacock stayed under the willow, watching me go. I found Cora snoozin' at the wheel with the door open. I yodeled back towards Lena.

"Jesus, Jimmie, how do you do that in your condition?" Cora acted all out of sorts but I didn't really believe she'd been sleeping.

"Lucky, I guess."

I was headed for the backseat when out of the corner of my eye I saw Cooper slow walking toward us coming from behind the station, cockin' a shot gun. Uh oh. I dove in the back and crawled out the other side, grabbin' for the pistol that had fallen out of my boot. When I got through, I thought I might have a shot. Maybe I could cut him off at the ankle. But who the hell was I hearing? Cora and somebody else. That's when I got sopped in the head. I smelled leather. Then a loud pop. And perfume. I saw Cooper's face hit the dirt hard in front of me from under the car, his dead eye square on my live one. The last thing I remember, I was face down, mouth wide open and my gullet full of dust, and a voice I'm sure was my girl.

BLUE YODEL No. 12

IN THE JAILHOUSE NOW

VICTOR TALKING MACHINE COMPANY

May 22, 1933.

In accordance with the resolution adopted by the Board of Directors at the Meeting held December 12th, 1932, authorizing the formation of an Executive Committee to function in accordance with the By-Laws of the Company, The THIRD MEETING of the EXECUTIVE COMMITTEE of the Victor Talking Machine Company was held at the principal office at the Company, Camden, N.J. on the above date, at 11.00 a.m. The following meeting was also recorded to direct-to-disc.

Present:
M. G. Screder, Chairman
C. O. Fuchs
G. B. Ryall
C. J. Baumer
E. J. Oberstein
E. K. Braxton, Secretary, Recordist.

The CHAIRMAN reported, on behalf of the Management, the following actions taken:

101 GEORGE GERSHWIN
Executive Committee CONFIRMED to pay Gershwin 1/2¢ per side royalty in addition to Copyright Royalty. No advance, in connection with record "An American in Paris."

Note: Mr. Gershwin would like his car horns returned. They are marked A, B, C, D.

102 PABLO CASALS
Pablo Casals has signed a one-year contract, $500 advance per approved selection against 10%; number of selections to be mutually agreed upon.

Note: Discourage Susan Casals (wife) from attending sessions.

103 <u>KING OLIVER & HIS ORCHESTRA</u>
Authority granted to enter into contract for services of this Organization on following terms:

1 year; 1 year option
16 selections per year
$150 flat per approved selection
(plus $25 per arrangement)

Exclusivity

104 <u>JIMMY ROGERS</u>
Reported that Jimmy Rogers (for whose services we have a contract through R. S. Peer) is dissatisfied with the terms of his present agreement viz.:

Option— 1 year from July 1, 1932, 20 selections at $150.00 per approved selection.

Authority was granted to enter into a new agreement on following basis:

2 years from May 26, 1933; 1 year option;
Guarantee of 6 or more selections per year;
Advance of $200 per selection, under usual conditions;
Against Artist Royalty of 1/2¢
Transfer to Bluebird division

NOTE: All future and past Master Recordings to be preserved by R. S. Peer

was APPROVED

Exclusivity

NOTE: (Approved by R. S. Peer on behalf of Rogers)

105 <u>SPECIAL EXPENDITURES ON BEHALF OF THE COMPANY</u>
The President reported that he has incurred expenditures on behalf of the Company of $5,000.

Eli Oberstein requests a break. On Motion, duly seconded, the meeting was adjourned for lunch.

Mr. Ryall: Is it true Sarnoff sold Peer back his publishing?

Mr. Fuchs: What with all the anti-trust issues in Congress he can't have both hands in the cookie jar.

Mr. Ryall: Tell that to Eli.

Mr. Oberstein: Excuse me?

Mr. Baumer: Why don't we own those copyrights. Who gave him that?

Mr. Fuchs: I think it's a smart move.

Mr. Screder (Chairman): Peer outwitted all of you. No surprise there.

Mr. Ryall: I don't remember approving that.

Mr. Oberstein: I think we should get out of the hillbilly business altogether.

Mr. Fuchs: Is that thing recording us?

Mr. Baumer: You'd vote yes to anything if he does.

Mr. Ryall: I just do what I'm told.

Mr. Oberstein: Mr. Screder, all due respect, is this $5,000 necessary?

Mr. Screder: No less necessary than the deals you're making with disc jockeys and publishers and all the other little games you got going on.

Mr. Ryall: I don't know why we're renewing this Jimmy Rogers fellow. I saw him yesterday and he looked terrible. He took my parking space. You know he drives a Duesenberg?

Mr. Oberstein: Mr. Screder . . .

Mr. Screder (quiets room): So, Eli, you want to put before the board, on the record for Mr. Sarnoff and all the world to see, the nature of the $5,000 I have incurred for services to the company.

Mr. Fuchs: It's for the company you keep, Eli.

Mr. Oberstein: I'm just saying I think it could have been handled differently. Dealing with these kinds of people . . . I mean what if word got out?

Mr. Screder: (sound of chair scraping floor) Now listen. Listen to me very clearly. All of you. Every simpering, stinking, sorry-ass, weasley, gambling, chicken shit, cotton-eye'd one of you. Your job is very simple. We are not dealing with intellectual giants. If we were, you wouldn't be here. Your job is to find talent, record the talent, manufacture records made by that talent, and sell them to folks. Then you sell folks something to play those records on. And when our records get played on the radio, you sell folks a radio. You raise your hand when I say raise it and you put it down when I say put it down. When I say shit, you shit! Like the dogs you are. And when I say pay up, you pay up. And when I say go home, you go home. Am I making myself understood?

(voices): Yes sir.

Mr. Screder: Eli? I'm waiting . . .

Mr. Oberstein: Yes sir.

Mr. Screder: Well, that's just fine. I'm glad we have an understanding. Miss Braxton over there is working very hard to get this all down, aren't you Miss Braxton?

Miss Braxton: Yes, Mr. Screder.

Mr. Screder: And are you getting everything, Miss Braxton?

Miss Braxton: Every word, sir.

Mr. Screder: Fine, fine. And Miss Braxton is

also recording this meeting on disc, aren't you Miss Braxton?

Miss Braxton: That's right, Mr. Screder.

Mr. Screder: And Miss Braxton will be bringing me both the disc and transcription straight to my desk.

Miss Braxton: Yes, Mr. Screder . . .

Mr. Screder: And there will be more than one record of this meeting. The one I enter into the official files and one I keep, right Miss Braxton?

Miss Braxton: Yes, Mr. Screder.

Mr. Screder: Very well. Now let's get back to business. Agreed?

Motion to continue meeting approved:

105(cont.) SPECIAL EXPENDITURES ON BEHALF OF THE COMPANY

The CHAIRMAN reported that he has incurred special investment expenditures on behalf of the Company in the amount of $5,000. Whereupon, the motion was duly made and passed that the President will be reimbursed by the Company for special expenditures on behalf of the Company in the amount of $5,000.

Approved $5,000

106 CUBA RECORDING TRIP

APPROVED plan for a Cuba recording trip, Summer 1933; 50 selections to be made; total talent costs and other expenses at $2,500 to $3,000.

A&R Supervision ~~Eli Oberstein.~~ R. S. Peer

Meeting Adjourned

E. K. Braxton, Secretary.

BLUE YODEL №. 13

A-SIDE: AWAY OUT ON THE MOUNTAIN

Today started out sunny. A bit windy. Nice though. The kind of day that if you weren't gonna live past it, you'd have no complaints. Other than not living to see past it. I spent the morning on the beach, lounging about in one of those canvas deck chairs with a hood on it. Cora took a photo. I hope it comes out. She and Carlos rode on the Human Pool Table, and I heard she got her skirt picked up by some little fella in a clown suit. The ocean serenaded me. And I yodeled back. We all saw the human cannon ball. Had a Nathan's for lunch and I drank a Boylan's. Celery! Who would think of such a thing? Pretty good though.

In the afternoon the breeze picked up. I put on some trousers and a shirt with Cora's help and sprang for an early supper at the Lobster, not far from the Taft. Had steak tartar. And it was fine. I nearly made it home on the walk back before I fell down hard. 'Bout put a fire hydrant through my chest. I don't remember anything after that. I told them to take me to Annie's in Washington. She'd know what to do. But they didn't. I'm still here. It's evening now. I'm sure to get knocked out again soon.

Lightening outside. Either that or a premier somewhere. I was dreaming my mother put her hand on my forehead. Something about the palm of her hand was just the right size. I've been carrying a letter she wrote me near all my life now. Pa tried to throw it away but I fished it out of the trash box before it got burned. I look at it on her birthday.

August 1, 1903

Dear James,
Out of all of my boys I think you are the one who would most appreciate a letter. You may read this many times before it makes sense. Letters are good for that. They grow as you do. And even though you are my

youngest, I think you are wise beyond your years. You pay attention to what people say. You listen.

I know a lot about you no one else knows. You were born with a veil over you. You were an anointed child. Only hours after you were born, we were resting in my room—just you and me. You father was far away. I could feel your breath on my chest. I looked at you and you not only smiled, you laughed. At 10 months you went straight to walking. Hardly ever crawled. You always seemed to know where you were going. You are my incomparably bright little child. I think if I had opened the front door you would have walked right out laughing and never looked back.

I'll always be with you. When you need a push, think of me as the person, arms outstretched, holding onto your shoulders as you go. Giving you a nudge. If there's a nagging voice in your head that says—"Are you sure you're sure enough?"—that's me, too. I used to ask you: Are you sure, James? You'd answer: "Mother, I'm one hundred per-sure."

I loved being your mother most of all. There are other things I loved. Sunflowers. I loved elephants. I loved music. I loved the banjo. I loved the smell of mint. I loved the 4th of July. I loved fresh bread. When you smell fresh bread, I am there.

Don't let your brothers tease you or let anyone put you aside if you grow up small. It's up to each of us to be decent to others. All scoundrels are alike. It's the decent people who are all different. The flowers of life. Be one of those. Different. Have pity on your father. He is a nervous man who sleeps only to wake up and worry if the two pennies he lost yesterday can be made up tomorrow. He'll probably marry again. You may forget me some days. But I'll remind you I'm still here when you least expect it.

Sometimes I worry your fate will be like mine. A flower trying to grow in barren ground. So live. Take chances. See the world. Sometimes when you think of me you might only remember the hard days. But there were not that many. James, you are my boy. And I am always with you, right there in your pocket.

Adieu
Your Mother,
Eliza

Gal could write. We finished at RCA last night. Fred was so patient with me. What a hoss. I can't remember if I said that or not. Tony and John, the guitarist and Hawaiian steel man who backed me, did all right. I think it'll be a long time before they can go in the studio again. I was in a bad way. But between 1:30 and 5 o'clock we took on four songs and got 'em all. I had my name on all of them so hopefully that will bring Carrie and Boots some cabbage. "Mississippi Delta Blues" was the best of 'em I think. I'd like to make it back in a few months and cut the Delmores' tune. Maybe a few more. The very last number we did was not much of anything. But I managed it on my feet in one try. Fred said I did good.

I went back to Lena's story. Almost got to the end. Seems these lava women from Venus can alter their shape as they go about the Earth searching for the "souls of light" who came from their planet centuries ago to populate the Earth. Naturally, the souls of light get chased and hunted down by the dark souls from Mars. All through this tale, the lava women are in a race to save the light souls from the combustible trash pit of eternity where lost souls languish. Kind of like my buddy Raymond who could write a good tune like "TB Blues" but couldn't keep from landing in the pen. Poor squash. Says in this issue that Bob Olsen's got a new one coming next month. I like him. The Crime Crusher. Acute intelligence vs. the powers that be who would save themselves at his expense. They got all kinds of funny ads, too. Says here you can learn to fly by mail. Earn $60 a week. I went up in Will's airplane once. I tell you that? Give me an old train anytime.

I always thought churches are train stations for God. All souls waitin'. Seems like it's always somebody else's train that's pullin' in. I suppose this story of mine is all about dreaming of leaving and dreaming of arriving. When you know you're gonna leave the party early you notice a lot more. You notice that people aren't paying attention to nothin' that's important. You can measure your life by how much you were wanted or how much you were welcomed. Up to you.

When I came to pick up Charley she was with him. Said she was just going to New York to see the sights. I only found out later Charley didn't have a session up there at all. He was there to make sure she got out of town. Out of the south. Away from me, maybe. I remember her fingers were pickin' at a pair of dark purply gloves. I can't imagine how her little hand could fit inside them. She tugged and tugged at those things the whole time we were on the platform.

"Where'd you get those?"

"Hey, give 'em back." I hardly ever saw her sore.

"I'm jealous. They get to touch your skin. What are you not telling me?"

She was teary. "Nothing, Jimmie."

"'Nothing, Jimmie.' That's all anyone says to me these days." I wanted to remember everything. But I didn't know where to look first. She had a spoonful of freckles on each cheek. I wanted to kiss them but I was afraid for her if I got close. "Will you come find me?"

"I'll find you." She patted the lining of my coat. "Are you staying in the same place? The Taft?"

"It's the only place I know how to find." I took out a $100. But she wouldn't take it.

"No, no," she said. "You keep it. You're gonna need it." She poked a finger in my belly and like a rag doll, I laughed. She kissed my eyes. She was clutching at the middle button of her jacket. Gold with a fella on a horse.

"Did I get you that coat?" I tugged at her cuffs. "It's nice."

"You did!" She blew her nose and sobbed and laughed again. "It's so nice. I thought you stole it. It was a little big on me."

"Not anymore," I said.

She touched my cheek and together we patted her tummy. "No, not anymore."

"You know I've probably worked this train. Do you want me to see if I know anybody?"

"Better not." And she wiped her nose. "They might throw me off if they find out I know you."

"They might anyway."

Charley came up and took her elbow. I nodded and he nodded back. She whispered something I couldn't quite hear and put her palm on my forehead.

As the train left the station, Haydee leaned out the window and waved. She had put her gluvss on// / the train slipped away, her outline
wz bleached out by the sun /// the train curved away and left the tracks white

. . . liiike they had never been there at ..a..l.l

jamz

BLUE YODEL No. 13

B-SIDE: HIGH POWERED MAMA

TRANSCRIPTION

Disciplinary Review—Ms. Cora Bedell

RE: Patient #6563595

July 3, 1933

Dr. J. Ferguson: This hearing will come to order. For the record, we are concerned with the treatment of Patient #6563595 deceased May 26, 1933, under the care of Nurse Cora Bedell formerly of Carthage, Texas. Present is Dr. Ferguson and Dr. Cooper of Meridian (MS).

Dr. Cooper: Miss Bedell. Thank you for coming. I know you're anxious to enjoy the holiday as we are. This is just a formality. We have your statement. I have a few questions. We are reviewing the death of Mr. James Rodgers of San Antonio, Texas who was under your care for some time.

Cora Bedell: Yes sir.

Dr. Ferguson: And Mr. Rodgers suffered from tuberculosis which he had contracted in . . .

CB: Mr. Rodgers told me he had been diagnosed in 1924. I believe his father was a railroad foreman and his mother had passed from it as well. He suspected he caught it working railroad jobs.

Dr. Cooper: I began treating Rodgers around the same time in Meridian. The last time I saw Mr. Rodgers in 1929 we had discussed increasing his dosage to a ¼ grain. That was the last time I treated him.

Dr. Ferguson: I see. How long was the patient under your care, Miss Bedell?

CB: From around February the first until May 26 of this year. Mr. Rodgers died in the early morning of May 26.

Dr. Ferguson: And what were the circumstances in which Mr. Rodgers entered your care?

CB: We had met last summer when he was performing. Mr. Rodgers was a musician. I should have said that. Mr. Rodgers had an engagement at a theater in Carthage. The manager called me as Mr. Rodgers was due to perform and was having terrible pleurisy spasms. I had helped out with emergencies at the theater in the past.

Dr. Ferguson: Yes, I wanted to ask about that. Seems you have a penchant for taking on entertainers.

CB: As I said, at that time Mr. Rodgers was traveling by himself. He was concerned about properly administering the morphine he required. He had a friend who had overdosed on a combination of morphine and cocaine administered by a doctor whose license had been revoked.

Dr. Ferguson: Eh, just a moment, Miss Bedell. It seems there was a review of your conduct in regards to this. You've had a number of persons in the entertainment industry as patients. Seems you were a favorite of that sort of group. You travel with musicians, circus people?

CB: I have, yes.

Dr. Ferguson: Freelance?

CB: I'm sorry?

Dr. Ferguson: Not associated with a hospital, in other words.

CB: Not currently, no.

Dr. Ferguson: You received your nursing degree in Austin, University of Texas in 1913. They don't have a record of you there, Miss Bedell.

CB: I was married at the time.

Dr. Ferguson: Ah, and what was your married name?

CB: Boasberg. Mrs. Mark Boasberg. I stopped using that name after the divorce.

Dr. Ferguson: I see. You noted that before being employed by Mr. Rodgers you were employed by the J. D. Morgan Players. And what did you do for them?

CB: They took me on as a company nurse. I believe Mr. Rodgers was under their employment when we met.

Dr. Ferguson: But you said Mr. Rodgers was traveling by himself when you first met him.

CB: Yes, he was. Let me clarify. Because of his condition, he was having some difficulty and had left to continue performing on his own. As you might know, he was quite renowned in his field. He could make more money that way. He had left the group when I came to his aid.

Dr. Ferguson: Funny how you should have worked for the same troupe but had never crossed paths, prior.

CB: He often traveled separately from the rest of the players. I imagine because of his condition. I'm sure he was aware of who I was. I know we met briefly in passing but I had not had any real conversation with him. When the Carthage theater called for me, perhaps he had suggested me?

Dr. Ferguson: So, let me get this straight. You worked for this J. D. Morgan players group but didn't actually attend to Mr. Rodgers during that time. But you left to go out on your own around the same time he left their employment and just happened to be close by when he played the local theater and required assistance with his morphine dosage.

CB: What can I say? It's a small world.

Dr. Ferguson: I also see here you were employed for some time by a Jack Sheehan of New Orleans, Louisiana.

CB: I worked for a time at the Jung Hotel in New Orleans, that's correct. Mr. Sheehan was a regular at the card table.

Dr. Ferguson: This Mr. Sheehan—it seems he has quite a reputation for mischief. And he kept a full-time nurse?

CB: Well, no. I'm not sure why my employment at the Jung would give that impression.

Dr. Ferguson: What kind of impression?

CB: Well, any impression. I knew Mr. Sheehan to be a professional gambler. That's why he came so often to the Jung. He excelled at excessive drinking. That's all. Not much I could do for him but tell him to take a cold shower.

Dr. Cooper: Dr. Ferguson, I came a long way for this meeting. Could we concentrate on how Mr. Rodgers fits into this?

Dr. Ferguson: Yes, let's do.

CB: Quite all right. As I mentioned, Mr. Rodgers was looking for someone who would administer the proper dosage for someone with his dependency without impeding his ability to perform. Mr. Rodgers was grateful for my help and said he might like to hire me to accompany him the next time he traveled. Earlier this year, Mr. Rodgers was admitted to Houston Methodist for quite some time. After he was released, he asked me to accompany him whenever possible. He was concerned his condition was progressing quickly.

Dr. Ferguson: Did you consult with Dr. Cooper before you began tending to Mr. Rodgers?

CB: Yes. When I met Mr. Rodgers, he referred me to Dr. Cooper, his physician in Meridian, who had been treating Mr. Rodgers on and off for a number of years. Dr. Cooper showed me the results of the x-ray he had given Mr. Rodgers. At that time, and this was quite some time ago, he noted Mr. Rodgers' life expectancy was a little over a year. Mr. Peer, his manager, helped Mr. Rodgers arrange for another x-ray last year for a possible tour of Europe. But he was too ill to make that voyage.

Dr. Ferguson: Did you relay your concerns about Mr. Rodgers' condition to any medical professionals prior to going to New York?

CB: Yes, both to Mr. Cooper as well as the attending doctor at Methodist in Houston.

Dr. Ferguson: Yes, I see that in his file. Mr. Rodgers was most dissatisfied with the staff at Houston Methodist and upon checking out he noted they were not, and I quote: "Doin' me right." Did you administer anything else to Mr. Rodgers during your time treating him? Do you find this funny, Miss Bedell?

CB: No sir. As noted in my summary, I sometimes would provide Mr. Rodgers a very small dose of Benzedrine prior to his recording sessions.

Dr. Ferguson: You must be aware of the danger of such an application to a patient in Mr. Rodgers' condition.

CB: Yes, and I was adamant with Mr. Rodgers that despite his determination to perform, I would not do anything that would further compromise his health or hasten his decline. But small doses, monitored carefully, did enable him to perform in the studio.

Dr. Ferguson: The pressure to do more must have been acute, Miss Bedell. He was getting paid for these recording sessions, was he not?

CB: Yes, he was.

Dr. Ferguson: Was there any kind of kickback to you?

CB: Absolutely not.

Dr. Ferguson: Why did you take this trip, Miss Bedell? Here was a dying man, an addict by any stretch of the imagination, who for all intents and purposes, was living hour to hour.

CB: At first, I politely declined. But at the behest of his representative at RCA Records, I changed my mind.

Dr. Ferguson: Why, may I ask?

CB: Well . . . I liked him. Mr. Peer had an excellent reputation as did Mr. Rodgers.

Dr. Ferguson: And they paid you I presume.

CB: Of course. But I was most struck that I couldn't find anyone who had a bad thing to say about either of them. I decided I would rather do the best I could to ensure Mr. Rodgers made his engagements rather than see him go to someone disreputable. I admired him. For many reasons. I wanted to help him. He was trying to earn money for his family. It was my suggestion that we travel to New York by boat, which we did from Galveston in early May. He made the trip without any issues.

Dr. Ferguson: And he passed away while still in New York?

CB: Yes sir. The day after his last recording session.

Dr. Cooper: In a hospital?

CB: No sir. In his room at the Hotel Taft.

Dr. Ferguson: Why was he in a public hotel in his condition?

CB: He was, to the end, quite strong minded. And probably not the only person with TB in that hotel. I did my best to keep us isolated. By any measure his effort over those last two weeks was heroic. He recorded 12 new songs on that trip, taking long breaks between sessions. Sometimes several days. After he finished on May 25, he was in terrific spirits. He gave me no cause to think he wouldn't return to Texas. In fact, he planned to visit his sister-in-law in Washington on the way back. The day he died, we had spent the morning at Coney Island, his favorite place. He could stay secluded there. He insisted, in fact, on riding the Ferris wheel. That afternoon we had an early dinner at the Lobster, downtown near his hotel. He was weak but otherwise under his own mobility. On the way back, he wanted to walk the two blocks from the restaurant instead of taking a cab. He collapsed near the hotel.

Dr. Ferguson: Were you by yourself in attending to Mr. Rodgers.

CB: I was often accompanied by an assistant from Mr. Peer's office. Mr. Carlos. Mr. Peer offered me any assistance I might need. We helped Mr. Rodgers back to his room. He rallied some that night.

Dr. Ferguson: Were you with him when he passed?

CB: I was. I first noticed convulsions while passing his room. My room was across the hall. I heard a coughing spasm about 10 o'clock but it subsided, and he was resting comfortably when I checked in on him around midnight. He liked to type . . .

Dr. Cooper: Type?

CB: Yes. Letters. Poems. Shortly after midnight I heard typing coming from his room. Then I heard him leave his room and return shortly thereafter. Sometime after 1 a.m., he had another spasm which did not subside. He became progressively worse. He was delirious and in terrible pain. He didn't recognize me. He thought I was from . . .

Dr. Ferguson: Yes?

CB: Such a strange thing. He thought I was from the planet Venus. Then he asked me to take him to his sister Annie in Washington. "Take me to Annie," he said, "She'll know what to do." He went into a coma shortly after that and slipped away around 3 in the morning. I contacted Mr. Peer and called the front desk who called an ambulance. Mr. Peer took care of all the arrangements.

Dr. Ferguson: It sounds most traumatic. Miss Bedell, were you aware that Mr. Rodgers wrote this board?

CB: I'm sorry?

Dr. Ferguson: Mr. Rodgers, it seems composed a letter to this board which was posted from New York on May the 26th. Were you aware of this letter?

CB: No sir. I was not.

Dr. Ferguson: It seems Mr. Rodgers must have a made a quick trip to the mailbox before he expired. And it so happens it was typed. I'd like to read it to you:

> May 26, 1933
> NY NY Hotel Taft
>
> To whom it may concern:
>
> I'd like it to be known for the record that Miss Cora Bedell, at the urging and full cooperation of the RCA Victor Corporation, has served as my personal nurse since February, 1933. During

> that time, Miss Bedell has shown me the utmost compassion, attention, and professional conduct. I'm convinced the quality of her care and dedication to my well being made it possible for me to fulfill important engagements in New York.
>
> These professional engagements earned much needed money for my wife and child. Miss Bedell accompanied me to all of my recording sessions and saw to it that I was cared for properly and was made comfortable. I have lived with TB for nearly 10 years. I have seen the writing on the wall. If the records I made in New York should prove to be of any success, I can largely attribute that to her humanity and care. Without Miss Bedell, I surely would have not lived long enough to make the trip. I owe her a dept. that can't be paid . . .

Dr. Ferguson: (spells out) d-e-p-t period. "Dept."?

CB: That's how he spelled debit. Like the abbreviation for department.

Dr. Ferguson: Hmm . . . (continues reading)

> Please see that my appreciation for Miss Bedell's (pronounces) exempla-o-rarity (Dr. Ferguson sighs) professional conducting remain part of her record.
>
> All my sincerity,
>
> Jimmie Rodgers
>
> The Blue Yodeler
> San Antonio, TX

On his own stationery, too. Very nice sentiments. Well, I don't think I have any more questions. Anything else you care to add Miss Bedell?

CB: . . .   . . .

Dr. Ferguson: Do you need a moment to compose yourself, Miss Bedell?

CB: Only that he was a gentleman in every respect.

Dr. Cooper: I understand, Miss Bedell, you will be relocating to New York to work as a midwife.

CB: Yes.

Dr. Ferguson: May I ask why you're leaving Texas?

CB: I just really grew to love the city. It seems like it would be a nice change of pace for me. Plenty of work. I'd like to adopt a child as well.

Dr. Ferguson: I have your forwarding address as 409 Edgecombe Avenue, Harlem, New York.

CB: Yes, that's right.

Dr. Cooper: Miss Bedell, we won't keep you any longer. Thank you for your time.

CB: Thank you. Thank you both.

(MEETING ADJOURNED)

CODA

MY LITTLE LADY

We always went to Coney Island on his birthday. It was very windy, I remember. I must have been 10 or 11. And Mama was calling for me. She'd say my full name when she wanted my attention.

"Eliza June Chatmon!"

Mama was running towards me, holding her hat as the wind swirled all around. I put my hands on my ears it was so loud. I knew she was calling but the wind blew her words away. I ran towards her to hear better.

"Baby, turn around! The pages!"

I was doing just like she asked. I had put the pages and the scrolls of paper down on the sand so they wouldn't get wet. But then the wind came. Both of us ran and ran trying to catch them, but they were flying everywhere in a cloud going every which way. And the more I chased after 'em, the farther they flew. Just when I bent down to get one it would tease me and pull away like it was attached to a string that kept getting pulled back. Sometimes they'd blow along the shore like I imagine a manta ray glides above the bottom of the sea. At first, I laughed. But then I could tell Mama was upset and so I began to cry.

Seagulls circled overhead, and one swooped down and landed on a page. The ocean kept coming for them, too, each time coming closer. We picked up what we could and stuffed them back into Papa's old briefcase where they belonged. A coast guard boat off shore honked its horn at us.

I used to trace my finger around and around his initials carved in leather around the buckle. Sometimes I'd write his name in the sand with a stick. That's what I was doing when the wind came. I used to think the briefcase must smell like him. He was in there. But now it just smelled like the sea. I was afraid it would never smell like him again. I wanted to make Mama laugh. "I guess he was tired of being in there. He was ready to fly away."

Mama sat down next to me with her legs straight out. She put her hand up to her forehead. She was breathing heavy. It was cloudy and I could tell it was going to be a hot day soon. I thought she might be mad. But she didn't want to be, so she wasn't. Mama pretended to count the freckles on my cheek with her finger. "It's gonna be pretty hard to read next year with so many missing pages."

But I told Mama Cora we didn't lose hardly any. She knew I didn't mean to make them blow away. Mama took the briefcase and closed it up. She was quiet for a long time. I stood up next to her and took her arm and started swinging it, all the while singing:

He floats through the air with the greatest of ease
This daring young man on the flying trapeze
His movements are graceful all the girls he does please . . .

But she wasn't singing. She held my hand, but she wouldn't swing with me.

"Mama Cora," I said, "Can we please go get a Nathan's?"

She let out a big sigh. "Sure, baby. Let's go. I'll race ya!" And we kicked up little clouds of sand as we charged the seagulls. And they flew all around our heads and laughed and laughed with us all the way up to Nathan's. Mama said we should try to write down what we could remember from any pages that went missing. I knew the beginning by heart.

The way I see it. Everybody is allowed one big break in life. One big idea. Sadly, most folks never know they got one coming. And even if they get a good one, they usually let it go, just to see if it might come back.

FINIS

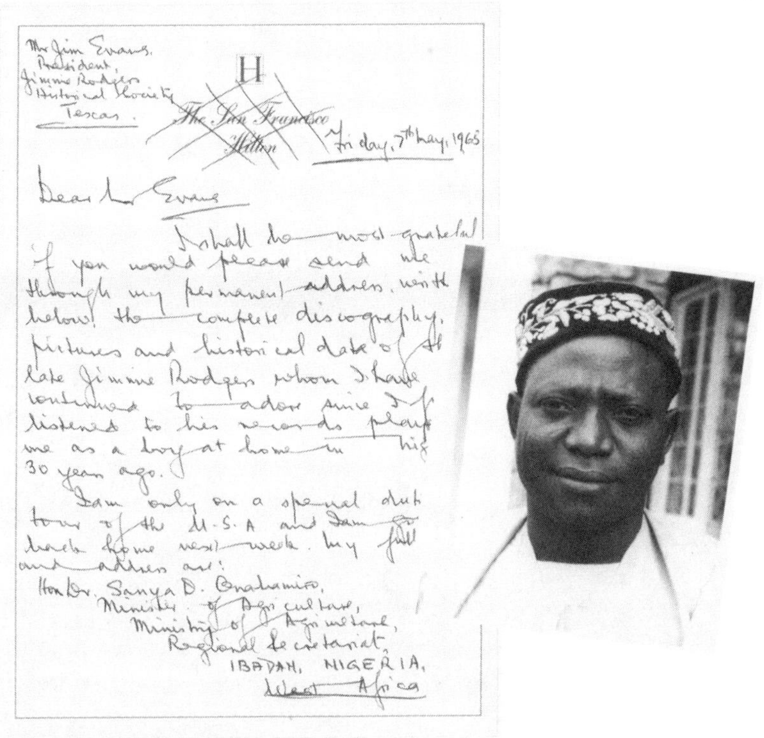
Mr Jim Evans,
President,
Jimmie Rodgers
Historical Society
Texas.

H
The San Francisco
Hilton

Friday, 7th May, 1963

Dear Mr Evans

I shall be most grateful if you would please send me through my permanent address, written below, the complete discography, pictures and historical data of the late Jimmie Rodgers whom I have continued to adore since I first listened to his records played for me as a boy at home in Nigeria 30 years ago.

I am only on a special duty tour of the U.S.A and I am going back home next week. My full and address are:

Hon Dr. Sanya D. Onabamiro,
Minister of Agriculture,
Ministry of Agriculture,
Regional Secretariat,
IBADAN, NIGERIA,
West Africa

Mr. Jim Evans President
Jimmie Rodgers Historical Society
Texas

Friday, 7 May 1963

Dear Mr. Evans,
I shall be most grateful if you would please send me through my personal address written below the complete discography pictures and historical data of the late Jimmie Rodgers whom I have listened to—adored—since I first listened to his records played to me as a boy at my home in Nigeria 30 years ago . . . I would like to place an order for as many Jimmie Rodgers Records as are available and I shall be grateful if you would please advise as to how much money to remit to you . . .

I am yours sincerely,

Sanya Dojo Onabamiro
Nigerian Copepodologist and Statesman

Credits and Acknowledgments

The author wishes to offer his sincere thanks to the following for their scholarship, archives, conversation, and enthusiasm for Jimmie Rodgers including the Country Music Hall of Fame, Barry Mazor, Richard Weiss, Steve Forbert, the Nolan Porterfield Archives/TSHA, Jimmie Rodgers Foundation, Martin Guitars, Scott Barretta, Jeff Rosen, MTSU Center for Popular Music, Gayle Dean Wardlow, Woody Guthrie Center, and Peter Guralnick. Images derive from the following sources:

p. 22: Jimmie Rodgers on tour, c. 1925. (Courtesy of Richard Weize and More Bears)

p. 37: Drawing by the author, inspired by a letter found in the Jim Evans Collection (former president of the Jimmie Rodgers Fan Club) at the Country Music Hall of Fame, that contained a floor plan of Yodeler's Paradise, the Rodgers family home in Kerrville, Texas.

p. 46: Jimmie Rodgers (*center, standing*) on tour with musicians, c. 1925. (Courtesy of Richard Weize and More Bears)

p. 49: Jimmie Rodgers, early professional photo, c. 1920–1925. (Courtesy of Richard Weize and More Bears)

p. 60: Blues talent scout H. C. Speir, c. 1930. (Courtesy of the Gayle Dean Wardlow Collection)

p. 69: Musicians, New Iberia, Louisiana, 1935. Photograph by Russell Lee. (Courtesy of the Library of Congress)

p. 73: Newspaper ad for Jimmie Rodgers's appearance at Speir's Music store, Farish Street, Jackson, Mississippi, January 1928. (Courtesy of *Clarion-Ledger*, Jackson, Miss.)

p. 84: Jimmie Rodgers and Will Rogers on their benefit tour for the Red Cross, 1931. (Courtesy of Fort Worth Star-Telegram Collection, Special Collections, The University of Texas at Arlington Libraries)

p. 107: H. C. Speir's music store, Farish Street, c. 1930. (Courtesy of the Gayle Dean Wardlow Collection)

p. 111: Street Musicians, West Memphis, Arkansas, c. 1935. Photo by Ben Shahn. (Courtesy of the Library of Congress)

p. 140: Jimmie Rodgers's business card, Washington, D.C., c. 1927. (Courtesy of Martin Guitars)

p. 145: XER, Villa Acuña, Coahuila, Mexico, c. 1932. (Courtesy of Library of Congress)

p. 159: Jimmie Rodgers, Maybelle Carter, Sara Carter, and A. P. Carter, Louisville, Kentucky, 1931. (Courtesy of Richard Weize and More Bears)

p. 196: Jimmie Rodgers family and Ralph Peer family, c.1930, Yodeler's Paradise, Kerrville, Texas. (Courtesy of Richard Weize and More Bears)

p. 232: *DeLa Mano's Great Magic Book*, c. 1880. (Illustrator unknown. Author's collection)

p. 262: Jimmie Rodgers on tour, c. 1925. (Courtesy of Richard Weize and More Bears)

p. 273: Children playing in the Surf, Sea Gate, Coney Island, New York, filmed by G. W. Bitzer, August 3, 1904. (Courtesy of the Library of Congress)

p. 277: Letter and photo by Sanya Dojo Onabamiro, Nigerian copepodologist and statesman, sent to Jim Evans, president, Jimmie Rodgers Fan Club, May 7, 1963. (Courtesy of the Country Music Hall of Fame and Museum)